T.L. BODINE

Nezumi's Children

First published by Glass Rat Media 2013

This novel is entirely a work of fiction. The names, characters, and incidents portrayed in it are the work of the author's imagination. Any resemblance to actual persons, living or dead, events, or localities is entirely coincidental.

Second edition

ISBN: 978-1-7374650-5-8

Cover art by Emz Warren & Martin Shannon

*This book was professionally typeset on Reedsy.
Find out more at reedsy.com*

To Andrew, for his enduring patience.
To the folks at the Rat Shack, for their endless knowledge.
And to all the rats, living and dead, whose brief lives have enriched this world.

And for Juliette. Happy birthday.

Content Warnings

This book contains sequences of animal death and violence, as well as instances of sexual assault and cannibalism (within the context of natural rat behaviors). Reader discretion is advised.

I

Faith in The Beyond

Prologue

Nezumi pressed her nose through the bars of her cage and felt the open air with her whiskers. She'd never been able to do that before. At her old home, in the pet store—and before that, in the breeding facility where she'd been born—the walls were made of glass and the air was close and thick with the smell of rat. Here, she could smell many different things: the woody smell of pine trees from the open window; the alcoholic under-scent of air freshener; the sizzling meaty smells from downstairs. But there was rat smell, also, and she squeezed a forepaw through the bars of her cage, snatching at the air as though she could somehow grab the scent, pull it inside and force it to explain itself.

She had been Named just a few days ago. It was a prestigious event, earning a True Name. That was the ultimate gift of the Great Ones—those whose hands open the sky, the bearers of food, they who walk in the Beyond. Nezumi, all her life, had heard stories of ascension into the Beyond, of being specially chosen by the Great Ones and endowed through True Names with amazing power unknown to any nameless rat.

She withdrew her black-and-white patched muzzle from the bars and sighed, running both paws over her face to clean her whiskers. She had been Named for days now, but she didn't feel any different.

"Hey. You. Hey!"

She flicked her ears, searching for the source of the voice. The rat smell she had caught on the air was suddenly thicker. It was muskier than she was used to, a thick oily odor that was simultaneously revolting and intoxicating. The scent was unfamiliar, but not entirely unknown; she had smelled one other like it before, and as the wild rat's scent clung to her nostrils a troublesome memory nagged at the back of her thoughts.

He's come back for me. The thought came to her, unbidden and unwanted, and she forced it away.

"Come over here."

She turned and caught sight of the rat. He was large, easily twice her size, and his brown fur was ticked with grey and black. Wild color. And solid, without the white blaze. *Not the same rat at all,* she realized, and she wasn't sure if the thought comforted or saddened her.

"Who are you?" she asked, taking a few tentative steps forward. She paused, sweeping her whiskers forward, nose twitching rapidly as she inhaled his scent. He was outside of the cage, without a Great One in sight. Only once before had Nezumi seen a rat outside, in the Beyond, without a Great One's guidance: that white-blazed male who had come to her before she had been taken from the pet store. "Why are you out there? The Beyond isn't safe without the Great Ones to watch over you."

"I don't know about all that," the rat said, clicking his incisors together. He laid his forepaws on the cage bars; his claws were long and curved. His nose twitched. His ears flattened to his head and he hissed, drawing away from the bars. "It's too late for you," he said, an accusation in his voice, as though she had deceived him. "You've already been taken."

She hesitated. She didn't know how he knew about her pregnancy. She gave him a long, appraising look, taking another tentative step forward. "Are you one of the Spirits?"

She had heard tales, in her infancy, of the Spirit Realm—the communal plane between life and nothingness where the souls of rats lingered after death. Sometimes Spirits would whisper things in the ears of sleeping rats, teaching them things they had learned in life, like how to recognize poison without eating it, or how to build a nest for unborn *jask*.

She hadn't quite believed in them until that rat had come to her, days ago, before she had been Named. She had been in an isolation tank, held in quarantine for a few days at her buyer's request, when the words came—not to her ears, but inside her mind. The rat with the white face. He found his way inside of the cage and inside of her mind and inside of *her*, before she'd even realized, and when he left a part of him lingered within her. Not just in her womb, but in her thoughts as well.

He grinned a mirthless grin, more a baring of fang than an expression of pleasure. "Sure," he said. "I'm a Spirit. Is that what *he* told you?" He snorted and backed away from the bars. "Pets," he muttered, his tone full of disdain. "You lot will believe anything."

He turned and trundled away, deftly climbing from the table her cage sat on down to a pile of laundry and then to the floor. He squeezed through a crack in the baseboard, sucking in his belly, and disappeared.

Nezumi touched her nose to the place his paws had been on the wire. It was still warm.

Weeks later, when her belly swelled and her nipples began to protrude from her soft, piebald belly, the Great Ones banished her from the Beyond. She went back to the old ways, living once more among her kin in the close air and the cool glass walls, laden with the understanding that her transgression had expelled her from paradise.

But she kept her Name.

II

Faith in Blood

Chapter One

Inside Rocco's Pet Emporium, Lori sat cross-legged on the tile floor of the leash aisle, carefully untangling the jumbled contents of a box of choke-chains and hanging them on hooks. From her position, she could see through the large bay windows and glass door that made up the storefront. Outside, it was dark—much darker than it should be for 4:30 in the afternoon—and it had been very long time since a car had pulled into the parking lot.

Mr. Haskins, the owner, was standing in the open doorway, puffing on a cigarillo and glancing intermittently between his watch and the ever-darkening sky.

They had only gotten one customer all afternoon—a guy a few years older than her, Lori guessed, maybe a college student—and he was still there. For the last five minutes he had been standing in front of the small animal display. He would look in at the hamsters and gerbils in the top shelves, then duck down to look at the rats, then straighten out again to look at the gerbils. Outside, a flash of lightning arced through the clouds, temporarily throwing the parking lot into sharp relief. Before Lori could finish counting a thousand one, thunder cracked and rumbled so loudly that the birds began squawking in their aviary. The lights flickered.

Lori climbed to her feet. The leashes in her lap slid to the floor, landing with brassy thuds against the tile. She crossed the center aisle to stand beside the customer at the small animal enclosures and put on a smile. "Can I help you with something?" she asked.

"Um, yeah. Can I see the rats?"

"Sure." She was relieved. She liked most of the animals in the store well enough, but the rats were her favorite. She always looked forward to the chance to visit with them under any pretense, especially since Mr. Haskins was always riding her about spending too much time playing around instead of working. Then again, she was the one trying to make a sale while he smoked and watched the clock, so she figured he didn't have much room to complain about anything she did.

She knelt beside the display and unlocked the cover, which allowed the cage itself to be rolled out like a drawer. The drawer was made from glass with a wire-mesh lid mounted on a wooden frame. She unsnapped the lid, opened it up, and lifted up the purple igloo-shaped nest box to reveal a furry pile of sleeping rats: black, fawn, white, and gray fur all blurred together like one strange, giant patchwork rodent. "Was there one you wanted in particular?"

The customer knelt beside her, peering over the lip of the container and down at them. "Are any of them boys?"

"No." Lori reached in, brushing her fingertips over the rump of one dark-furred rat, who froze in place under her hand, waggling her ears. "We only keep girls, so we don't run the risk of any pregnancies. And girls don't fight as much as boys do."

"Oh." He raised his hand as though planning to reach in to touch the rats as well, then apparently changed his mind and set his hand back on his thigh. "You don't breed your own?"

"We have a distributor up-state," Lori said. In one corner of the cage, the white one looked like she might try to jump out, so Lori swept a hand over to knock her gently away from the glass. "Some of ours are related, though. This one," she pointed to a white-and-black patched female, "is the mom to about half of these. All the little black ones, that cream-patched one, and this one with the brown-gray hood are all hers. We sold her to some people, but they brought her back a week later, demanding a refund because she was pregnant. Obviously they must have had her in a cage with a boy or something, there's no way she could get pregnant here."

But they had given the refund anyway, because Mr. Haskins wouldn't turn down a chance at a litter of free babies, especially considering how pretty the rat was. It had been a disappointment when most of her babies had turned out to be plain black berkshires.

"She looks sick."

Lori scooped her up, and was surprised at how light she was. She didn't squirm or attempt to get away, and she leaned against Lori's chest and groomed her face feebly with one paw. "You're right," Lori said, smoothing the fur on her side. "That's odd. She was alright this morning."

The customer's eyes narrowed and he started to stand up. "That one's sick, too," he said, pointing to one of the little black rats. Unlike her sisters, this one—who had a white dot on her forehead, between her eyes—had not scattered when the igloo had been moved, and instead sat hunched-over and taking deep, heaving breaths. "She's bleeding out her nose."

"No, she's not," Lori said, patiently. "That's just porphyrin. It makes their mucous look pink or red, but it's harmless."

She didn't know how many times she'd explained that to customers in the year she'd worked at the pet store. All the same questions came up often enough that she could almost answer them before they were even asked. "She's always been kind of sniffly. Some rats get chronic respiratory infections on and off throughout their lives. She won't get the other rats sick."

He looked unconvinced, and Lori was starting to feel both defensive and embarrassed. She wished Mr. Haskins would come over to make the sale. She'd always hated the selling part of her job, and it was even worse when the animals seemed to be in such poor shape.

Another clap of thunder rattled the roof, and a parrot squawked loudly in dismay.

"Did you still want me to get a rat for you?"

He looked back into the cage. "Um. What's the story with the patchy one?"

"Oh, that one? She's my favorite. Here, watch." Still cradling the sick rat in the crook of her arm, Lori reached into her shirt pocket, where she kept treats to give to the dogs that sometimes came into the store with their owners. She broke the corner off of one of these biscuits with one hand and then reached into the cage, holding it between her forefingers. "You want a cookie?" she asked, in the voice people use with small children.

The rat—who looked identical to her mother, except that her patches were cream-colored and she was nearly three times as fat—rose up on her hind legs, sniffing at the treat. Then she grabbed it with her teeth, dropped back to her paws, and scurried into the back corner of the cage. She ate with a gluttonous expression, her eyes boggling in her head as her jaw muscles worked. Her ears waggled.

The customer laughed. "Okay, that's pretty cute. I guess I'll take that one, then."

"Alright." Lori tried to hide the disappointment in her voice. She really was very fond of her, and had often considered buying her herself—if only her mom would allow it. Her mother had never approved of animals in the house, and would certainly never accept a pet rat. As far as her mother was concerned, animals belonged in barns, and rats belonged in traps.

But it wasn't so bad. Lori could spend plenty of time with the animals here. And in just a few weeks, Lori would be moving into a dorm room and then she could easily sneak in a caged pet. Who would ever notice?

She lifted the rat from her elbow and set her down inside the cage by the water bottle. "Here. Keep an eye on them, I'll get the adoption paperwork. And watch out for the white one, she's always trying to climb out."

"…Adoption paperwork?"

"Well, yeah. Just a little contract saying you won't use the rat as snake food or anything. We don't do live feeding here anymore."

"Anymore?"

"I've never thought it was a good idea. But we made it store policy a few months ago. That rat there," she pointed back at the cage at a very large white rat with a caramel-colored hood over her head and chest, "somebody bought her to feed to their snake. But she was too big, the snake wouldn't eat her, and she ended up attacking the snake and hurting it pretty bad. The customer came back and threw a huge fit over it and returned her."

She realized, sometime during the story, that Mr. Haskins would probably not approve of her telling all of this, but it was too late to stop.

"But there's not a lot we can do with her. She's kind of a monster, she won't let anybody touch her at all. Anyway. That's what the paperwork is for. So that if you do decide to try and feed your rat to something, we're not responsible for what happens. But, um…please don't do that."

His expression was inscrutable. Lori really wasn't doing so well. She glanced once toward the door, noticing that Mr. Haskins had disappeared—probably into his office—and breathed a sigh of relief. At least he wasn't listening to her botch this sale.

"I'll be just a second." She walked to the back of the display and opened up the door. The display was encased in a movable shelving unit, and inside there was a small storage space where they kept paperwork and extra bits of bedding and food that didn't make it back to the stock room. One side of the display had rats, hamsters, and gerbils. The other side had guinea pigs, mice, and the occasional chinchilla, although more often than not that cage was empty as they were pricier than Mr. Haskins liked.

Lori dug around in a stack of papers, trying to find the rat information packet and adoption agreement she was supposed to make every buyer sign.

"Ow! What the hell?"

Outside—Lori could just make him out, heavily distorted, through the glass of the gerbil cage—the customer reeled back from the unit. He had a finger in his mouth.

"Sorry!" Lori yelled and, flustered, dropped all of her papers. She rushed out. "Are you okay? What happened?"

"It bit me!"

The customer withdrew his finger from his mouth, looking down at it. Blood beaded up at the edge of the torn skin on his first knuckle.

"Are you okay?" Lori repeated. "How bad did she get you? It wasn't the patched one, was it? She never bites."

"No, it was the other one, that brownish gray one," he said. "She's vicious! Vicious rats, sick rats, adoption paperwork, what a fucking joke." He huffed, put his knuckle back into his mouth, and stormed out the front door.

"…That could have gone better," Lori said to herself, watching hopelessly after him. She caught the white one in her peripheral vision trying once again to make a break out of the cage, and she nudged her back inside. Doing a quick check for errant paws or tails, she closed the top of the cage and slid it all back into the unit, locking it up behind her.

"I can't be having the livestock biting customers," Mr. Haskins said.

Lori jumped. She hadn't realized that he was standing behind her, and she dropped her keys in surprise. She bent down to pick them up again. "Sorry, sir," she mumbled. "I didn't think…"

"Don't leave customers alone with the animals," he said. "They always do something stupid and then it's my insurance claim to make. Now, come on. Help me close up."

Lori peered around the corner of the animal exhibit to look outside. Through the glass door she could just make out the gray vacant parking lot, the empty street and, beyond it, the horizon—also gray. "Is it time already?"

"It is today," Mr. Haskins said, placing a hand in the small of her back. His fingertips lingered there a moment and then he withdrew his touch, replacing his hand in his pocket. "We're closing up early. Just heard on the radio, this storm's going to be a bitch. They're forecasting hail and rain all night. Flash flooding, too."

"Oh. Okay." She shifted away from his touch and bit her lower lip as she ran through her mental checklist of everything she was supposed to do before they closed. "Just let me change out the food right quick—"

"No time. Come on. Nobody's going to starve missing dinner for one night."

"Well, alright, but the black-and-white one is sick, and that little black one seems to be getting worse…"

"We'll deal with it tomorrow," he said, firmly. Outside, as though to accent his point, the first hailstones began to fall. They pounded against the cement and gathered in small piles in the parking lot. The roof rattled with the wind. "And you're not riding your bike home," Mr. Haskins said, before Lori could say anything. "Now go grab your backpack. I'll give you a ride."

"It's just a few blocks," she said. She bounced on the balls of her feet, forming her hands into fists and then relaxing them.

"In case you didn't notice, it's hailing outside." His bushy gray eyebrows rose up toward his receding salt-and-pepper hairline. "I have a bike rack."

She bit her lower lip, then said, reluctantly, "Okay. I'll just be a second."

She turned for the break room—really a glorified broom closet with a couple of lockers and a microwave—and Mr. Haskins waited for her. The hail fell harder and faster, pounding down onto the roof, mingling with fat drops of rain. When Lori returned, they both pulled their coats up over their heads and ran outside. Despite her coat, Lori's shirt was still soaked through by the time she made it into his passenger seat, and she sat uncomfortably with her arms over her chest, painfully aware of the transparency of the cotton work shirt. She realized, too late, that she'd forgotten to load her bike, but it was too late to go get it now: Mr. Haskins was already starting to back up.

The car pulled away from the lot and splashed through a puddle.

Behind them, the door—which, in his rush, Bob Haskins had neither locked nor latched properly—rattled on its hinges, and finally swung open.

Chapter Two

Outside, the rain fell in fast, piercing blades, as though the heavens had opened up and spilled a thousand tiny glittering knives toward the earth. Droplets didn't hit the asphalt: they exploded upon impact, shattering like glass. The few unlucky folk who had been caught outside would swear, later, that it was sleeting; but it wasn't sleet that fell, only an uncharacteristically aggressive pelting rain, as though the clouds sought to wreak vengeance upon humanity for some unspoken wrong-doing. The wind, too, seemed part of the conspiracy, tearing through trees and howling between buildings with mounting ferocity. Tree limbs snapped beneath the strain of the wind. Already, the gutters filled with rainwater; sewers overflowed, backing up into streets and basements; mud and debris swirled and combined and crept toward the streets with ominous inevitability. The promise of devastation lurked in every clap of thunder, and still the storm had not truly broken.

Inside, the animals of Rocco's Pet Emporium knew nothing about the weather—and yet, they still felt a creeping agitation, like mites burrowed beneath the skin, a restlessness that spread through them and made the already-small confines of their display seem maddeningly cramped.

Rats, being a burrowing animal, experience claustrophobia differently from humans. The terror of confinement for a rodent is not the tight space or the pressure of a nearby body; the terror is knowing there is nowhere to run to. In the wild, rat colonies build their tunnels with multiple side-exits so that, in the event of disaster, there is always at least one way out. Here, far removed from nature by circumstance and years of selective breeding, the so-called "fancy" rats still felt that instinctive desire to run—to bolt—and realized there was nowhere to bolt to.

Instead, they huddled together, drawing comfort from the proximity of other bodies. If there was nowhere to run to, at least they could face this unknown fear together. Strength in numbers. That, above all, is the guiding principle of rat-kind; notions of individualism play a minor role beside the greater good and—more importantly—the security of the crowd. A lone rat is exposed, and an exposed rat is, almost always, a dead one.

"You shouldn't have bitten that Great One's hand," Top Ear said, for what must have been the hundredth time that night. She and her twin, Dumbo, were indistinguishable except for the placement of her ears; while Dumbo's were large and set low on her skull like their mother's, Top Ear's sat atop her head.

"I thought you were sleeping," Bitey said, irritably.

"I mean it, Bitey," Top Ear pressed. "You can't be biting hands. You saw what happened. The Great Ones went away without taking any of us with them."

"And we didn't get fed dinner, either," Dumbo pointed out.

"Quite right. We didn't. And now both Mother and Sniffles are sick; they shouldn't be missing meals."

"What do you want me to say, Top Ear?" Bitey felt the fur along her shoulders begin to raise in annoyance. "It happened. I won't do it again."

"You will, though," Top Ear insisted. "You spend too much time with Monster. You'll never find a home with the Great Ones and if you keep this up, none of us will either. She's insane, Bitey. You have to accept that whatever happened to her before, it's driven her mad, and if you decide to waste your life following in the footsteps of a lunatic—"

"I don't want to get into this." Bitey rose deliberately to her paws and headed toward the mouth of the nest box. "I'm going to go check on Mother."

Truthfully, Bitey didn't know why she had bitten the hand—or why she had ever bitten other hands—or why she was always so quick to defend Monster. She had been raised by her mother, Nezumi, to believe the same things as all of her other siblings: the Great Ones were their providers and saviors; pleasing the Great Ones brought rewards of good food and soft touches; all rats should aspire to one day be taken by the hands into the Beyond, from where no rat had returned.

Well…no rat aside from Nezumi. And Monster.

"What's up?"

The voice broke her thoughts, and she froze for a moment, ears laid back as though confronted by *ushu*, before she recognized the voice. "Oh, hey White One."

White One was perched atop the nest box, seated back upon her haunches, her head inclined toward the wire mesh ceiling of their enclosure. Her whiskers periodically swept the ceiling, as though investigating it for a hitherto undiscovered weakness, but her ears were clearly trained on Bitey. "You're distracted by something. Do you feel it, too?"

"Yes. I don't know what it is, but I don't like it. Feels funny, like dirt on your whiskers." She sat back onto her haunches and groomed herself, reflexively. The idea of dirty whiskers was unbearable even to think about. "Even Sniffles feels it. Nobody can sleep."

White One lowered herself to all fours, directing her attention to the corner of the cage by the water bottle. On one side of the bottle, Cookie was munching at what was left of the dog biscuit Soft Hands had given her, eyes boggling in delight. On the other side, Nezumi had pressed her thin piebald form against the glass and was staring glassy-eyed at nothing in particular.

"She's not doing very well," White One said, gesturing with her nose.

Bitey swept her whiskers forward and back and dropped down to all fours once more. "I know. I was planning to check on her. Squeaker said she would come, later this evening, once Sniffles settles down."

Squeaker was what the rats called a *nosobo*, or a nurse-rat. Literally the word meant "one who licks and touches the wounded" but there was more to it than that. Any rat can clean the wounds of another, but a true *nosobo* has restorative powers, the ability to soothe pain and even bring rats back from the edge of death.

"Might be a while, though. You want to come with me?"

White One flicked an ear, but said nothing.

Bitey sighed. White One was a strange rat. She wasn't unfriendly, precisely—and certainly not as antisocial as the likes of Monster—but she was aloof. Her pale fur and red eyes made her stand out from the others, but not as much as her constant nervous energy did.

"All right," she said, at length. "I'll come, if you'd like."

They made their way across the cage to the water bottle. Opposite the bottle, pressed against the rear wall, Monster and Smeeze spoke together in low voices. Bitey turned an ear toward them, but she couldn't make out what they said, and they fell silent as she walked past them. She wondered if they were talking about her. Smeeze, catching Bitey's eye, looked away suddenly and interested herself in digging into the bedding.

"White One…you're always trying to get out in the Beyond," Bitey said, hesitantly. "Without the Great Ones."

"I am," she agreed, without adding any further comment.

"Didn't you even manage to escape once?"

"For a few minutes. I didn't see anything, though, if you were wondering. Just Soft Hands dropping me back into the cage."

"Oh."

Silence feel between them for an awkward moment. Bitey started again.

"Do you…do you ever want to bite the hands?" Bitey asked, and then winced, wishing she hadn't said anything. It sounded so much worse when she said it aloud.

"Not usually," White One said, and smiled, her whiskers twitching. "But I don't think any less of you, if you're concerned about that."

Bitey laughed. "It wasn't really your opinion I was worried about. But thanks." She paused, a few inches from her mother, and peered sidelong at White One. Somehow, it felt safe to confide in the pale little rat—as though nothing she said to White One really counted. "I just…when the hands come, something inside of me tells me that…that they're not welcome. That they're intruding." She cast an uneasy glance back at Monster and Smeeze. "Monster says that the Beyond is a lie, that the Great Ones only take us to…to hurt us. But I don't know if that's quite right, either." She dropped her voice. "It's like…it's like they're just animals. The same as you and me."

"That's blasphemy," White One said, matter-of-factly.

"It's the Spirits." Nezumi's voice—a little unsteady, but still as lyrical as it had ever been— broke through their discussion. She struggled to her paws.

"What?" Bitey trained her ears and whiskers on her mother.

"In your head. Making you question. It's the Spirits. They play tricks, sometimes."

Nezumi smiled, and walked a few steps in an awkward, tottering gait to the nozzle of the water bottle. She touched it with her nose, and a droplet of water beaded up and dropped, splashing against her forepaw. She stared at this for a moment, then rasped her tongue against the nozzle, drinking in rapid, desperate gulps.

"I hear them, too," she said, after she'd finished. "They scratch in your brain like suckling *jask* and sometimes you can't make out what they say at all."

Bitey and White One exchanged a worried look.

Nezumi had never been entirely normal, by rat standards. She was an *usoothe*, or spirit-talker—a rat who could commune freely with the Spirit Realm. Rats believe that after death, a rat's consciousness is absorbed into a communal plane of knowledge, accessible to all but fully understood only by a select few. The Spirit Realm accounted for all the knowledge that rats had but could not explain as they had never actually been taught: knowledge of reproduction, of finding food, of enemies. The rats of Rocco's Pet Emporium had—except for Monster—never been face-to-face with an *ushu*, but all of them had an instinctual understanding that such things existed in the Beyond.

The Spirits told Nezumi about quite a bit more than *ushu*, however. She always knew things that rats should not know. When the Great Ones would open up the sky. Whether they would get carrots or lettuce as a treat. Once, a new shipment had come in while Nezumi's kits were very small, and the night before their arrival she had gathered her weanlings and explained how they should behave when the newcomers arrived.

Bitey remembered it clearly. She had stared in confusion at her mother, not understanding at all what she was talking about or how new rats could just materialize among them. And yet, the morning after, the new rats arrived. Bitey had befriended one, the same ruby-eyed Siamese that Monster had adopted as a daughter. Smeeze was the last of the shipment to remain, due in part to her tendency to lunge and bite.

"I don't think the Spirits talk to me quite the same, Mother," Bitey said, gently. "I'm not an *usoothe* like you."

Nezumi withdrew from the water bottle and cast her daughter a grave look. "You'd be surprised what the Spirits will do," she said. Her eyes were heavily crusted with porphyrin and her fur stood up along her body in ragged clumps. She clearly had not been grooming herself. "They told me a terrible thing was coming," she said. "But they won't say what it is. The words they use don't make any sense."

Bitey glanced back at White One. White One scratched her ear with one hindpaw.

"A terrible thing?" Bitey crept forward a few steps, extending her nose to sniff at her mother's side. She could smell no disease upon her, but she was hardly a *nosobo*. "I think you're sick, Mother."

"She was fine before the Great One got hold of her," Monster said. She crossed the cage to the water bottle, shifting around Nezumi in her path. Monster walked with a swagger, her haunches held high and tail aloft behind her. "You saw that as well as I did, Bitey. Whatever's wrong with her, the Great Ones did it."

"No they didn't!" Cookie said, dropping the last crumbs of what she had been eating. Her ears swept back, indignantly. "The hands don't do bad things like that."

"Just because they're fattening you up," Monster said, coldly. She took a long, rattling drink from the water bottle. The ensuing clatter drowned out any attempts at conversation until she was finished. "I'm sure the snake will appreciate their efforts."

Monster was always talking about the snake. Bitey didn't know exactly what a snake was, but she knew it was *ushu*—a great enemy, or predator. The word Monster used specifically was *ushuzu-sim*, which meant something like "crawling death-bringer." The image that conjured wasn't pleasant.

Cookie grumbled in displeasure but said nothing. She shoved the last bit of food into her mouth and bounded away to the other side of the cage, clearly eager to put some distance between herself and Monster. Of all Nezumi's children, only Bitey was unafraid of the surly old female—and her choice to listen to Monster's opinions about the world had been a source of ample fights between her and her sisters.

Bitey looked back at Nezumi, who lay once more on her side, her eyes open and staring at nothing. "Mother…Is that true? Did the Great One make you sick?"

"When the hands touch me, I can almost see it," she said, and then she smiled. For a moment, her expression cleared, and she gave Bitey a lucid, piercing look. She struggled to sit up, but fell back into the bedding, looking exhausted. "Cookie was going to be *churzu* today," she said. *Churzu*, or "gone above," was the Ratspeak word for being adopted, or taken by the hands into the Beyond, never to return. "Before you bit the hand."

Bitey looked away, pawing at the bedding. "I don't know why I did that," she said. "I didn't want to do it. I can't help it…"

"It's the Spirits," Nezumi repeated, and her eyes were clear and bright. If she was taken by some sickness-induced madness, it was impossible to tell: she looked as lucid and intelligent as she ever had. "Cookie was not meant to go Beyond today. She has a part to play in what is to come."

"What *is* to come?" White One asked. Bitey jerked; she had forgotten that White One was still with them, as she had been so silent until now. The pink-eyed-white rat took a few steps closer to Nezumi, brushing her whiskers over the *usoothe's* haunch. "You said they showed you a terrible thing, and Cookie is part of it? What have you seen?"

Nezumi said nothing further, however, and the lucidity in her eyes faded. She lay on her side, looking thin and tired, and Bitey moved to lay beside her. She rested her chin atop her mother's bony shoulders and licked at the back of her ears.

"Careful," Monster warned. Her voice was cold and it made Bitey's fur bristle. "You might catch whatever curse the hands put on her."

"If it's contagious, I'm sure we all have it already." Squeaker had emerged from the igloo and now made her way across the cage in her usual halting, fidgeting gait. "Sorry I've taken so long, Bitey, your sister was having a terrible wheezing fit. She's better now, I think. Sleeping, anyway."

Bitey lifted her chin from between her mother's shoulders. Nezumi's eyes were half-closed now and though her breathing was still quite normal, her tail had begun to go cold.

"It's bad," Bitey said, and her ears folded back to her head as she said it. She was suddenly aware of how many eyes were upon her, and she rose to her paws, withdrawing from her mother's side to allow the *nosobo* plenty of room to examine Nezumi. "Do you think the Great Ones could have done this?"

Squeaker laid her paws on Nezumi's side, sniffing her over thoroughly, her whiskers twitching. "I don't know," she said. "The Great Ones can do many things, good and bad. Who are we to say what is or isn't possible?"

Bitey shifted from paw to paw, unbearably restless. Somewhere in the Beyond, that rattling noise was growing louder and more insistent and Bitey wished she could go out and see what the sound was. White One, apparently also struck by the same restlessness, withdrew from the others and crossed back over the cage, passing the igloo to jump instead onto the wheel. White One was one of the only rats who liked to run on it—her and Top Ear both said it helped them think.

"Go rest," Squeaker said, lifting her eyes to Bitey. "I'll call for you if anything changes."

She hesitated, glancing across the cage to the igloo. She didn't want to go back in there and deal with any more of Top Ear's lecturing. She took a tentative step forward, changed her mind, and instead walked to the rear corner of the cage. She pressed herself against the glass, cocking an ear toward what little sound she could make out through the walls of the cage, and tried to sleep.

* * *

Sleep did not come easily to Bitey. Just as she began to nod off, some small noise would catch her thoughts, amplified by the heightened senses that come at the edge of sleep. The wheel squeaked. Sniffles had a sneezing fit. Someone drank in loud rattling sips from the water bottle. With each noise she jerked, casting bleary eyes about for the source of the disturbance, and then fall uneasily back into slumber.

When she did sleep, she dreamed. Odd half-formed snatches of images and voices flickered through her mind, old conversations dredged up from childhood, playing over and over yet feeling somehow ominous. She ran on a wheel. It squeaked and creaked under her paws and though she tried to get off, she couldn't stop running. Everywhere, rats were talking, a dozen, a thousand, their voices all too jumbled to make out. Then everyone was silent, and the wheel was gone but Bitey was still running, running through darkness, suspended in time. Beside her, Nezumi ran as well—Nezumi as she had never known her, young and sleek-furred and playful. "You'll need to ask them for help," Nezumi said, conversationally. "When the time comes."

Because it was a dream, Bitey said, "But why will they help me?"

Nezumi didn't answer, but instead bounded forward. She was on a wheel again—both of them were, Bitey running inside and Nezumi running, desperately, to stay on top. Bitey tried to stop running but her paws wouldn't listen to her, and

Nezumi, unable to keep up with the pace, stumbled. The wheel swept her underneath, pinning her, and she screamed, a blood-curdling scream that shook Bitey's thoughts.

She jolted awake and realized that her mother was still screaming.

Confused, half-asleep, heart thudding in her chest, Bitey scrambled to her paws and bounded across the cage. From the other end, Top Ear and Dumbo scurried out from the nest box. Sniffles followed behind, looking bleary-eyed and miserable; porphyrin dripped from her nostrils.

Nezumi continued to scream.

She thrashed, throwing herself headlong at the glass. Squeaker tried to stop her, but Nezumi kicked out at her, forcing her back. She charged, again, for the glass, and hit with a hard thud, reeling back. She clawed at it, desperately. "Out!" she cried. Her eyes rolled in her head. "We have to get out! It's coming!"

"Mother!" Bitey yelled. Everyone froze, staring in shock, as Bitey tore herself away from the crowd to thrust herself between Nezumi and the glass. "Mother, stop it! You're hurting yourself."

Nezumi's nails, torn loose from the nailbed, oozed blood onto her white paws. Her head tilted to one side, and her eye bulged. Burst blood vessels clouded the lens, the pupil grown nearly to the size of the eyeball itself. She looked crazed, and she hissed and threw herself once more at the glass.

Bitey grabbed her scruff between her teeth and tugged her back, but Nezumi rounded on her, sinking her incisors into Bitey's shoulder. Bitey yelped in pain as her blood pooled around her mother's teeth and dribbled down her chin.

This roused the others into action. Smeeze leaped forward,

taking Nezumi's other shoulder, and between the two of them they managed to muscle her away from the glass. Smeeze forced Nezumi down, planting her forepaws on either side of the rat's bony chest, and she lifted her eyes to meet Bitey's, casting her a questioning look.

"We have to get out!" Nezumi said, again, and with surprising vitality she squirmed free of Smeeze's hold and made another desperate bid for the glass wall of the tank. "Before the Big Water!"

Bitey jumped, trying to head her off before impact, but received another bite, and she reeled back. Nezumi, too, sprawled on her side, thrashing her legs and tail. In the chaos, someone collided with the water bottle and it broke free of the casing that held it against the wall. It crashed against the floor, kicking up a fine dust of bedding, and water poured out in waves. Bitey struggled to her paws, her side soaked from the sudden onslaught of water, her chest stained from her wound and the blood from her mother's claws.

Nezumi lay unresponsive on her side, her bulging eye fixed and glaring, jaws slightly agape and teeth stained with blood.

Bitey didn't need to be a *nosobo* to see that she was dead.

Chapter Three

Across town, Lori sat cross-legged on her bed, watching the rain beat against the windowpane. Dawn had come and gone, but the sky was still a deep velvety black. It had been raining on and off throughout the night, but sometime after four it had begun to really come down. Now, at six, the rain increased in its intensity, pouring from the sky in heavy sheets that crashed against the earth like breaking waves. The gutters overflowed; rivulets ran across the streets, trash swirling in the rapid flash-flood current. There was no more earth-shaking thunder, no more brilliant lightning coloring the sky—only rain, a constant torrential downpour that showed no signs of relenting.

She'd called Mr. Haskins to see if he wanted her to come in. He hadn't sounded very happy about being woken up.

"I'm not going anywhere in this rain," he'd said, sounding groggy.

"But the animals," Lori had insisted. "They didn't get fed last night...I could just swing by your house to get the keys..."

"They'll be fine. We feed them too much anyway."

She tried to push the issue, but it was pointless. She wouldn't be able to go out today, anyway, not with her bike still chained out in front of the store and the rain pooling in the streets.

She had considered sneaking out, before her mother woke, to borrow the car, but that would cause even more trouble. Though she'd completed her driver's education class almost a year ago, her mother was always too busy to oversee the mandatory practice hours that were required for her full license. If she got caught driving by herself, any chance of getting a license before college was long gone.

I'll wait a few more hours, she decided, watching miserably as the rain sheeted down past her bedroom window. She could hear her mother's snores, faintly, through her room's thin wall. If the rain lets up by noon, I'll have Mom drive me to the store so I can feed the animals.

That made her feel a little better. Now all she could do was wait and hope the storm wouldn't get any worse.

* * *

Inside of Rocco's Pet Emporium, the first leak had started. The ceiling above the aviary had begun to crack, a thin hairline fracture of drywall that grew dark with the moisture that gathered behind it. Droplets escaped, slowly at first, but gaining momentum until a puddle formed just in front of the aviary. Water gathered in the parking lot and flowed slowly toward the center, pulled into tiny rivers by gravity. One of these made a deliberate, meandering course for the door, which stood open, creaking uselessly against the wind.

* * *

"Nobody is blaming you, Bitey." Smeeze nudged her friend on the shoulder with her chocolate-smudged nose, her ruby eyes gleaming with sympathy. "Things like this happen all the time. It's just bad luck."

"Bad luck," Bitey echoed and laughed a barking humorless laugh.

The last few hours of night seemed to stretch on forever. The rats mostly huddled together in the rearmost corner by the wheel, as far from the corpse and the soaked bedding as they could get. Top Ear and Dumbo pressed into the corner of the cage with two of their sisters. Sniffles was inconsolable. She buried her nose into Cookie's side, staining her sister's pale patched fur with rust-colored porphyrin. Squeaker pressed against her other side, head rested atop Sniffles's shoulders, silent—an interloper to the family grief.

Yet Squeaker was more at place there than Bitey was.

Twelve inches away, in the opposite corner of the cage, Bitey curled into a tight ball, head tucked under her chest. She trembled. Smeeze had been sitting by her side for at least an hour now, talking steadily, but the mink-hooded rat refused to look up at her.

White One lay curled atop the igloo. She could have been asleep, except for her open eyes and the calculating look on her face. Occasionally she would run a paw over her whiskers, or nibble at her flank, but otherwise she had been perfectly still and contemplative all night.

Monster stopped her pacing. She alone had dared venture across the cage where Nezumi's body now lay—empty eye staring in eternal terror at the ceiling—and she had not lingered long before shuffling back across the cage, where she had taken to walking from one wall to the opposite, wearing a small path into the bedding.

"Nezumi and I had our disagreements about the Great ones,"

she said, gently—and this, the uncharacteristic softness in her voice, pierced through Bitey like teeth. "But I never wished this upon you. I'm sorry."

Bitey shifted her weight away from Monster's voice; she had no words. She felt, irrationally, insanely, that she should have prepared for this, memorized a speech, rehearsed her emotions. She wondered why the Spirits had never come to her in her dreams to teach her how to handle this—why they had wasted their time making her bite the hands when she could have been shown the clear, unobstructed path through this treacherous emotional terrain.

"I hate to interrupt," White One said from her perch atop the igloo. Her voice was soft, but in the funereal atmosphere of the cage it seemed both piercing and out of place in its frankness. "But breakfast is past due."

Bitey lifted her head to glare at White One. She might have expected such callousness from Cookie—maybe even Dumbo—but from White One, it was insulting. How could White One possibly be thinking of food at a time like this?

White One squeaked in alarm. "Oh, no, I didn't mean…I'm not complaining that I'm hungry," she said, her tone both exasperated and embarrassed. "What I mean is…the sky should have opened by now. The Great Ones are late."

"The Great Ones can't be late," Cookie said, indignantly. "They're…they're…"

"Infallible?" Squeaker suggested. She was always using strange words that the others believed were made up on the spot.

"Yes. That. They don't make mistakes. They own the Beyond."

"Maybe it isn't a mistake," Top Ear said, lowering herself back down to her haunches. Her voice held an undercurrent of a growl, a dark sullen tone that swept over her entire demeanor. She cast a cold look at Bitey, then swept her eyes past her to Nezumi's cold body across the cage.

"They can't have abandoned us?" Cookie said. She ran her paws over her face and whiskers, clearly distressed at the idea. "What would they do that for?"

"First we miss dinner," Dumbo said. "And now, breakfast. We've never missed two meals in a row. Ever."

"I wonder whose fault that could be," Top Ear growled.

"Hey!" Smeeze whirled around on her paws, fur on end. "Careful where you're flinging accusations!"

Bitey rose wearily to her paws. Her bones ached. The corners of her eyes were crusted in porphyrin from grief and exhaustion. "Even if it is all because of me," she said, feeling suddenly as though she were a hundred lifetimes old. "Why now? It's not like Soft Hands hasn't been bitten before. Monster bites all the time. And Smeeze. It's not just me."

"It was a different hand this time," Cookie said. "Not Soft Hands. Maybe that's why."

Top Ear had left her spot to come closer to her mink-furred sister, aggressively pushing into her face. Anger seemed to radiate off her. "Squeaker told me what Mother said. That Cookie was meant to be *churzu* before you messed it all up. She would have gone away with that hand if you'd just kept your teeth to yourself!"

Nose to nose, Bitey could just feel the tip of her sister's whiskers against her own. Her fur rose and she stiffened, baring her teeth in warning.

"Are you going to fight me?" Top Ear taunted. "You want to do to us what you did to Mom?"

Bitey lunged before she knew what came over her.

They tumbled in a frenzied ball of fur and paws and tails. The fight was quick and brutal, the way rat fights always are. Bitey screamed, a wordless expression of rage, and forced Top Ear down on her back. Her own flanks were bleeding now from dual bites on either side of her hips, and the ache in her haunch met with the ache in her shoulder. She wondered how many times her skin would be broken today by the teeth of her own family.

Beneath her paws, Top Ear squirmed and hissed a long stream of obscenities, most of which she seemed to make up on the spot. Dumbo bounded forward to rescue her twin, but was stopped abruptly in her tracks. Monster sidled up to Bitey, blocking Dumbo's approach. Bitey was a large rat, but Monster was twice her age and easily double her size. She displaced her with one smooth push of the shoulder, and stood between the siblings, casting a warning look from each ruby-colored eye. "Enough. All of you."

"You're not our *Usim-li*," Dumbo muttered, mutinously. "You're not our alpha."

"Your alpha is dead," Monster said, bluntly. "Either someone needs to step up, or this colony will be ripped apart."

"We're not following you," Top Ear said, rolling to her paws. She limped back to Dumbo's side.

White One had not moved from her place atop the igloo. Now, as the uncomfortable silence spread between the sisters, she spoke up. "Look. I know everybody's scared and upset right now, and I appreciate that you need time to grieve. But the fact is, Nezumi's dead and the Great Ones aren't coming. The water bottle is empty. We have no food. And we're all trapped here."

"Very encouraging, White One," Smeeze muttered. She bumped her nose into Bitey's side and Bitey sighed, leaning back against her.

"Alright. So we're trapped," Top Ear said. "What do you propose to do about it?"

White One ran her paws over her face. Her whiskers twitched forward, back, forward once more, and her ears flicked. Then she said, "...I think I found a way out of the cage."

Chapter Four

"So. I guess now we're all blasphemers," Bitey said, in an attempt to lighten the mood. She, Smeeze, Monster and White One had retreated to the far corner of the cage—giving a wide berth to the soaked-through circle of bedding and Nezumi's body—and they huddled together. Bitey's sisters and Squeaker had retreated back into the nest box. *If this doesn't work,* Bitey mused, *there will be two new colonies, rather than one.*

She didn't welcome the thought. The idea of two *usimli* sharing such a small territory was madness; they'd fight constantly. Still, she couldn't shake the image from her head, of herself nosing off against Top Ear—who, she assumed, would be alpha of the opposing group.

Her daydream flattered her, however. If any rat alive was an alpha, it was Monster. After all, she was the biggest, the strongest, and the only rat left alive in this world who had ever seen the Beyond. Bitey turned her eyes toward the huge fawn-hooded female, seeking comfort, guidance, answers—anything to validate her faith in the older rat, to prove she hadn't been a fool for standing by her.

"It's hopeless," Monster said. "There's nothing for us in the Beyond. It's their world, and it's full of pain and *ushu.* Even if it were possible to escape, there would be no point. We'd die within a matter of days."

That was not the encouragement Bitey had been hoping for.

"So what do you suggest?" White One asked. Her tone wasn't aggressive. Indeed, it was respectful—almost reverent. Bitey thought she too had cast her vote for new alpha. "A colony can't last without food or water, Great Ones or not."

Monster's tail thrashed, but she said nothing.

"Look. I'm not saying we have to stay out there. We'll send out just…one or two. A…" she cast about for the word, "a scouting party. Whatever we find, we bring back here, to the colony."

Monster nibbled at the wrist of her forepaw. Her ears flicked. "If you have willing volunteers," she said, in a voice hardly above a whisper, "I won't stop you."

White One, apparently appeased, turned eager eyes to Bitey and Smeeze. "Well?" she demanded. "Are you in?"

Bitey cast Smeeze a sidelong look, and the Siamese-pointed rat rose to her paws. "I am," she said. "…And, Bitey. Come on, before we try it. I want to show you something."

Bitey's ears flicked. She trailed after her, a tail's length behind. What could Smeeze possibly have to show her? They'd lived together in this cage their entire lives. Bitey was quite certain that she knew every inch of it. There just wasn't much room for secrecy or surprises in a two-foot by three-foot universe.

"Here. Look."

Bitey swept out her whiskers, casting a glance around. "What?"

Smeeze sighed. "You're standing on it. Look down."

Puzzled, Bitey peered below her paws, finding—after a

moment of hard searching—a small dark-colored patch in the bedding. She sniffed it. "What is this?"

"Blood," Smeeze said, triumphantly. "It dripped from the finger of that Great One's hand, when you bit it." She stared at the others, then snorted in annoyance. "Bitey, don't you see what this means? The Great Ones, they bleed. Like us. Like animals. You were right all along."

"Well." White One nudged Bitey's flank—which was beginning to scab over from the fight but still stung terribly—as she passed. "That's plenty of evidence for me. Now let's go. I'm getting thirsty."

Bitey ran her tongue over the dried blood. All her life, she had suspected the Great Ones of being animals. Giant, powerful animals, and residents of another world…but animals, all the same. Now, faced with powerful evidence, she hoped she was wrong. If everything Monster said was true—if there were really *ushu* everywhere in the Beyond—then the Great Ones must be the worst of them all. *Even greater than the ushuzu-sim,* she thought, and she shivered, halting her steps.

She had never seen a snake herself, but she'd heard the story at least a hundred times. The eyes, the great hypnotic eyes that stared unwavering into the hearts of its victims; the muscled, coiling body that stretched forever into infinity; the long, sharp, plunging teeth. *Nothing could possibly be worse than that,* she thought.

Nothing—except for the very masters of the Beyond.

Realizing that the others had gone on ahead, Bitey tore herself away from the drop of dried blood, forcing the thought from her mind. She had dealt with the Great Ones every day of her life—until today—and though she had often had the urge to bite them, to chase them away from her territory, she had no reason to think that they were particularly dangerous. Besides, Nezumi had never talked about *ushu* from her time in the Beyond. Then, Nezumi had never talked about a lot of things. Who the father of her litter was, for example, or why she had been sent back.

"Bitey?" Smeezed asked, from a tail's length ahead. "You coming?"

Bitey shook herself all over. "Yes." She took a deep, steadying breath and bounded forward a few steps to catch up with the others. White One was once more at her usual place atop the igloo, standing on her hindpaws and sniffing at the wire ceiling of the cage. Inside the igloo, Bitey could just make out the dark shapes of her siblings and Squeaker huddled together. She paused, one paw raised, ears cocked forward listening for any sound—any indication that the others knew she was here—but no one said anything. She jumped up onto the igloo beside White One. "Well?"

"We have to go up there," White One said. Her whiskers swept forward and back, and she swayed slightly, unbalanced on her hindpaws, but she did not come down. "Do you see it? The hole in the wire?"

The ceiling of the cage was made of thin mesh wire stretched taut over a frame set on hinges so that it could be flipped open to allow access. Beyond the wire was a gap, barely two inches, between the top of the rat cage and the bottom of the cage above it—a gap to allow the cage to roll out easily from the unit. In the corner of the frame, just above their heads, a few staples had come loose and the wire sagged, slightly, revealing an open corner that led up into the dark crawlspace above.

"It's not very big," Bitey said, dubiously. She leaned forward and sniffed, but smelled nothing out of the ordinary. "Do you think we could get through it?"

"I think so," White One said. "Especially if we could just…" she trailed off, and rather than finish her thought she dropped for a moment back to her paws, coiled her muscles, and jumped.

Bitey squeaked in alarm and nearly tumbled off of the igloo. White One had disappeared!

No…that wasn't right. White One was still here—but she was hanging, upside down, from the wire of the cage ceiling. Bitey stared at her. Her muscles bulged with effort beneath her pale coat and she moved, paw-over-paw, to maneuver herself below the gap. She wrapped her jaws around the loose corner of the wire and tugged, straining to pull it free. It budged slightly, maybe a few centimeters, and White One let go of it and clung panting to the ceiling. Then, moving swiftly and determinedly, she set her paws on each side of the opening, pressed her nose through the gap, and squirmed up and out.

Bitey watched, shocked and confused, as White One's haunches wriggled, paws scrabbling against the wire mesh until her tail was the only thing visible and then that, too, was gone and White One had disappeared entirely, swallowed up by the sky.

Bitey gaped.

Below, Smeeze squeaked and scrambled up onto the top of the igloo, pressing close to Bitey. She was shivering. "Did the sky just eat her?" she asked, incredulous. "Did I just see that?"

"I'm fine, you guys." White One's voice came from nowhere and everywhere at once, and Bitey froze, flattening herself against the roof of the igloo, her fur standing on end. "But I appreciate your concern. Bitey, stand up, you look ridiculous."

Bitey's ears flicked, trying to pinpoint the source of the voice.

She could still smell White One, and that was the strangest part—that her scent would be so close, so prevalent, when the rat herself had disappeared from the world entirely. A disembodied voice and an insistent lingering odor.

"Bitey! Look." Smeeze nudged her, and she winced as her friend bumped into her wounded shoulder. "Look up."

The mink-hooded female tilted back her head, staring straight up, and for a moment she wasn't sure what she was looking at as her brain worked to process what her eyes were seeing. Then it came into focus, and she squeaked and rose up to her hindpaws, half defensively, half in shocked curiosity. "White One?" Above her, a few inches over Bitey's head, white fur poked through the fine mesh of the ceiling and pink toes curled over the wire. "How are you doing that?"

"I'm on top of the ceiling," White One said, patiently. "You can see me because there's gaps in the wire, but it's close enough together that it holds me up."

Bitey cast a bewildered look at Smeeze, who was staring dumbfounded at the ceiling. Below them, a black nose-tip poked out of the igloo opening, sniffed a few times, and then retreated back inside.

"You'd best come up here. I could try to explain all day and you won't understand until you try it for yourself."

"I'll stand guard," Smeeze said, immediately. She sneezed, a nervous tic, and made quite a show of cleaning her face.

Bitey huffed. She extended a forepaw up, over her head, but the ceiling was just out of her reach. She lowered herself back to all fours, trying to remember how White One had done it, and tensed the muscles in her haunches. They seized, painfully, from her wounded flanks, but she gritted her incisors together and jumped.

She caught hold of the wire in her forepaws and hung there, dangling, feeling the joints in her fingers popping from bearing too much weight. Her haunches writhed and swung almost of their own accord, tail spinning like a rotor in a desperate attempt to regain some sort of balance. Her paws slipped, and before she could try to catch herself she tumbled down and landed heavily on the floor next to the igloo. Bedding rose up in a small cloud around her.

"Bitey, are you okay?" Smeeze asked, peering over the edge of the igloo.

She snorted and rolled to her paws, giving herself a violent shake. Bits of aspen clung to her fur. "I'm fine," she said, jumping back onto the roof of the igloo.

"You have to move faster, to get your hind feet up there to help grip," White One instructed from above their heads. "You've only got a second, really. You have to use your momentum from the jump to carry your back end up."

"Easy enough for you to say," Bitey grumbled. "You hardly weigh anything. I'm too big to be playing at this."

But already the muscles in her haunch were tensing.

She jumped, again, and this time when she caught the wire she swung her tail up in a smooth arc. Her haunches followed and her hindpaws brushed the wire. She clawed for a foothold, managing to catch the wire with just two toes of one paw—but it was enough, and after a moment she was able to procure a firmer grip. The wire bit into her paws. Blood rushed to her head and she closed her eyes, warding off the sensation that the world had turned upside down and that any moment she would go tumbling endlessly into the sky.

"You're halfway there," White One said. The wire vibrated, slightly, and then Bitey felt warmth and fur pressing against her belly and she dared to open her eyes. White One poked her nose through the mesh, managing to just touch the fur at Bitey's throat. "Now you just have to crawl forward a few inches to get to the opening. One paw at a time. Come on."

Bitey realized she was shaking—with the effort of holding herself up, she amended hurriedly to herself. She was shaking because she greatly outweighed White One and because holding her body weight in this unnatural position with an injured shoulder and two torn flanks was difficult. That was the only reason.

Her whiskers brushed the opening, and she wrapped one paw around the lip of the loose wire as she had seen White One do. She edged forward, reaching her other forepaw through the gap, and realized she could grip it from the opposite side. She pushed her head through the opening, pulling herself forward with her forepaws, and cleared the wire with her shoulders. The scab of her wounded shoulder caught on the wire and tore open, and she cried out. Her hindpaws slipped and she dangled, held up only by two quivering forelimbs.

"White One, this is impossible!" She kicked, uselessly, with her back feet, but she had no way of regaining her hold on the wire. Her shoulder burned.

"It's not!" White One shifted from paw to paw, centimeters from Bitey's nose. Their whiskers touched, entangled. "You just have to pull. Go fast."

"I can't!" Bitey wailed, but she was already doing it. She tightened her grip on the wire with one paw so that she could release her hold with the other and extend it fully forward, wrapping her fingers over the mesh. Her body moved upward and, with a pop, her shoulder broke free of the wire prong.

"There you go. You're alright. Come on, you're almost

here…"

She sucked in her belly as she writhed and pulled herself upward. Her knees caught on the wire and she kicked with her hindpaws, seeking leverage. One hindpaw caught something solid and she propelled herself forward, breaking the last of her body through the opening in a single lurch.

She collapsed against the mesh.

"See? That wasn't so hard."

Bitey glared at White One with one dark eye.

"Bitey?" Smeeze called, tentatively, from below. "Are you up there?"

"Yeah, Smeeze. I'm here."

She took a deep breath and tried to steady the rapid pounding of her heart. She rolled to her belly but realized there wasn't enough room to stand, and instead flattened herself in a crouch against the wire floor which had, moments ago, been the ceiling.

"White One…what happened? Did the world turn upside down?" Bitey tilted her head back, brushing her whiskers at the low ceiling overhead. The tight quarters were comforting—close, like a tunnel to a burrow, and reassuringly solid. As long as she could feel the solidity above her, she knew she wouldn't tumble away into oblivion when she fell into the sky.

"No. We're outside."

Her ears flicked. Bitey knew something about the world outside her cage. The sky had opened, after all, twice a day every day all of her life. Sometimes she was picked up and briefly transported by the Hands, sailing through the great openness of the Beyond. She had never seen anything like this tunnel-like place before.

"I know it's strange," White One said, apparently sensing Bitey's uncertainty. "But you'll have to trust me. Come on—I feel open air on my whiskers. This way."

Body pressed to the wire, Bitey crept forward. She kept her eyes firmly fixed on the darkness ahead of her; spying the world below her through the gaps in the wire only made her dizzy and frightened. It brought back that awful feeling that she would lose her hold on the world and tumble off into eternity.

White One stopped up ahead, and Bitey came up beside her, moving with painstaking slowness. "Well?" She asked, pressing in close to the smaller female. "What now?"

White One swayed, slowly moving her head from side to side as she peered into an expanse of seemingly endless dark. Rats, whose eyesight is generally very poor, are excellent judges of depth and distance; by moving their heads and calculating the subtle shifts in position, they can nearly always gauge how far something is and whether they can make it across.

Here, however, there was nothing to look at.

"We'll just have to jump down," White One said, more cheerfully than was appropriate for the occasion.

"Jump?" Bitey asked. "Jump where? White One, you're insane."

White One swept her whiskers forward, into the nothingness, then—without further warning or discussion—stepped forward and disappeared off the edge of the world.

In hindsight, Bitey wanted to believe that she acted out of bravery and loyalty, that she followed White One over the edge in an act of blind faith and rodent solidarity. But the truth was, she was driven by cowardice. There, huddled atop the fine mesh of the cage roof, crouched below the low ceiling and with her nose to the abyss, Bitey was overwhelmed with a sudden feeling of complete isolation, as though she were the last rat left alive in a world forsaken by the Spirits and rat-kind and Great Ones alike. She wanted to turn and run back to the safety of the cage. But truthfully, she didn't know how to go back, and she couldn't trust her shaking paws to carry her that far.

She jumped off the ledge.

The fall was shorter than she had anticipated, maybe eighteen inches, and her fall was broken by something soft—a bag of bedding. She sank into this and then rolled free, landing crouched on her paws. The air here felt more open than what she was accustomed to in the cage, and it smelled strongly not just of rat, but of other creatures. The scent was vaguely familiar, something she had caught on the hands of the Great Ones from time to time, but she had no words for it and no image to associate. Animal-smell; that's all she knew.

"Oh, of course *you* would fall on something soft," White One muttered beside her. She moved gingerly and held up her forepaw, fingers clenched into a fist and wrist tucked against her chest.

"You're hurt."

"I'm alright. Just a little jolted, it'll be fine once I walk it off." She reclined back on her haunches so she could relieve the weight from her sprained paw, and took the opportunity to look around. Bitey followed suit, turning eyes and ears and nose and whiskers all toward this new location.

They were inside of the small animal unit. It was a narrow storage space, just large enough for a grown human to move around in, but it was the largest place the rats had ever occupied. Inside was a small file cabinet filled with adoption papers; a plastic bucket full of some lemon-smelling liquid and a large sponge; a metal three-step-ladder on wheels; a bag of aspen shavings; and a half-empty bag of hamster food.

White One's nose twitched and she dropped back to all-fours, bounding unevenly on her hurt paw to investigate the bag of food. She nudged it, rose to her hindpaws, tugged at the bag with her teeth, and then jumped back as it fell over in a shower of seeds and corn and small kibbles. She picked up a dried corn kernel and nibbled at the corner, then clicked her teeth together appreciatively. "*Uchu*," she said—the rat word for particularly good food. "Come try some."

Bitey didn't need the invitation. As soon as the food spilled across the linoleum, she found herself in the middle of it, pawing through the seeds and nibbling at the corners of everything. Having grown up on lab blocks—hard, nutrient-packed grain kibbles that all tasted very much like nothing—she was intoxicated by the sudden variety of foodstuff. Not that it would have mattered; yesterday's breakfast was so long ago now that her grumbling stomach would gladly have accepted anything she fed it.

"We've done it!" she said, excitedly. She held a peanut between her forepaws, puzzling over how to crack open the shell. "We'll just carry all this up to the others."

"It won't last," White One said. She ran her tongue over her injured forepaw, then flexed her fingers a few times before setting the paw down. She tested it with her weight. "Besides, it doesn't solve our water problem—and there's more, I think. I think…the world is much, much bigger than this."

Bitey looked at her dubiously but she didn't argue with her. She cracked open the peanut shell and gobbled down one of the nuts inside, then nudged the remainder across the linoleum.

It rolled to a stop at White One's paws, and she gave a grateful smile and ate it in three big bites.

"This way," she said, and started forward. The limp, as she had said, dissipated with each step, and by the time they reached the wall she was walking almost normally again. She paused, sniffing, and then dropped to her belly. "It's narrow here—like the gap up there was," she said, pressing her nose into the two-inch gap between the floor and the bottom of the mobile small-animals unit, which was up on castors. "So we should be able to squeeze through it, and then jump down again. Or maybe up. I'm not sure."

Bitey pressed her own nose into the gap and took a deep whiff, trying to make sense of the odors that assailed her. She smelled dust and shoe-leather and floor polish. She also smelled animal smell, too rich and omnipresent to attribute to any single creature or pinpoint to any particular location. She flattened herself to the linoleum and crawled forward, belly sliding on the smooth floor and claws digging at the tiny imperfections of the flooring for a grip. The alien quarters were much less frightening with solid ground beneath her, and she made her way out a nose-length ahead of White One.

Out in the open, she rose to her full height and shook herself, sneezing the dust from her nose. She waited a moment for her senses to acclimate; it was brighter out here than it had been inside, and the air was more open on her whiskers. Sounds, too, were clearer, not muffled by glass or plastic. She could more clearly make out the rattling treat-can sound of the rain pounding against the roof, of the wind howling outside, of the front door swinging freely on its hinges as it knocked against the door frame and then bounced back.

Standing now on the very edge of her known universe, Bitey

was overwhelmed with its enormity. She quivered, and her fur stood on end. The irrational urge to bite and attack swept over her. But bite what? Attack what?

"It's enormous," White One said beside her. "I didn't expect it to be this big."

"It is," Bitey agreed. Her heart thudded in her chest. She smelled Great One smell, but it was distant, stale. If the Great Ones had forsaken them, they had abandoned their hold of the Beyond as well; Bitey knew, without question, that she and White One were totally alone. She took a tentative step forward, then another, and released a few droplets of urine onto the linoleum floor. "And it's ours."

Chapter Five

An explorer can only be timid in a newly-discovered paradise for a short while before the seductive qualities of a place take over the mind and crowd out anxiety. Bitey and White One, standing in the shadow of the small animal unit, were not just explorers: they were conquerors of worlds.

Beside the unit that housed their cage was a tall glass-and-wire enclosure full of various types of birds. These puzzled White One, who sat back on her haunches and stared up and up at the colorful creatures. She watched with rapt attention as they groomed their feathers by combing their sharp beaks over them, and as they flared and flexed wings that were of no use to them in such a small space. The birds, for their part, paid no attention to the rats. They groomed themselves, or tucked their beaks beneath a wing to sleep, or climbed restlessly up and down the bars at the top half of their cage and flitted from one roost to another.

"Come on," Bitey said, nudging her companion's shoulder. She couldn't imagine why White One found them so interesting. For one, they were in a cage—unlike them—which in Bitey's mind made them immediately irrelevant. For another, they made her fur bristle. She didn't know why, but the sight of them, of the sharp curved beaks and scaled talons and piercing eyes, stirred something in her chest. They weren't *ushu*, but they felt like they could be. "I found some water."

The roof had begun to leak just above the aviary, and rain came through in a steady drip, pooling in a shallow puddle on the tile. Bitey made her way to the edge of this and swept her whiskers over it, feeling droplets cling to them. She had never drunk water from a dish or pool before, but the action was intuitive, and she lapped up the water in big messy gulps. Water clung to her whiskers and chin, soaked into the fur of her throat. When droplets fell from above they splashed up, spraying her with a fine mist, and when she had drunk her fill she found that her face was quite damp.

She rolled back to her haunches to groom herself. Her stomach, awoken by the nibblings they had done inside of the small animal unit, gave a twinge and she winced. "Think there's more food out here?"

White One pulled reluctantly away from the foot of the aviary and padded to the puddle, sniffing the water before taking a few tentative sips. "Almost certainly," she said. "And lots of other things, besides. I wonder what else lives here?" She glanced back over her shoulder to the birds.

"*Ushu*," Bitey said at once. "At least, that's what Monster has always said."

"Yes…" White One lapped up a bit more water, then cleaned her face. "And we would be wise to keep an eye out for *Ushuzu-sim*. But…I can't help thinking…I don't think this is quite the same as what Monster or Nezumi experienced. Do you think the Beyond is different for everyone?"

"Maybe," Bitey said. She shook herself and dropped down to all fours, scenting the air and turning her ears in every direction. Sitting still so long in the shadow of the aviary was beginning to make her restless. "Come on—this way. I think I smell something."

That wasn't entirely true. Her nose had caught nothing of particular interest from that direction, but her whiskers had felt a movement in the air from the other side, and she shied away from it instinctively. Somewhere, some distance from where they stood, the air was moving very quickly. It smelled wet and cold and Bitey didn't want to see for herself what could make air run away like that. She didn't know for sure if there could be *ushu* that hunted air—or light, or sound, or any of the other features of the world that she had so far always taken for granted—but it didn't seem unreasonable.

So, in favor of playing it safe, she turned away from the wind and moved closer to the heart of the store.

"What's that?" White One paused for a moment at Bitey's side, one paw raised, and then she bounded forward. They had, until that moment, been hugging close to the sides of the displays, but now White One ran across a patch of open ground, apparently oblivious to anything but whatever had caught her eye.

Bitey huffed and looked around, verifying that they were alone, before reluctantly following the smaller white rat. White One might not believe in Monster's warnings about *ushu*, but Bitey wasn't willing to take chances yet. "Don't do that!" she admonished, coming to a halt beside White One. "We should stick to the walls, at least until we know..." she trailed off, then, as she became aware of what had caught White One's eye.

Before them, rising up infinitely into the sky, so tall that the top was completely outside of their line of vision, was a shelving unit. The shelves, spaced in eighteen-inch intervals, were packed full of colorful packages—but beneath the shiny plastic skin was the overbearing scent of food.

White One jumped up onto the bottom-most shelf, which stood just inches from the ground. She gnawed a corner off of a bag, and it burst open with an intoxicating odor, seeds and pellets spilling out over the shelf and onto the floor. White One gave a delighted laugh and jumped into the midst of the spilled food, her eyes bulging in her head with sheer joy at the bounty they had discovered.

Bitey nosed through the stack. Peanuts, corn, sunflower seeds, rolled oats—it was a venerable cornucopia of *uchu*, free for the taking. She gnawed open a sunflower shell and relished the oily taste of the seed on her tongue.

"There's so much," White One said, speaking around a mouthful of food. "This will last an eternity. We should go get the others."

Bitey swallowed. She dropped the empty shell and licked her lips. "Yes," she agreed, after a moment of hesitation. "We should. Do you know how to get back inside?"

"I think so. When I fell, I noticed that there were ledges beside me. We should be able to climb up those to get back inside, and I think if we worked at it a little we could tug the wire looser so the others could get out more easily. It will be a tight squeeze for Cookie and Monster, but the others should be alright."

Getting back into the cage proved to be much easier than escaping had been now that they knew the rough layout of the unit. Together they squeezed under the gap between the unit and the floor, and White One led the way up the step ladder, bounding up each step with ease. Once at the top it was easy to slip back into the narrow crawlspace between the top of the cage and the bottom of the next shelf.

Between her paws, Bitey could make out the others, their forms only slightly obscured by the wire mesh in her line of sight. Smeeze paced back and forth beside the igloo, casting occasional glances up at the hole in the wire. Top Ear sat on top of the igloo, watching her with dark eyes.

"I'm telling you," Smeeze said, with the air of someone who had been saying the same thing over and over. "I don't know where they've gone. They're outside."

Top Ear shifted her weight on top of the igloo and looked up, fixing her gaze on the hole in the wire. She did say anything for awhile, but bruxxed slowly, grinding her incisors together with meditative slowness. "We are going to be in so much trouble," she said, at last. "When the Great Ones come back."

"They're not coming back, Top Ear." Bitey poked her head through the hole in the ceiling, and Top Ear and Smeeze both jolted in alarm at her sudden appearance. Top Ear nearly tumbled from her perch atop the nest box, but managed to regain her balance. "Trust me. We were out in the Beyond, just now, and it's totally empty."

Bitey pushed through the wire and twisted her body so she could get hold on the ceiling with her paws. It was strange how quickly she had adjusted to the concept of the floor turning into a ceiling now that she had a firm grasp of "inside" and "outside"; the initial inversion of the world still made her dizzy, but she closed her eyes against the vertigo and managed to crawl out into the open and drop beside her sister on the igloo.

"That's it," Smeeze said, looking from Bitey atop the igloo to White One, who was now hanging deftly from the ceiling. "Next time, *I'm* going outside on the grand adventure and you two are standing guard and arguing with Top Ear. What was it like?"

"No point in telling you," White One said as she dropped down onto the now-crowded igloo roof alongside the sisters. "You won't really understand until you see for yourself. So we'll just show you all instead."

"I'll get the others," Top Ear said.

Bitey was surprised. She had expected skepticism or violence at her return, and Top Ear's sudden resolve struck an uneasy chord with her. She began to say something, but Top Ear had already jumped down from the igloo roof and disappeared inside. Within moments she appeared with Dumbo, Cookie, Sniffles, and Squeaker. All five of them looked up expectantly at the rats on the igloo as they settled down in its shadow. Smeeze crowded in next to them, rolling back onto her haunches and training expectant ruby-red eyes on them. Monster, who had been on the opposite side of the cage, crept in closer, but kept a distance of at least six inches from the others, creeping around them in a slow, uneasy semicircle.

Bitey cast a sidelong look at White One. She had hoped the other rat would've prepared some sort of speech, as now that she stood with all these eyes upon her, Bitey didn't have any idea what she was supposed to say. An uncomfortable silence settled over the cage like a fog. Sniffles sneezed.

"We've been outside," Bitey said, finally, realizing that White One wasn't going to make the first move. "Into The Beyond. It's bigger than anything I can describe, and there's fresh water to drink and a *chusim* greater than any you can imagine. We can show you how to get out."

"And what about the Great Ones?" Dumbo asked.

"They're gone," White One said. "Or gone into hiding, anyway. There's no trace of them, only an old scent." Her brow furrowed, as though she were about to say something further. Bitey wondered if she was considering mentioning the birds. If so, she changed her mind, as she said nothing else.

"For whatever reason, the Great Ones have deserted us," Bitey said. "Maybe they're testing us. Maybe they've decided we're ready to take over the Beyond. Or maybe something else has happened altogether. But whatever else is going on out there, the whole world is ours for the taking." She tried to relay this news as calmly as she could, but her limbs trembled with excitement. Already she ached to go back outside and forage amongst the endless *chusim* and explore.

"And the *ushu?*" Monster asked.

"We didn't smell any," White One said.

Monster snorted. "You never do, until it's too late."

"*Chusim* greater than I can imagine?" Cookie interrupted. "Are you sure?"

"We both ate our fill. There is enough food there to feed us for an eternity." White One ran her paws over her whiskers, and glanced up at the ceiling before looking back down at the others. "Every rat in the world could eat there, and there would still be plenty left over."

Bitey squeaked in agreement. She didn't know how many rats there were in the whole world, but she supposed it couldn't possibly be enough to eat everything they had seen. "Now, come on. I know everyone is hungry and thirsty. Climb up here and we'll show you the way out."

White One illustrated for the others how to jump up and grab onto the wire, and then how to move paw-over-paw to the opening. She shimmied through the gap and waited at the top so she could show the others how to get down onto the step ladder and out into the open. Bitey stayed behind on the igloo roof, helping the others as they lined up for their chance at escape.

Top Ear was the first onto the igloo. "You'd better be right about this," she muttered. She was thin and sinewy, built like White One, and her slim body lent itself naturally to the acrobatics needed to climb through the ceiling. She vaulted herself up and over the opening within moments, her sleek black form disappearing completely into the darkness overhead. Dumbo followed after; though to an untrained eye the sisters were nearly identical, Dumbo was a few grams heavier than her sister and the small bit of extra weight caused her more difficulty in maneuvering. She had to jump twice. The first time her nails caught at the wire but her grip slipped and she fell back with blood pooling around one torn nail. The second time she managed to hold on, swollen nailbed and all, and heaved herself through the opening.

Squeaker helped Sniffles, who was so thin that she could slip through the gap without needing to suck in her sides, but too weak to hold herself upside down for long periods. The two rats ascended the wire together, Squeaker pressing her steely-gray body against the other rat's for support as they crossed the tail-length distance from igloo to wire-hole. Sniffles collapsed against the wire floor when she managed to make it through, and she lay gasping on her belly for a few moments, Squeaker at her side licking the fur behind her ears and chittering a low, constant stream of encouragement. Once she caught her breath, Sniffles rose gingerly to her paws and tottered off into the darkness, black fur disappearing into oblivion as quickly as her sisters had.

Smeeze hauled herself up laboriously, catching on the wire and leaving chunks of white fur behind. Cookie barely made it through the wire at all—despite it being much loosened now from all the bodies that had gone through it—but with some heaving and lots of gut-sucking she managed to writhe up into the crawlspace. Her fat squished down through the mesh of the cage as she crawled out toward the step-ladder, and the wire sagged slightly with each step. White One peeked down, hanging her head through the gap.

"We'll catch up," Bitey said, shooting her a glance. "Get the others out. I'm sure everyone is hungry and thirsty."

White One squeaked an acknowledgment and disappeared into the darkness.

Monster watched all of this with cold, introspective ruby eyes. She huddled defensively against the far wall of the cage, and she breathed faster than she should. Her sides heaved and her fur stood on end; porphyrin dripped from her nose and the corners of her eyes.

"Monster?" Bitey dropped down from her place on top of the igloo, taking a few halting steps toward the larger rat. She had never seen her mentor look like this. It reminded her of the panic that had overtaken Nezumi, and it filled her with cold dread. "Are you alright? You look like you're getting sick…"

"I'm fine," Monster said. She shifted away from Bitey, hunching her caramel-colored shoulders. "Go join the others."

"I'm not going to leave you here," she said, feeling as though she had missed something, somehow, some key that would decode Monster's actions. "We're all going out. Together." She forced a brave smile. "Besides—I would have never thought to leave if it weren't for you. It's everything we could possibly want. Paradise, with food and water and plenty of space. We could have two colonies, if that's what we wanted to do. Me and you and Smeeze. White One, too, if she wanted to come. We could do whatever we wanted, and there's no hands. No hands, Monster!"

Monster rubbed her paws over her muzzle. Her face had a lean, raw look, and when she spoke it was weary. "I've already told you. It's a trap." She shivered, irritably, and nibbled at the fur on her upper arm. "It's always a trap."

"There is no snake—" Bitey began, but stopped; Monster flinched at the word as though she had been bitten. She lowered her voice. "You'll die in here. I can bring you food, but I can't bring water."

Monster snorted and tucked her head under her body. "I'll come when I'm ready. Let me rest."

She hesitated. Monster had looked quite healthy yesterday; she had no idea what could have happened to her overnight. *Maybe she has what Nezumi had,* she thought, and shuddered. In the excitement of discovery, she had almost forgotten about Nezumi and the terrible pain of loss and the role she may have played in it—but now, seeing Monster curled up defensively, clearly ill, memories of the last twenty-four hours flooded into Bitey's mind.

She focused her eyes and ears entirely onto Monster so that her senses wouldn't stray to her mother's body. "Alright," she said, finally. "I'll be back for you, once the others are settled. I'll bring Squeaker, so she can have a look at you." She hesitated. Overhead, and some distance away, White One chirped at her to hurry up. "You have to get well, Monster. This colony needs an alpha."

She touched her nose to Monster's shoulder and turned,

reluctantly, to make her way back into the Beyond.

* * *

It was eight o'clock.

The lightning had ceased; the hail and the wind and the earth-shaking rumbles of thunder had disappeared, and though the rain no longer fell in violent knives, it continued to pour from the sky. Slow, steady, fat droplets of rain hit the water-soaked ground and rolled off of it like so many marbles. Water pooled in the streets. It crept up over the curb and flowed downhill, congregating in the hollows of parking lots. The river, having drunk its fill, bloated and expanded past its banks, tumbling deliberately over the rain-soaked earth, gaining speed as it absorbed the run-off in its path.

Inside of Rocco's Pet Emporium, the first of the floodwaters began to trickle over the threshold, spilling from the parking lot into the front of the shop.

* * *

Tentatively, the rats spread out along the aisle, growing bolder with each passing minute that they enjoyed their freedom. At first, they had remained huddled together in the shadow of the bottom shelf, peering around at the infinitely expanded world with a mixture of awe and consternation, uncertainty causing them to freeze and press close together against the overwhelming newness of the situation. Rats are naturals at adaptation, however, and they react quickly to change; within twenty minutes, most had followed Bitey and White One's example and begun climbing the shelves, nibbling intermittently at the corner of bags and sampling their contents.

Although the food supply seemed limitless, the instinctive need to hoard and stockpile was still firmly affixed in many of them. Once they had eaten their fill, Cookie and Dumbo set about building *chusim*, or food caches, throughout the aisle. They had figured out quickly how to climb from one shelf up to the next, and the pair of them managed through their efforts to scatter small piles of feed pellets, seeds, dried corn and kibble throughout the five-foot-tall shelves. Sniffles and Top Ear huddled together on the bottom shelf, nibbling at the corner of bags and talking among themselves; Sniffles had perked up substantially with some food and water. Squeaker, satisfied with her recovery for the moment, made her way from rat to rat, examining the scratches from the wire and tending to wounds as she found them.

White One perched on top of the highest shelf. She peered over the edge, weaving her head from side to side in an effort to get a clearer view of this newly-discovered, enormous world that they had inherited. Her nose twitched rapidly and her whiskers swept the air constantly. Smeeze stood next to her, though she clung more carefully to the shelf and didn't lean out quite so far.

Bitey nosed through a pile of food that had fallen from a bag she'd gnawed open, debating how best to get it into the cage for Monster.

"You should let me take a look at you." Squeaker's voice broke into her thoughts, and Bitey dropped the pellet she had been holding in alarm. "You're covered in wounds."

"I'm fine," Bitey said.

Squeaker gave her a hard look. "If you catch a fever from an infection—"

"I'm fine," she repeated. "But I'd like you to come help me with Monster, if you can. I think she's come down with something. What Nezumi had, maybe."

"I don't think so," Squeaker said. She touched her nose to Bitey's flank, running her tongue over the scabbed-over bite wound. Bitey's skin twitched at her touch but she didn't resist her; the *nosobo*'s touch was both gentle and warm, and instantly soothing. "Whatever was wrong with Nezumi, it was something…inside of her. It had been there a long time I think. I suspect if Monster's acting out of sorts, it's a more… psychological…problem."

"You think she's crazy."

"No. I think she's frightened." Squeaker nipped down on Bitey's haunch, tugging at the scab that had formed there.

Bitey cried out. She felt blood flow from the wound in her haunch and she wheeled around, baring her teeth at the blue-furred rat. "What was that for?"

"The tissue was dying," Squeaker replied, matter-of-factly. If she was concerned that Bitey would attack her, she showed no sign of it; she advanced on the larger rat and licked the now-bleeding wound until the blood had stopped and the stinging had died down. "Sometimes you need to bite away at the bad parts so that it can heal properly. Now. Sit still and let me do your shoulders…"

Smeeze climbed down from the top shelf, leaping from perch to perch and following the path they had already begun to mark. White One bounded down after her, both of them coming to a halt near Bitey.

"Bitey," Smeeze said, panting a little with the effort of scaling down the shelf. "Something's come up. We thought you'd want to know right away."

Bitey withdrew from Squeaker, brow furrowed. "What is it?"

"*Ushu*," White One said. "I've found where they are. At least, I think I have. The air is running this way, and I can smell them on it."

"Are they close?" Bitey demanded.

"Hard to say. But I think someone should go look. We can't defend ourselves if we don't know what we're dealing with." White One paused, then, nose wrinkling. "I...I don't know why the air is running away," she added. "But I don't think it's being chased by *ushu*. I think...I think it's something else."

The terrible thing, Bitey thought—the thing Nezumi had been screaming about before she died. But she had warned them to get out before it came, hadn't she? Why would she warn them to go out where it could get them? Unless perhaps they were supposed to meet it head-on and fight. "*Liso*," she said. "White One, stay here and help the others. Find cover, just in case. I'll go out to see what I can find."

"I'm coming with you," Smeeze said. "And we should take someone else, as well. In case something happens."

Bitey hesitated. She wished Monster were here. "Top Ear," she called, after a moment. "Come here."

Top Ear, who had been busy gnawing the corner off a bag of chinchilla food on the bottom shelf, lifted her head, sweeping her ears forward at Bitey's voice. She touched noses with Dumbo and Sniffles, who were on either side of her, and then climbed down onto the floor and scurried to where the others had gathered. "What?"

"White One's just told me she smells *ushu*. We need to investigate before they are able to creep up on us. Are you in?"

Top Ear glanced over her shoulder. "Dumbo—"

"—Should stay here, in case something happens," Bitey interrupted. "We can't leave them here without a fighter. White One is staying too." She offered a brave sort of smile. "Hopefully she's wrong and we don't find anything at all."

"We'd better get going," Smeeze said.

Taking a deep breath, Bitey crept away from the shelves and started forward, Smeeze and Top Ear following behind, none of them knowing what they would come across.

Chapter Six

Rats never travel in the open if they can help it. Instead, they prefer to move along walls or under cover—both, if possible. One lesson the Spirits teach rats at an early age is to know, at all times, what is happening on all sides; the fewer sides one has to worry about, the easier that task is.

Bitey led the expedition cautiously, as there were no walls to cling to here. She paused at the edge of each shelf they came across, lifted onto her haunches to sniff the air, and then darted forward to the next shelving unit to press herself against the metal and wait for the others to follow.

They passed the unit that held their own cage, and she had to tear herself away to resist the urge to try and go back inside to talk to Monster again. They passed the aviary, and she had to double-back to grab Top Ear by the scruff and drag her away from the birds. Now they crouched in the shadow of a plain shelving unit, and Bitey tried to sort out all the smells that assaulted her nose so she could try to make sense of them.

"Maybe White One was wrong," Smeeze said. She, too, stood on her hind legs and sniffed the air, her whiskers working rapidly. "I don't smell any *ushu*, and I don't feel any running air."

"It's because we're on the ground, I think," Top Ear suggested.

"Didn't White One say she smelled it when she was up high?"

Bitey fell back to all four paws. "Maybe…" she said. She had to admit Top Ear had a point. Things smelled different from the ground than they otherwise would. Right now, she smelled dust, and the lingering odor of shoe-rubber, and some bitter-tasting clean smell. There were other odors, but they were so jumbled and confused that she couldn't tell them apart, much less identify them.

"Here—we can climb up this," Top Ear said. She moved around the corner somewhat, and jumped onto the bottom-most shelf, climbing atop a bag of cat litter. "It's just like the other one, except I don't think there's any *uchu* here."

Smeeze sniffed experimentally at a bag and nibbled the corner. A sandy substance spilled out over her paws and she backed away in alarm, sneezing. "No…definitely not."

Bitey climbed up beside Top Ear and, silently, the two made their way to the top. Smeeze scrabbled behind them. The cat litter on the bottom shelves gave way to toys and collars on the middle shelves. Many of the packages jingled when they were touched, and each time the rats froze in place, waiting for something to happen—but nothing did. A feather on a string, ruffled by the wind, bobbed in Bitey's peripheral vision, and she lunged at it, nearly losing her balance on the shelf.

"I don't think it was going to eat you," Smeeze said, dryly.

Bitey dropped the feather—what was left of it—and looked sheepish. "It might have been something else," she said, reasonably. "Better to bite it first."

"…What else would it have been, precisely?" Smeeze asked. "We're completely alone up here."

"Not quite," Top Ear interrupted from the shelf above them. "I can smell it now. I don't know how we missed it before. Get up here."

Bitey heaved herself up onto the top shelf and was immediately assaulted by two completely alien sensations.

The first was the feeling of wind—or, as White One had described it, of running air. It swept over Bitey's whiskers and ruffled her fur, and she understood immediately how the feather had moved on its own. The air was cold when it hit her face, and it smelled so wet that she felt a spray of water on her whiskers.

The second was an animal odor: thick and oily, not unlike rat musk but much richer. The smell made her fur stand on end and the muscles in her jaw tightened with the sudden urge to bite. But bite what? They were still totally alone.

"Down there," Top Ear said, staring down from the shelf to a black metal-and-glass apparatus in the aisle below. It was smaller than the unit that held the rat's cage, but there was only one cage in it. The base was made of painted metal, with an octagonal glass tank situated on top. The access point was a flip-top door, also made of metal, which was scored with a series of vents; the oily smell came up through the vents. "That's where it's coming from. What is that?"

"*Ushu*," Smeeze said. "It's gotta be. What else could possibly smell that bad?"

"Shh!" Bitey said. She leaned forward, wrapping her claws around the top of the shelf and holding her tail out behind her for balance. Her ears perked forward. "They're talking."

She hadn't noticed it, at first, because they were speaking a different language and the voices were muffled. But as she listened, amidst the chirps and squeals, she began to make out the gist of what they were saying; the dialect was different, but it was close enough to ratspeak to catch every few words. She looked back to her companions, questioningly—wondering if she was the only one who heard this. The shocked, baffled expressions on Top Ear and Smeeze's faces were enough to show that she wasn't.

"Hungry!" a voice said. "Hungry! Hunt, play, kill!"

There were other words, besides, but these four seemed to be repeated over and over, more like a chant than anything. Bitey caught a tone of desperation in their voice; they were screaming for help, knowing that there was nobody who could hear them.

"…They must not have been fed either," Smeeze said, brow furrowing. "They sound like they're starving, or something."

"If we're even understanding them right," Top Ear said, quickly. "Who knows what they're actually going on about?"

"Or you just don't want to admit you were wrong about why the Great Ones abandoned us," Smeeze shot back. "Couldn't very well be Bitey's fault if they didn't get fed either."

"Shut up, both of you," Bitey snapped. She leaned out again, over the ledge, and trained her ears on the sound.

She didn't want the others fighting over it, but Smeeze had hit on precisely what she was already thinking: if rats were not the only animals kept by the Great Ones, and if those animals had also been abandoned, then the world was not only much larger than she had anticipated but also much further removed from her influence. The knowledge was both humbling and hugely relieving. But she had to be sure—had to know, without question, that she was right—because there were other possibilities that played at the back of her mind. What if, as Monster had said, the Beyond was just a trap? What if all of this was an elaborate set-up to lead them all to their deaths? Or, even worse, even more impossible to consider:

what if the Great Ones weren't keeping these animals at all? What if they were, as she'd always suspected, only animals themselves? Maybe they were kept in a cage also, and maybe *they* had been abandoned by whatever was greater than *them*.

Maybe this whole huge, new world she had discovered was nothing more than a cage constructed to hold the Great Ones, and whoever owned it was lurking just out of sight—a huge race, unfathomably massive, big enough to hold Great Ones in their hands and cause the wind to run in terror.

"Out! Out! Out!"

The voices below cried out now, in unison, this single frenzied word. Perhaps they had caught the rat's scent. It rang in Bitey's ears and her heart clenched in her chest. They cried out the way her mother had when she threw herself at the glass. Maybe whatever malady had taken her life had descended upon these unseen, potent-smelling creatures...

"Bitey, what are you doing?" Top Ear's voice broke through her thoughts. She sounded scared and skeptical.

Bitey was used to the skepticism, but the fear startled her and she froze, coming back to herself from her thoughts. She hadn't realized how far she was leaning over the edge of the shelf. Subconsciously, she weaved her head from side to side, watching the way the shadows shifted so she could gauge the distance down to the top of the cage below. The cage was shorter than the shelf, but only a foot or two away—a distance she could probably travel, she thought. The fall wouldn't be any longer than the one she'd sustained climbing out of her cage the first time. She hadn't planned to jump, but she realized that she could, and suddenly the desire overwhelmed her and she tensed her muscles. Smeeze realized too late what she was doing and snatched at her just as her paws left the ground. Her tail brushed past Smeeze's outstretched paw and she felt the scrape of nails against the scales on her tail, but then she was clear and she was falling toward the cage.

"Bitey!" Top Ear yelled. "Bitey, what do you think you're doing?"

"Are you okay?" Smeeze asked, leaning out over the edge of the shelf.

Bitey landed hard on all fours, bending her legs on impact to help displace some of the jolt. Her joints screamed in pain and her paws gave out below her and she rolled onto her side, totally winded. "I'm fine," she panted, and found that she couldn't say anything more for a time as she tried to catch her breath.

Below, poking up through the vents, she felt a cold nose press against the fur of her underbelly.

"Who are you?" she asked.

This apparently was too difficult a question for the creature to answer. It let out a shrill chittering noise, a series of words she didn't understand. Then it said, "Out. Out, out. Eat, eat, *eat*?"

Her brow furrowed. She wondered if an *usoothe* would be able to understand them, and then remembered that it wouldn't make any difference if they could—their *usoothe* was dead. She struggled to get her paws back under her and pressed her nose through the vent, touching noses with the other.

The creature lunged, trying to nip her. Bitey jerked back and the creature, unable to get at her through the thin slit in the metal, fell back.

"None of that!" Bitey said, wrinkling her nose. "I know how you feel. I'd probably try to bite me, too. But don't. I want to help you."

Through the vents, she could make out a half-dozen of the creatures. They all pressed together atop an igloo very much like the one in her home cage, and from there they could brace themselves against the side wall in order to sniff through the ceiling. Bitey got the feeling that they weren't very good at standing on their hind legs; they kept falling over on top of each other, and they seemed to need the glass to hold themselves steady.

"Okay. So. You're hungry, right? Because you didn't get fed?" She thrust her nose back into the vent, trying to get a better idea of what their cage was like. She couldn't make out much of anything over their rank, oily scent. "I don't know how to get you out. Your cage is different from mine so you can't get out the same way we did."

The creatures, clearly not understanding a word of this, chittered back at her.

"Bitey, I'm glad you're alive," Smeeze yelled down, "But what are you doing?"

"Trying to help these creatures get loose," Bitey yelled back, a little irritated. Wasn't it obvious? "The jump isn't so bad. Just be sure to bend your legs when you land and –"

"—Get loose?" Top Ear interrupted. "Bitey, have you lost your mind? They're *ushu*! If they get loose they're going to eat you!"

Bitey paused. She settled back on her haunches and ran her paws over her whiskers. She had been so caught up in her sudden curiosity about their relationship with the Great Ones, and about their current plight, that she'd quite forgotten they might kill her. "I don't think they will," she said, with more confidence than the situation warranted.

"I hate to break it to you," Smeeze said, "But two out of the five words of theirs we understand are 'hunt' and 'kill', remember?"

"They're *shu*," Bitey said. "But I don't know if they're *ushu*."

The distinction was minor, but significant: all predators are *shu*, but only those who are a risk to rats are *ushu*. Rats, after all, sometimes prey on mice or other rodents—so they, sometimes are *shu* of a sort as well.

Top Ear let out an exasperated noise.

Bitey ignored her. "Where does the cage open?" she wondered aloud, turning to peer back across the black roof for some detail she had missed. *From the top*, she thought; the Great Ones always come in through the sky, so something on this roof would have to show her the way into the cage. The roof was an octagonal piece of black metal, around two and a half feet in diameter. A line bisected the top, a thin gap in the metal like a seam, and there were hinges along this seam— small bumps in the otherwise flat surface. Across the cage, on the opposite side of the roof from where she sat, something silver sat above the top of the black metal—a knob, just a few inches long, that jutted up an inch above the flush surface of the roof. She crept forward to investigate, moving slowly because her paws slid on the smooth metal of the roof and her nails caught in the vents. It was a short journey, though, less than the length of her own cage, and then there she was—nose to knob.

"You can't use that!" Top Ear wailed. "That's made for Great Ones. Rats can't figure it out."

"Just like rats can't climb out of their cage and feed them-selves?" Smeeze shot back.

Top Ear hissed.

Bitey nudged the knob with her nose. It didn't budge. She tried to bite it, but it was cold and too hard for her teeth. She circled it, sidling up next to it as though it were another rat she challenged for dominance, and then tried to nudge it from the opposite side. It rattled, but didn't budge. Below, the creatures—no longer able to reach the ceiling without the aid of the igloo to stand on—stared up at her from the cage floor, and chittered what she hoped was encouragement. She nudged the knob again. She stepped back a few inches, lowered her shoulder, and shoved her body into it, thrusting all of her weight against the silver-colored handle.

This time the latch turned and she spun out with the force of her push, nearly skidding off the roof of the cage. She caught herself, at the last moment, on a vent and winced as her nails strained with the effort of pulling herself away from the ledge.

The roof remained closed, and she growled.

"I bet it lifts up," Smeeze called.

"Then get down here and help me lift it," Bitey yelled back. She shook herself and then peered down through the vents. "Try pushing it from underneath," she said, hoping they could make out the meaning of at least something she was saying. She scratched at the roof, then looked down pointedly through the vent. Then, remembering that the creatures couldn't reach on their own, she bounded back across the roof to stand above the igloo.

One of the creatures, a sable-colored one, followed her back and climbed on top of the igloo, pressing its nose through the vent. Bitey touched noses with it. She couldn't tell if this was the first one she had met or not; it was too hard to make them out in detail through the vents. The creature bumped the ceiling with its nose, but the roof didn't budge.

"No…maybe it's only on one side?" Bitey said. She bounded back across to the opposite half of the lid, across the bumps of the hinges, and scratched at the roof. Then she went back to the side where the igloo was and looked at it pointedly.

The sable-colored creature stared up at her with dumbfounded, dark eyes. Bitey had to repeat this pantomime three times; by the third, she was panting a little with all the running back and forth. Each time, the creature followed her, and at the end of the third it stopped at the igloo and a sudden look of understanding dawned on its features. It let out a delighted bark, circled around the igloo, and gave it a hard shove. It squeaked against the floor as it moved forward a few inches.

As soon as this happened, all half-dozen of the creatures seemed to realize in unison what was happening, and they swarmed around the igloo, shoving each other out of the way and crawling over each other in their excitement. They talked among themselves in excited high pitched-chatter, words Bitey didn't understand but which sounded slightly obscene to her ears. She watched this in bafflement, entranced by their odd mannerisms.

Somehow, despite their bickering and shoving, they managed to maneuver the igloo against the opposite wall of the cage. The sable-colored one, who appeared to be the leader, climbed up onto it, balanced itself against the cage wall, and climbed up onto its hind legs. It thrust its nose against the ceiling at the place where the lip of the ceiling met with the side wall of the cage—and the ceiling cracked open. Letting out a shrill, delighted nezise, it jumped, wriggling forward, scrabbling at the glass wall, and then it emerged and twisted its lithe little body out onto the roof.

Bitey stared at it, now that she could see the whole creature at once. It stared back at her, and for a moment neither of them moved.

"Play?" it asked, tilting its head.

It was larger than she was. Longer, at least, and built like a furry tube, its long body slung low to the ground and covered with long, bristly hairs. Its face was rat-like, but rather than large gnawing incisors its muzzle was filled with small pointed teeth, the kind of teeth made to tear into flesh. Its body was sable with white accents on the face and paws; a dark mask laid over its eyes, which were large and liquid brown.

"You're welcome," Bitey said. "What do you call yourselves?"

Behind the sable-colored creature, a white nose pressed out through the opening. It crawled free and came to stand beside its companion, looking Bitey over intently. Neither of them responded to her question.

"*Shujisk*," she decided. "That's what I'll call you."

"Bitey—" Top Ear called.

"I'm almost done!" Bitey yelled back, irritated. She didn't want to move too quickly, in case it triggered a predatory instinct in the *shujisk*.

"No, Bitey. You don't…look!" Top Ear's voice had a terrified edge, and the words tumbled out in a screech. "It's here! It's here!"

"What in the Beyond are you talking about?" Bitey asked, sweeping her whiskers toward the shelving unit.

"Turn around!" Smeeze yelled.

Another *shujisk* had managed to free itself, and now all three stared with sudden intensity, not at Bitey, but at something just beyond her shoulder. She turned to peer that way herself, whiskers and ears swept forward to see what the commotion was about.

Outside, the river had swollen past its banks; the rivulets of water in the flooded parking lot had gained both volume and momentum. Now, crashing over the asphalt and spilling against the wall of the pet store, the floodwaters invaded the building with the power of a tidal wave. The water poured through the open door, spreading out across the floor like an ominous shadow.

The shadow came toward Bitey, and she stared dumbfounded and heard an echo of her mother's voice in her head. *The Big Water*, she thought, and shivered. It was here.

Chapter Seven

White One sat up on her haunches, whiskers and nose twitching as she tried to sort out the sensory input that assailed her. She rubbed her forepaws together, then ran them over her face, then dropped down to all fours. She took a few tentative steps forward, stopped, then darted back into the shadow of the shelf, tucking her slim white body into the two-inch gap below the bottom shelf. She had done this particular dance a half-dozen times so far, but had always reined herself in at the last moment—had always darted back into the shadow before her paws had the opportunity to carry her away.

If Bitey had a problem with impulse-control, White One suffered the same affliction. It was, perhaps, the reason why White One had accepted the hot-tempered mink as her comrade-in-arms for this adventure. White One had come to the store in the same shipment as Squeaker had, making them the newest wave of arrivals to the shop; like Squeaker, she tended to speak in a way that often made the others tilt their head in incomprehension. They may in fact have been sisters, or half-sisters, or perhaps cousins. She hadn't weaned with her, she remembered that much—they had found each other some time later, perhaps in transit to the shop, perhaps when they were two satin-furred hoppers huddled together in a transport cage in the back of a dark, rattling truck. But she didn't remember the exact moment she had met Squeaker, much as she didn't remember precisely what her mother had smelled like or exactly how many others had been in the shipment with them. Even as an infant, White One had her whiskers trained on a larger world, and she had never bothered with details.

Squeaker made friends quickly. Well—*a* friend, at any rate. She had imprinted strongly on the little berk with the white star on her forehead, the one the others called Sniffles. White One had never fully understood the reason for the friendship—Sniffles was, after all, very likely to die young, and even more likely to be in ill-health until then—but then, White One had never understood friendships in general. She often sat in her perch atop the igloo, or in the shadow of the wheel, and watched the others with the sort of diffident curiosity that a foreigner might regard the locals of some obscure town. Relationships among others intrigued her, but she'd had no desire to take part in them herself.

She wasn't antisocial. Not like Monster, at any rate. She would chat, amiably enough, share food with Cookie when asked and share the wheel with Top Ear when she was of a mind to run. She didn't scuffle for position, didn't fight for anything; if someone wanted something she had, she politely turned it over to them and found something else to occupy her time.

No…the reason White One had never bothered with making friends was that she knew, from the moment she was first capable of independent thought, that she was destined for a different life. Not greater, perhaps—but different.

"White One?" Dumbo asked, hesitantly, from the shelf above her head. She leaned over, her nose centimeters from White One's. Their whiskers touched. "Are you alright? Do you smell something?"

How to answer that, precisely? Of course she smelled something. She smelled a whole universe of somethings: feathers and birdshit, rainwater, car exhaust, mud, a thousand other smells. The problem was, she didn't know what any of them were, what any of them meant. "No *ushu*," she said, because she knew that's what the big-eared berkshire was trying to ask. "Not down here, anyway."

"I hope the others get back soon," Dumbo said, drawing herself back up onto the shelf.

"I'm sure they're fine," White One said. "But—you should go help Cookie put together some *chusim* up there. The more places we can hide them, the better. Just in case."

Luckily, Dumbo didn't ask "just in case what," because White One didn't know. Instead, she said, in the slow but well-meaning way she tended to speak, "…You're probably right. Yes…that's a good idea. Just in case."

White One reflected, not without bitterness, that Dumbo also would not be able to answer "just in case what." But it didn't matter. Dumbo pulled away and made her way up the shelf, climbing bags and squeezing between the rear of the shelves and their corrugated backing, to go and speak with Cookie. White One was, once more, alone with her thoughts, at least until another interruption came.

She crept away from the shelf and rose, once more, to her haunches.

She could smell better from the top of the unit, of course. From up there, she had sensed the wind and the *ushu* smell on it. She had also gotten a clearer idea of just how large the world was. Unfortunately, while it made for a great lookout, the stronghold atop the shelf had a greater weakness: it was isolated. There was no way off except for the somewhat laborious climb down to the floor, and that was a major hindrance to running.

So she sacrificed her superior look-out in favor of a more accessible location.

When they'd first climbed free from the cage and squirmed their way out into the Beyond, Bitey had looked so astounded—so overwhelmed—that White One didn't have the heart to tell her that she had seen all this before. She had been out here twice, in fact, in her life. Once, she had climbed over the lip of the cage when it was open for the Great Ones to choose others to *churzu*. That time she had made it only out onto the floor before she was caught. She had hit the floor and, realizing she was free, had frozen in terror and awe.

The second time she made it a bit further. Knowing a bit better this time what to expect, she had squirmed free of the Great One's hand when she was lifted out of the cage; squirmed free and fallen to the linoleum with a hard thud that sprained her paw and bruised her ribs, but it didn't matter. She hit the ground running.

That time, she had been loose in the store for nearly a quarter of an hour, darting in blind terror from the Great Ones that pursued her. They caught her, of course, and dumped her unceremoniously back into the cage with her companions—most of whom had viewed her with an uneasy curiosity which had, in time, faded into denial, the natural response of animals faced with incomprehensible realities—and White One had never succeeded in escaping again.

But while she had been free, she noticed a great number of things. She had seen the enormity of the world; had witnessed some of the wonders laid out upon the shelves; had scented the myriad scents that clung to the linoleum. She also got a good look at the feet of the Great Ones, which had been particularly interesting as they were so much different from their hands—blunt and clumsy instruments that clumped over the ground. White One pitied them, a little, because of the feet. She intuited that Great Ones must be terrible climbers, having no gripping capability in their hindpaws, and that suggested to her that they were at a terrible disadvantage. Perhaps this inability to climb, to explore more than the most base levels of whatever type of world they inhabited, was responsible for their obsessive tending of the rats. Perhaps they envied them.

Their feet had, in fact, been White One's downfall. While she was in hiding beneath a shelf, a rubber-smelling black club of a foot passed next to her hiding place, and she could not help but creep forward to investigate. Within moments the hands—soft, articulate, claw-less lands, each twice the size of her whole body—had swooped down and caught her in their woven cage of fingers.

So. This was the third time White One had seen the Beyond, or at least this corner of it. She had seen the tall shelves, the rows of food. She had seen the birds, though she didn't know what they were. What she had not seen was the rest of the Beyond, the part that Bitey now explored and whatever lay past that. White One was quite sure that there was a lot of Beyond left to discover.

She flicked her ears back, listening for the others. They didn't seem to take notice of her. She heard low talk between Sniffles and Squeaker; she heard Cookie gnawing on something; she heard Dumbo rustling between two bags, chewing a plastic wrapper. She could slip away now, and no one would notice.

She had every intention of coming back when she was done exploring. Once she determined that the coast was clear, she would return and report what she had seen and they would all decide together what to do with that knowledge. But first, she needed to ascertain precisely what the Beyond was like, without being slowed down by the others—others who would stop to gawk and wonder, who would freeze in terror at things they didn't know, who would run off on their own. White One didn't need the distraction, and she certainly didn't need the liability.

Her heart thudded quickly in her chest. She felt it in her paws. The blood was pumping so hard through her body that she felt like she was vibrating all over, and it took everything in her power to remain cautious as she pulled away from the shelf: she wanted nothing more than to dart out into the open at full speed and run until her nerves had settled. But running over open ground wasn't the same as running on the wheel, and excitement or not she couldn't risk being spotted by *ushu*. Just because she hadn't smelled any nearby yet didn't mean one couldn't come as soon as she dropped her guard.

She moved quickly but quietly, scurrying across the gap between the pocket pets shelf to the aviary. She paused here, in the shadow of the bird's enclosure, and listened to the rustle of feathers. A bird squawked—and then it spoke.

White One froze, squeaking in alarm, and pressed herself flat to the ground. The bird had spoken in a strange, strangled high-pitched voice, but the words had been human words, the sort of words that Great Ones said in their deep rumbling voices. The bird made another strange noise, like the rush of air through a narrow gap, and then repeated itself. What concerned White One was not really that the bird had spoken—rats after all comprehend their names, even if some of the human mouth-sounds are hard to mimic in ratspeak—but what the bird had said.

"Cookie!" it said, and squawked, then whistled. "Cookie! Cookie! Pretty bird."

"…What about Cookie?" White One asked, thoroughly unnerved. Was this green-and-red winged beast prophetic in some way? Had it somehow seen their arrival? And if so…why was it asking for Cookie, in particular?

The bird didn't seem to understand White One's question. Instead, it replied, "Pretty bird!" It then fell abruptly silent and began to use its beak and talons to climb up the wire side of its cage. The other birds in the aviary, housed in other wire enclosures, paid no heed to White One or the parrot.

White One puzzled over this. She laid her paws on the bottom lip of the cage—it was plastic at the bottom for about six inches before it turned into glass, which became wire about two feet above that—and craned her neck back to look at the bird, which was now ignoring her. "I'd really love to talk to you," she said, hesitantly.

She wondered if all creatures aside from rats spoke the Great One's language, or if the bird was simply bilingual. If it was adept with two languages, she wondered if perhaps it knew a third, a fourth, even a hundredth. Maybe the creature would understand ratspeak after all? Maybe it knew all languages. That was certainly within the realm of possibility, and quite sensible in White One's estimation, especially if it was a prophet as she suspected it was. "Pardon me, do you know anything about the Beyond, or the Great Ones? My companions are very worried. We were supposed to get breakfast this morning, but it never came, and now it seems there are no Great Ones to be seen. Do you know where they've gone?"

But the bird, if he understood anything she said, didn't seem interested in talking.

White One sighed and contemplated what other way she could try and communicate with it. She opened her mouth to try again, but an odd sound caught her ear and she pulled away from the aviary, ears pricked forward. Her whiskers trembled; something about the quality of the air had changed. And there was a sound like she had never heard before.

Frightened but intrigued, she crept around the corner of the aviary, craning her neck to peer out into the open space of the center aisle. She stared for a moment, not fully understanding what she saw. Some huge, dark thing was slithering over the ground, approaching from very far away but coming closer at impressive speed. Was it a snake, she wondered? She had heard Monster talk of the *ushuzu-sim*, of its giant tubular body and black staring eyes. Monster had said it was large…but she didn't think it was *this* large.

The slithering thing slammed against the table that held the cash register, and White One heard a crash and a muffled crumpling sound as many bags of chips and candy were knocked from the check-out shelf and hit the floor. The slithering thing rippled but didn't stop, and White One realized what it was.

Get out, a voice in her head, Nezumi's voice, echoed as though from the Spirit Realm itself. *Get out before the Big Water.*

"Dumbo!" she yelled, wheeling around and running full-tilt for the shelves she had left the others on. "Dumbo! Squeaker! Everyone, get off the ground!"

She screamed the words, but they were drowned out by the dull roar of the thing that followed her. Water tumbled through the building. It stripped away merchandise from bottom shelves, boxes and bags clattering to the floor before being swallowed by the rising flood.

White One didn't bother to hesitate before charging into the open. Her paws skidded on the linoleum. She lost her footing, slid sideways on her belly, and clawed at the floor to get her feet back under her. She could hear the water behind her, moving much faster than she possibly could.

Dumbo and Cookie were on the middle shelf of the unit, each gnawing opposite corners of a bag of food pellets. Dumbo peered down at White One as she rounded the corner. "What—?"

"No time!" White One yelled, skidding to a stop. Sniffles and Squeaker were on the bottom shelf. Sniffles was asleep; Squeaker lay over her, chin rested between her ears, her eyes half-lidded and expression content. They both had the distended bellies of the recently well-fed. White One ran to them, taking the shelf in one jump. They were less than six inches from the floor. "It's coming! We have to move!"

Squeaker lifted her head sleepily. She blinked, stifled a yawn. "…What's coming? What are you talking about?"

There was no time to explain. White One jumped, catching hold of a bag of feed, and scrambled up on top of it. "Come on!" she said, heaving herself up onto the next shelf. "It's coming."

She could hear it, the dull roar of its approach, the sound of splashing and tumbling merchandise. It was louder, closer, than it had been just moments earlier.

The sound threw Squeaker into motion. She nudged Sniffles to her paws and pushed her up the bags, climbing behind White One. White One felt whiskers on her tail, warm breath against the bristly hairs of her tail tip. She reached the top of the bags and grabbed hold of the lip of the shelf, pulled herself up, and turned to help the others—

"—It's here!" Dumbo's voice called from above.

White One braced herself. The floodwater rushed down the center aisle like a river. It spread as it came, sending tendrils of muddy liquid to probe between the aisles and swirl around corners, but the central force remained powerful as it slammed against the shelf. The metal shook, and water rose, folding over the shelf like a wet blanket. For a moment, she was certain that the water would wash over her entirely—but it didn't. It stopped level with her paws, soaking into the fur of her underbelly, but rose no higher.

Two dark shapes materialized in her line of vision: Sniffles and Squeaker, swept clear from the shelf and floating now across the aisle, buffeted on the water like so much debris. Without thinking, White One leaned over the edge of the shelf and snatched at them with one paw, balancing precariously on the other three. Sniffles floated into her reach. She swept her paw once, twice, and on the second attempt her claws caught fur and she curled them down and back, dragging the other rat toward her.

As soon as she was within biting distance, she caught Sniffles by the scruff and dragged her up onto the shelf beside her like an overgrown infant. Sniffles clawed weakly at the shelf to help pull herself up, then collapsed onto the damp metal, wheezing with the effort.

"Squeaker, hang on!" White One called as she leaned out again over the edge of the shelf. "Squeaker?"

Where there had been a flailing silver-blue rat, now there was only a flat, rippling expanse of muddy water. Her eyes scanned the surface, but it was no use—Squeaker was gone.

Chapter Eight

Floodwater burst through the door and spread across the store like a living entity, a giant slithering creature whose body was made up of brown liquid and debris. Bitey watched from the top of the ferret cage, and the world around her seemed to twist and shrink until the only thing she could see or hear or smell was the flood. The ferrets, just inches behind her, no longer mattered. Distantly, she could hear Top Ear and Smeeze yelling something, but it didn't matter. Their voices were small and inconsequential.

Bitey watched the water pour in from the outside, the level rising up and stripping merchandise from shelves and knocking displays askew. She imagined the rat cage, once a safe-haven, now filled with water. She could see it clearly in her mind's eye: water spilling over the wire roof, dripping down like a miniature waterfall into the glass tank, Nezumi's body floating up as some ghastly marker of the water level. Was this what Nezumi had seen? Was this what the Spirits had warned her about?

Monster.

The fawn-hooded rat was still in there. There was no way she would know what was coming until it was too late. Bitey imagined her clawing at the glass as water poured in over her, screeching for help from anyone who would listen.

She ran to the edge of the ferret cage—the roof now stood two feet from the water line—and jumped, plunging into the floodwater without a second thought.

At first, all she could feel was the shock of cold. Water clogged her ears and nose and blurred her vision. Then she felt the world tumble away at her feet, and when she tried to regain her footing, her paws met with resistance as though this wet, cold air had grown thick enough to touch.

Then she understood.

Bitey had never experienced water outside of what was given to her in the water bottle, but she was a smart rat. She remembered clearly the way the water had gushed and spurted from the nozzle when the bottle had been knocked over, remembered the way it first spread over and then soaked into the bedding all around Nezumi's body. Suddenly that seemed like a terrible omen.

She tumbled end-over-end and when she righted herself, her head broke through the surface and she gasped, inhaling sweet fresh air into her burning lungs. She was surprised to discover that she was suspended in the water, floating on the surface alongside broken tree branches and empty wrappers. Her paws churned at the water reflexively, her body instinctively understanding the mechanics of swimming without her brain delivering the order, and she uttered a short silent prayer of thanks to the Spirits for instructing her.

Rats are excellent swimmers. Bitey had no way of knowing this herself, but centuries ago her ancestors had once crossed continents; they swam in writhing brown-bodied masses across rivers and lakes out of Asia and across Europe on their initial conquest of the world. Now, the collective memories of millions of Norway rats filled Bitey's mind. They instructed her paws and showed her how to use her tail as a rudder. She learned, in the span of seconds, how to swim, and she pressed forward because the only alternative was drowning.

The water buffeted her aside, but the current moved in her favor, and she only had to work to keep herself straight: the current itself moved her forward toward the rear of the store, toward the cage and Monster. The current was strong and she crossed the aisles much faster than she had by foot. She swam past the aviary, heard the angry sound of squawking birds and rifling feathers. She tried to smell the others, but it was no use—her nose was clogged with muddy water and her whiskers were damp and drooping. In her peripheral vision, she thought she saw someone in the water, a bobbing dark shape, but she blinked and it was gone. No time to wonder about it. She pressed on.

The small-animal unit loomed before her and she twisted her tail to bank a hard turn. The water shoved her roughly and she spun around, making a neat semi-circle in the eddying current. It tugged her back, and for one desperate moment she was certain that she would be torn away into oblivion before she could get her paws back beneath her. She paddled furiously, kicking with her hindpaws and clawing at the air before her, and fought the current with painstaking effort. She moved at an angle, and realized that there was a little triangle of stillness directly in front of the cage; water rushed in from either side, but the cage itself blocked the direct flow of water and created a relatively tranquil shadow. She swam for this.

Before her, the water was nearly to the top of the cage. Inside the cage was dry—for now—but as soon as the water line broke over the wire ceiling it would begin to invade it just as she had imagined it would. Inside, Monster was not pressing herself desperately against the glass; she was not crying for help. Instead she lay curled in a ball, her head buried beneath her body and her fur on end. It was impossible to say whether she was even aware of the outside world.

"Monster!" Bitey yelled, dog-paddling toward the cage. She put her paws on either side of the wooden flap that folded over it, keeping it from being opened without a key. "Monster, can you hear me? You have to get out of there. You're going to die."

Either Monster did not hear, or Monster wasn't listening—either way, there was no response.

Cursing, Bitey clung to the inch-wide wooden lip and tried to think. How could she get Monster out? There was no way back inside of the cage without breaking the glass. She would have to go under the display again, and come back up on the other side.

Was that even possible?

"Only one way to find out," she muttered. Her heart thudded and her thoughts swam with the intoxicating effect of adrenaline. There was no time to hesitate, no time to think, and so she acted on instinct—the same instinct that told her to bite the unknown, the same instinct that had driven a wedge between herself and her family. She took a deep breath and, uncertain of what she was doing, not sure if it would even work, dove beneath the water's surface.

It invaded her nostrils immediately and burned her eyes. She fought against the water as it tried to work itself inside her lungs, closed her eyes tightly against the searing pain of grit and debris, and forced herself down through the floodwater toward the floor. Water pressed in around her. A terrible pressure filled her ears and the burning in her nostrils spread into her nasal cavity and she wanted desperately to sneeze but she couldn't. She swam hard, and found her forepaws scratching at linoleum; her eyes opened, and she propelled herself forward with a kick of the haunch and a flick of the tail, dragging her body through the floodwater. There! The bottom of the display was before her, and she drug herself along the linoleum, finding footholds as best she could to launch herself forward without bobbing back up to the surface.

She had to turn herself sideways to grab hold of the bottom lip of the display, and for a few terrifying moments she felt utterly trapped. The ceiling pressed down on top of her, water crowding her from every side, and there was no way out but to press forward. The tight space, usually a comfort for a rat, had become tomb-like, and she dragged herself forward as quickly as possible. Her lungs burned. She released a bubble of air, to relieve the pressure in her chest, and her brain screamed for oxygen. Stars burst into her vision. For one terrible moment she thought she would lose all consciousness and simply surrender to the terrible cold of the flood.

But, then, she was through it. She became aware of open air above her, and she turned upward, propelling herself towards the dim gray surface with desperation. She broke the surface and gasped for breath, swallowing water and choking and gasping. She bobbed uselessly for a moment, her thoughts a jumbled daze, and then she remembered what she was here for, and why, and she made for the top of the cage display.

"Monster!" she called, in a hoarse, waterlogged voice as soon as her paws hit the grating of the cage's ceiling. "Monster! Are you alright?"

"I'm fine!" Monster called back, sounding uncertain and

defensive. She raised her head and peered upward at Bitey's dripping underbelly through the mesh ceiling. "What's happening?"

"I don't know. I don't understand it." Bitey found her way to the opening in the wire and poked her head through it, peering down at the once-familiar cage. Monster sat below, a puffed-up irritable ball, and did not move toward her when she spoke. "It's the bad thing that Nezumi warned us about. Monster, we have to get you out of here or you'll die."

Monster gave her a long, uncertain look—a look that said she was struggling with the decision, a look that said *if I go outside, I'll die too*. Then, without speaking, she crossed the enclosure and climbed up on top of the igloo as she had seen the others do. She stared up uselessly at the opening, standing on her hindpaws. She was tall enough that her nose touched the wire. "I can't fit through there."

Water rose up from below and washed over Bitey's paws in waves. It slid down the inner wall of the cage and stirred up the bedding, which rose to the surface of the water in a loose mass like quicksand.

Bitey could scream with frustration, but she held herself back. "Yes you can. We got Cookie through it, you'll be fine." Silently, she wondered if Monster were right; she was larger by far than any of the others, and built of solid muscle, not flexible rolls of fat. What if she couldn't climb through the opening? What if she got stuck? What if she couldn't make it out before the water level rose and they were both washed away or drowned? But thinking these thoughts wouldn't help either of them, so Bitey kept them to herself. Instead she said, "Just put your paws through and I'll help you."

Monster tentatively grasped at the wire opening with her

paws, pulling herself up. Her limbs quivered with the effort, but she held her weight. Her head and shoulders cleared the hole, and she heaved, letting out quiet grunts of effort as she attempted to squirm forward, clawing at the mesh ceiling which was now the floor. Her hindpaws couldn't quite reach the nestbox anymore, and they flailed uselessly behind her as she tried to pull herself forward through the hole.

"I'm stuck," she said, and an edge of panic crept into her voice. The wire caught at her sides and tore into the caramel-and-white fur around the edges of her hood, digging into the vulnerable flesh at her elbows. She squeaked in pain and her limbs trembled and for a moment Bitey thought she would let go and fall back entirely, but she didn't.

The water skimmed Monster's curled tail. The nestbox, now filled with water, floated up and drifted slowly across the cage, scraping against the wall with a muted thump.

"You're not stuck," Bitey said, reassuringly, and didn't believe it for a moment. She wished they'd had time to widen the hole, but it was too late now—they wouldn't be getting a second chance. "Come on. Just push yourself through." She tried to keep her voice steady.

Monster squirmed, still scrabbling for a foothold with her hindpaws, her nails threatening to come loose from her fingertips as she pulled herself forward. Her sides caught on the wire and she squeaked in pain. She was stuck. Water spilled over into her face from the lip of the cage and she sputtered and nearly let go.

Bitey leaned forward and clamped her jaws over Monster's nape, digging her heels and tugging. She tasted blood. Monster screamed and struggled against her, and Bitey felt Monster's teeth dig into her neck and shoulders as Monster's panicked blows struck her—but Bitey did not let go, and Monster in her desperation flailed free of the wire and fell against her, snarling. They were both bleeding from a number of deep gouges and scratches, and Bitey was soaked and shivering—but they couldn't pause here, not yet. "We'll never make it back out," she said, forcing herself back to her paws. Her muscles trembled and ached and water sloshed over the top of her feet and fell like rain into the cage below. "We have to climb."

"What are you talking about?" Monster asked, baffled and angry and reeking of blood and porphyrin. "Climb where?"

There was no time to explain any of it. There was no way to convey to Monster about the enormous world they had discovered without wasting valuable time, and even if there were, she wasn't sure she'd believe it. "Never mind now. Just follow me." Bitey took off, guided once more by instinct and now memory as she crawled through the narrow space between the cage and the one above it and toward open air. The water level was maintaining at the top of the cage— temporarily being diverted into the cage itself, and saving her some time —and it allowed her a moment to get a survey of her options. "Here—this way," she said, and hid the uncertainty in her voice as best she could. Climb where, indeed. Three times now Bitey had come in here, but every time she had gone down to the floor, not up. She had no idea what was up here, if there was anywhere for them to hide. And what if the water came up level with it?

Bitey peered out of the gap, craning her neck to try and see what was above her. Overhead a wooden ledge marked the bottom of the cage above hers. The ledge was narrow, only an inch at best, but just beyond it was a file cabinet. She thought they could probably reach it if they walked to the far side of the cage. "There's a tall place, this way," she said. "We should be safe here."

"If you say so," Monster muttered in a way that suggested neither of them would ever be safe again.

When they had reached the far side of their display, she squirmed between the roof and the ceiling and jumped, landing on top of the file cabinet. Papers fluttered to the floor and disappeared into the water. The metal was smooth and cool, and she shivered against it. She caught a faint earthy scent below of some animal she didn't know; the scent was familiar enough, having been living in proximity to her. She remembered the smell from the Great One's hands, but she didn't know what it was. It wasn't *ushu*. It wasn't water. That was all that mattered.

Monster thudded beside her and collapsed. She lay on her side, wheezing with effort and fear. She reeked of blood and her fur, wet with floodwater and bodily fluid, was stained in pinks and browns and yellows. Bitey, too, was covered in blood and filth, and the two rats were hardly recognizable as rats at all, much less as individuals. Even their scents had been washed away and replaced with the bitter acrid odor of sewage and rainwater.

But, they were alive, and that was more than Bitey could have hoped for. She shivered, and laid her head on her paws, and prepared to wait. She had run as far as was possible; now, it was up to fate whether she would be washed away. She groomed herself half-heartedly, moving one paw over her face with sluggish pained movements, as a distraction from the slow and inevitable approach of disaster, and waited for the flood's next move.

* * *

Midday was approaching, and it became quite clear that the rains would not relent. The power had been flickering on and off, so Lori's mother pulled out an old crystal radio so they could keep up with the news. The weather reports were saying that the storm was predicted to last throughout the day, even well into the night, and that parts of the city were being evacuated.

Frightened, Lori called Mr. Haskins to see what she could do about the shop. When he answered, he sounded just as groggy as he had that morning, and it took Lori a few minutes to realizing it wasn't sleepiness that slurred his speech, but liquor.

"It's fine," he kept reassuring her. "If the whole town floods—so what? That's what the flood insurance is for."

"But the animals…"

"Fuck the animals," he said, and laughed without humor. "They'll give me a good price for them. Hell, that python cost so much that nobody was going to buy him anyway, insurance would be a better deal."

Lori swallowed hard to keep herself from saying something she would regret. *He's just saying that*, she thought. *He's just as upset as you are. That store is really important to him.*

"Seriously, though," he said, when she didn't respond. "There's nothing either of us can do, so why bother worrying? Tell you what. If we do lose the shop, I'll give you a cut of the insurance money. We'll call it severance pay for all your hard work."

Lori thanked him politely and hung up the phone, feeling shaky and helpless.

Downstairs, her mother packed their bags for the evacuation. She loaded up on canned tuna fish, crackers, bottles of water. When Lori came down, she asked, "Are you packed? Get together whatever valuables you have so we can get going."

"But I don't have any valuables," Lori said. She thought of the things she'd bought from the store over the past year, the things she'd been hiding away in preparation for college—the rat cage, the toys. She had been planning to take some rats with her at the end of the summer, when she was going away to school and had her own place to live. But what was the point now?

"Then go pack some clothes," her mother pressed. "We need to be ready to go if they evacuate our neighborhood."

Lori wanted to talk to her about the shop, her worries about the rats and all the other animals, but she knew better than to expect any sympathy. Her mother was fiercely practical and had no patience or affection for anything as silly as a few rodents.

Lori went upstairs to pack so that she wouldn't need to talk to her.

She pulled down a suitcase, but left it open on the floor, unable to concentrate. She watched the rain outside her window, hoping it would stop, and said a small prayer for the animals.

III

Faith in Kindness

Chapter Nine

Outside, the darkness became absolute. The sky, overcast by a thick layer of cloud cover, was an inky blanket; no sign of moon or stars shining through in the night. The rain, finally, had begun to let up, relaxing from a torrential downpour to a steady drizzle. Rain dripped down from gutters and floodwaters swirled and washed out the roads and invaded every home and building at ground level, but the weather's rage had subsided. Most of the homes nearest to the river lay empty and dark, long since abandoned as the occupants searched for high ground, warm clothes and working electricity. Besides the constant spattering of rain against the earth, all was silent and still. The birds that had hunkered amongst the limbs and weathered the storm now slept in miserable heaps of sodden feathers, beaks buried beneath wings, feathers ruffled in agitation.

Inside of Rocco's Pet Emporium, it looked like a disaster area.

The door, broken down by the constant pressure of water and wind, hung lopsided and useless on its hinge. Just under two feet of rainwater had settled inside the store, once the initial wave had subsided, and it covered the linoleum in a gray-brown overgrown puddle. Debris from outside mingled with the sodden remnants of swept-up merchandise: broken bags of food, grooming supplies, dog toys and cat beds floated side-by-side with newspapers, fast food drink cups and severed tree limbs. The power was out, and the building was cast in utter shadow and silence, save for the sounds of the rain.

Some of the animals had managed to escape. The ferret enclosure was empty, its occupants gathered in an oily pile on the roof, clustered like refugees as they waited for the water to clear. Of the small animals, none but the rats had escaped; the others huddled together inside their enclosures, feeling the pang of hunger and suffering confusion in the aftermath of the disaster. Most weren't even sure what had happened. Luckily, the water level had stopped just above the lip of the rat tank, so the hamsters, mice, gerbils and guinea pigs were dry—but they were in poor shape otherwise. Most were running low on water, and all of them were out of food.

The aviary fared a bit better. The water had invaded the wire of the cages, but it had also jarred the frame of the aviary itself just enough to pop the lock on the door, and the birds had taken the first opportunity to fly away. The rafters now were filled with birds: the little zebra finches, the lovebirds, rock doves, the cockatiels and even the one large parrot had all taken refuge amongst the beams of the ceiling. The parrot would, occasionally, call out, "Pretty bird! Pretty bird cookie pretty bird!" but even that sounded forlorn from the rafters.

The fish and the reptiles were suffering the most. The fish, especially, were feeling the effects of the power outage; filters ceased working and the water quickly became stale and rancid on their gills. The lowest level of tanks were flooded, and the feeder-fish that were kept there had swum upward into the swell of floodwater and escaped, swimming now amongst the tepid pool that covered the floor, unable to get back into their tank even if they had wanted to. The reptiles, too, were faring poorly in the cold water; most were still caught, without heat or light, inside of their tanks. They slept, unable to gain energy for much else, and resigned themselves to sit out the disaster with sluggish exhaustion. They, at least, wouldn't go hungry for a few days.

One tank was empty, though. A certain large-bodied python, a tremendous specimen that had been purchased with no intent to sell, a store mascot of sorts. The tank lay empty, the lid pried open, its occupant long gone with no indication of its whereabouts.

* * *

'Do you think Bitey made it?" Smeeze asked. Her voice sounded odd in the gloom; now that the initial rush of the water had passed, an eerie silence had descended over the building. Her thoughts were far from quiet, though. The same questions has rolled over and over in her mind, growing louder and more insistent with each pass like a snowball gathering size as it rolled down a mountain. Her thoughts were deafening, but she couldn't find the words to say them aloud. It was as though something between her brain and mouth had disconnected. "And Monster?"

"I don't know," Top Ear replied, wearily. She began licking her paw and was silent for a long time. When she spoke again, her voice sounded faraway and hollow. "They're strong. Maybe."

Silence descended upon them once more as Smeeze tried again to reconcile the gap between her mind and her mouth.

Her head buzzed. When she closed her eyes, she saw the same scene played over and over: Bitey leaping into the floodwater, dog-paddling toward the cage they had abandoned Monster in. The image was burned so indelibly in her mind that when she opened her eyes the image persisted, the ghost of a memory.

It should have been me, she thought, over and over as she watched the image replay in her head. *Why didn't I think about saving Monster? Why didn't I jump in after Bitey? Why am I still safe and dry?*

"We should eat," Top Ear said, in the same dull, flat voice she had spoken with earlier. She didn't look at Smeeze when she spoke; her dark eyes were fixed on a distant part of the building, at the pale rectangle of light that marked the gaping door.

"I'm not hungry," Smeeze replied. Her stomach grumbled a loud refutation. She wondered how long they had been up here, and how long they would continue to be trapped by the dirty brown water. She thought of the others—of White One and Dumbo and the rest—and wondered if they were huddled on a high shelf also, staring down at the devastation, or if some other fate had befallen them.

"Me, neither," Top Ear said. "But we should eat, all the same. Eat, and then figure out a way back." She peered over the edge of the shelf. "We can probably jump down and swim back, just like…" she caught herself, then, with the embarrassed look of someone who knows they've said a terrible thing, and went back to licking her paw.

Smeeze spared her a curious, sidelong glance. She had never had much opportunity to get to know Top Ear—a strange fact, considering the size of their shared living quarters, but true. The colony had been united uneasily under Nezumi, but it had really been two separate groups: those who lived to be chosen by the Great Ones, and those who distrusted them. Smeeze had always belonged to the second group. Bitey, also. But she was the only one of Nezumi's children that had, and the tension between her and the Berkshire sisters especially was impossible to deny. "You said yourself that she probably made it."

"We should get back to the others, if we can."

Smeeze understood that 'the others' meant White One and Dumbo and all the rest they had left at the other shelf. Did that mean she had given up on Bitey? "Alright," she said. She rose wearily to her paws. Her joints felt like they were filled with sand. "…And then we go to look for Bitey and Monster?" Her voice sounded smaller and more pathetic than she liked—petulant, even—and she winced as the words crept from her mouth. When the question had formed in her mind, it had been both confident and forceful, an order rather than a plea.

Top Ear closed her eyes, looking suddenly old and weary. "We'll see what happens first. Then we'll go, if we can." She opened her eyes and swallowed. "We really should eat before we go, but I don't think we'll have time. Come on. Plenty of food back there. Not all of it can be wet."

Again, the suggestion of food seemed blasphemous, sacrilegious somehow, and Smeeze balked at the notion. She tried to think about the food-filled shelf, the paradise that they had discovered and claimed all for themselves, but the thought didn't bring her any comfort. Their sanctuary had been flooded, their Eden defiled, and it didn't matter whether the food was dry. Smeeze had an idea that it would all taste like sand.

Top Ear paused at the edge of the shelf, peering over it. Her whiskers swept forward and she tasted the air, licking her lips. It was a very long drop. The floor had disappeared under the rippling brown water. "Should be alright to drop down into it," she said, mostly to herself. "When Bitey jumped in, it seemed to catch her. I think it will do that for us, too."

Smeeze pressed in beside her, staring down with a gathering feeling of miserable terror in her gut. Her eyes swept over the ruins of the store, searching for another route. The ferrets, below, had stirred from their frightened pile, and began to move on the island of their cage roof. "Wait!" She nipped Top Ear's shoulder, just in time—Top Ear was midway to leaping down into the water. "We don't have to jump."

"Well, no," Top Ear replied, crossly. She shoved Smeeze off of her and bristled, but did not attack. "I suppose we can climb down first. But what's the point?"

"No," Smeeze said, backing away a few steps in case Top Ear decided to attack her after all. A sudden, vivid image sprang into her mind of the two of them tumbling ears-over-tail into the water and she shivered. "I mean, we don't have to go into the water at all. Look." She gestured with her muzzle to the ground below. Cat furniture had been swept from the bottom shelves of the display, and now lay scattered in the water, half-submerged like carpeted logs in some very strange swamp. The ferrets, once over the initial shock of the flood, had discovered these unorthodox stepping stones, and were making short work of escaping their island.

Smeeze watched as one of the weasels slid down the side of the cage, plopping unceremoniously onto the upright end of a carpeted cat post. It hesitated there for a moment before jumping to the next one, running along its length, and then leaping to the next. The furniture bridged the gap between the ferret cage and the side wall, which was filled with empty cages, and the ferret jumped from the last carpet-covered post onto a cage, deftly climbed the wire, and disappeared into a shadow between two cages.

"If they can do that," Smeeze said, "so can we."

* * *

White One opened her eyes with tremendous effort. They felt glued together, and she had to blink away the crusted porphyrin that had sealed the lids. She had tried to sleep, for a while, but sleep had brought dreams: half-formed sensations of the world spinning away from her; dark shapes moving in murky, dim light; a silver-blue rat tumbling ears-over-tail through a gaping chasm into emptiness. When she woke, the dreams refused to release their hold on her, and she struggled with shadowy memories that mingled with dreams until she could no longer tell which what had been real, and a short-lived hopefulness flooded into her. *Maybe it had all been a nightmare,* she thought. *Maybe I'll open my eyes and realize that everything is fine.*

She blinked, clearing away the grit, and reality swam into focus in slow waves. Her underbelly was damp, but not soaked. Her nostrils burned with unfamiliar odors, but they mingled with scents that she recognized, and she tried to sort them out, to make sense of what had happened. "Dumbo?" she asked, rising to her paws to shake herself all over, then ran her paws over her face. She seemed totally alone. "Sniffles?" Then, hopefully, "...Squeaker?"

"You're awake." Dumbo's voice broke from closer than White One had expected. Dumbo crept out from hiding, appearing from between two bags of chinchilla food. She had a harrowed, worn expression that suggested she had gone too long without sleep, and her ears swept constantly forward and back. "How are you feeling?"

"I'm fine." White One paused in her grooming, forepaws raised, and cast a shrewd look at Dumbo. "What's the matter? Why are you looking at me like that?"

"You've been out for awhile," Dumbo said, hesitantly. "I was starting to think…"

"I'm fine," White One reiterated. What else was she going to say—that she'd allowed herself to sleep so that she could hold out hope that what had just happened had been a dream? That she'd hidden inside a nightmare rather than face responsibility for what she had done, and what she had failed to do?

"I'm glad," Dumbo said, quickly. "With everything that's happened, Nezumi, and…well. I was scared maybe you'd gotten sick." She paused, her expression grim. She busied herself looking everywhere but at White One.

"What is it?" White One shot her a sudden, piercing look.

"It's just…well, Sniffles is in a bad way."

White One lowered herself back to all fours, systematically testing each joint and muscle with long, deliberate stretches. She was stiff from sleep and cold. Her joints ached from the abuse of landing on them—how long ago had that been now?—and the strain of reaching and grabbing Sniffles from the flood. But she would be fine. "How bad?"

"…Bad," Dumbo said, and sighed. "They're the next shelf up. Cookie's keeping an eye on her. I helped drag her up there. It's warmer, see, since it didn't get wet at all." She offered a confident, bolder-than-she-felt smile, and crept forward. "Now hold still, and let me groom you. You're filthy."

White One and Dumbo had never been friends, and this sudden showing of kindness made White One stiffen with unease, but she didn't draw away. Certainly, the black rat had never been unkind. But she had always lurked in Top Ear's shadow before. Now she laid both paws on White One's back and began grooming her with rapid nips of the teeth and gentle strokes of the tongue, washing the filth and grime from her pelt, and White One realized that no one had groomed her so attentively since her childhood. White One remained still and silent throughout, wincing slightly as Dumbo pulled out matted hairs and occasionally releasing small peeps in protest of the intermittent pain of the procedure.

When Dumbo was satisfied with her work, she withdrew, giving White One a final once-over before allowing her back to her paws. "You hungry?"

"Not particularly," White One said, gratefully nudging Dumbo's shoulder, running her tongue over the hollow where her neck connected with her shoulder. "I'd like to go see Sniffles, though, if that's alright."

Dumbo's brow furrowed, and she hesitated a moment, but relented. "Of course." She started to say something, thought better of it, and fell silent. After a moment, "It's easiest to go up this way." She led the way to the corner, where there was a gap of a few inches between the shelf and the pegboard it was attached to; multiple bags of food lay upon each other at a bias, creating a sort of stairway, and Dumbo clambered over these and leaped up through the opening and onto the next shelf with ease. White One followed suit, squeezing through the gap and heaving herself up onto the shelf with minimal effort, the soreness in her body dissipating slightly now that her muscles were being put to use.

Atop the shelf, the others had built a makeshift nest between two bags of food out of miscellaneous shredded bits of packaging and timothy hay. Cookie sat at the mouth of their cubby hole, absently munching at a pumpkin seed. Her expression was distant and thoughtful and not at all at home on her usually pleasant face. She ate mechanically, in a way that suggested she was eating more from compulsion and stress than hunger, and White One offered her a meager smile as she approached. Inside, sheltered between the walls made by the food bags on either side, was Sniffles.

She was barely conscious. Her eyes were open, but they had a glazed, distant look. Her breath came in rapid, rasping gasps that heaved her sides and rattled through her throat like the sound of leaves in the wind. Her body was limp, and her sides were sucked in uncomfortably, as though it took everything in her body to make her lungs function. Death hung in the air, hovering over them like a miasmic cloud.

"What's the matter with her?" White One whispered, lowering her nose to touch it to Sniffles' flank, nuzzling her tentatively. There was no response, only a wet "pop" as she exhaled.

"Her lungs are just…they've had enough, I think," Dumbo said, and her voice was a quiet, flat monotone. "She's been bad before, but not like this. I think the water, and the stress, and the cold…" she trailed off.

"How do we make her better?" White One asked, nosing her flank again, desperation welling up inside. White One was a problem solver, but this was a problem she had no idea how to solve. That filled her with far more dread than she had felt at any time before. The cage, the rushing current, the cold wall of water. All of that had been something she could endure or escape. This…this was entirely out of her depth, and the look of resignation on Dumbo's face was infuriating. "There's a way to make her better, right?"

"I…I honestly don't know." Dumbo's whiskers drooped. "I don't…I mean, I'm not a *nosobo*. Maybe Squeaker could have…" she trailed off,

"Nobody blames you, White One," Cookie said, from the opening of the impromptu nest. Her whiskers twitched. 'Sniffles told me, when she got up here, before the cold set in. She told me what you did for her. She appreciates it, you know."

"Yeah," White One said, drawing away. She didn't trust herself to say anything else. Thoughts buzzed through her mind, a constant chatter that made it impossible to understand anything clearly. The nest felt suddenly over-crowded, and she felt that, maybe, she could think things through if she could just get away.

She nosed past Dumbo and Cookie and made her way out onto the shelf. She climbed wearily to the top of the display, pulling her sore body upward with tired, trembling limbs. Maybe if she got high enough, she could see things clearly, or sort out the jumble of thoughts in her brain. Maybe she could figure out a way to make this better. Settling down between two over-stuffed bags of food, she cast a look over their ruined paradise.

It was a mess. Every sensory input available to her told her that much: the store was in shambles and chaos. She sniffed at the air, searching for any sign of Bitey and the others, but the reek of floodwater was too overpowering and drowned out all other odors. She called out, a loud, long series of desperate chittering yells, and awaited a response, but there was none.

She settled back to her belly, curling up between the bags, and tried to think up a plan.

Somewhere nearby, something rustled. She jerked back to her paws, ears and whiskers pinned forward. "Who's there?" She called, and sniffed at the air. There it was—faint, poisoned by the acrid smell lodged in her nostrils, but obvious. Rat-smell. Unfamiliar rat-smell.

She wheeled around, hissing, and lunged at nothing. Somewhere to her left, she heard a low snicker. "Who is it?" she asked, again, aggressively, with more dominance than she felt she could maintain. "Who are you?"

"Who?" an unfamiliar voice said, appearing—not from the left, where White One was now staring, but from her right, approaching from the flank. "What sort of question is 'who'? What does it mean by 'who'?"

White One wheeled around, hissing at the intruder. She found herself face-to-face with a small brown-colored rat, built similarly to herself except for a certain hardness and sturdiness, a sinewy quality. Its face was wizened and shrewd, and White One was puzzled by the odor, for there was something peculiar and strong about it that stirred her senses, resonated with something inside of her. It smelled earthy and wild, intoxicating and dangerous and undesirable all at once, and she was simultaneously attracted and repulsed.

"We have no who," another voice said, appearing from the left where the snicker had come. It approached White One from the other side, and she backed away uncertainly, finding herself at the edge of the shelf, unable to back away any further. This other rat was brown-furred also, but the fur was a bit darker and there was an uneven splash of creamy yellow-white along its underbelly. It, too, had that odd scent that White One could not place. "We have only what, and what you are is an intruder. Explain yourself."

White One had never met a wild rat, and it had never occurred to her that such a thing could even exist. She had also never in her adult life encountered a male rat, and the combination of these two new experiences was intriguing and frightening and fascinating all at once. She knew what males were, of course, and had a vague idea of the mechanics of reproduction, but nothing she had learned had prepared her for the actual confrontation with one. She planted her feet, staring down the males, fur on end and tail slowly lashing behind her. They were both larger than her, and they bore down on her intimidatingly, but she stood her ground out of necessity. "I don't mean to intrude. My friends and I were caught in the Big Water, and found our way here from necessity." Her ears pinned back to her head, but she made no move toward the offensive. "Please. One of us is very ill."

The lighter-colored of the two weaved a little, regarding her thoughtfully. He seemed to be the less dominant one, and held himself with a nervous uncertainty, the same ill-contained energy that White One herself was known for. She sensed that they were all, at their core, the same type of rat: rats who felt the urge to escape, to run, to explore. Feeling that they might have something in common, she pressed on, boldly filling the awkward silence that had settled between them.

"We come from inside a cage," she said, trying to keep her voice well-reasoned and keep the pleading tone out of it as best she could. "If this is your territory, we're sorry. We don't know the rules here."

"Cage?" the light-colored one asked, brow furrowed in confusion. He glanced at his companion, perhaps hoping the darker one could shed some light on the situation as he was clearly unfamiliar with the term.

The darker one, who was a bit larger and carried himself with confidence, pressed his shoulder into the lighter one and bared his teeth at White One. He reminded her somehow of Bitey. "You say you have friends," he said, ignoring the cage conundrum. "Where are they?"

She fidgeted with this for a moment, indecisive. Should she tell them? She didn't want to expose them to harm—but she also didn't want to find herself thrown over the edge for lying. And what if they could help her?

Before she could think up the right response, Dumbo poked her head over the edge of the shelf. "White One?" she asked, her voice sounding both baffled and amazed. "Is that you? Who is that you're talking to?"

Both males lunged for her, moving nearly in unison. The darker male sidled against her, pressing her to the wall, aiming bites for her haunches. She flipped, rolling to her back, guarding against his onslaught by thrusting her paws into his face. The smaller of the pair slipped behind her and tore at her neck and shoulders.

"Stop it!" White One yelled, bounding across the shelf, launching herself into the fray because there was nothing else she could think to do. "Leave her alone! We mean you no harm, please!"

Not sure what she was doing, or if it would help at all, she leaped on the back of the dark one and aimed a bite for his haunch. She scratched and dug her claws into his flesh as much for a foothold against his thrashing as to attack. They screamed and tussled and hissed and he threw himself onto his back in an attempt to dislodge White One. This opened him up for attack from beneath, and Dumbo pressed her sudden advantage.

White One had never seem Dumbo assert her dominance before. She had, for the most part, been satisfied to live beneath the authority of the others, submitting to Bitey and even Top Ear when confrontations came. But now that she was in action, White One couldn't help but marvel at the amazing speed and power she possessed.

In rat society, it is often the lower subordinate that takes the alpha position once it becomes open. They are, after all, well-adapted to the defensive arts as a matter of survival, and are able to competently turn the tables upon their aggressors because of their experience under the paws of bullies. Now, Dumbo was displaying that fact gloriously. She wheeled around, launching an attack on the dark-male's underbelly. She tore at his most sensitive places—attacking his joints and groin with lightning speed, her aim guided by instinct and desperation. The lighter one attempted to leap upon her exposed back, but Dumbo was too fast for him, and kicked out with a hindpaw, sending him reeling into the wall of the shelf. He hit with a clang and crumpled, temporarily dazed.

The dark one finally managed to unseat White One from his back, but he wobbled unsteadily on his paws and fell to his belly. He exposed his neck to her in sign of submission.

"Alright!" he squeaked, and he sounded both confused and impressed. "Please, stop."

Dumbo showed no signs of wanting to cease her onslaught, but White One pushed her back. "Stop," she whispered, intently. "There must be more. Let's not be hasty until we know what the situation is."

Dumbo grumbled a little, dissatisfied, but relented. She

fell back to her haunches and groomed herself in a show of bravado, though her eyes lingered distrustfully upon the beaten males. She had a wide, shallow scratch down the bridge of her nose, and her white-cuffed paws stained crimson from blood as she cleaned her face.

"As you can see," White One said, feeling much more confident than she had moments prior, "we are capable fighters, and will not be easily forced into submission. There are more like my friend, here, and we will not hesitate to kill you if we must."

She smirked a little, unable to help herself. If the males could be so easily bested by Dumbo, she could only imagine what would happen if they ran into the likes of Bitey or Monster.

Bitey. Where was she now? And Monster…had she made it out, or had she fallen victim to the Big Water?

Unexpected pain welled in her chest, and White One was forced to pause and gather her thoughts. Something hard formed in her throat when she tried to speak. The dark rat, sensing weakness, began to stand, but found himself quickly subdued by Dumbo's weight pressed against his shoulders, a warning bite delivered to his nape. The scent of freshly-spilled blood was heavy on the air.

"Don't even try it," Dumbo growled into his ear, tail lashing behind her. "White One may be willing to hear you out, but I'd just as soon see your insides."

He peeped, now utterly cowed, and White One continued. "There are two of you, but I know there are more. You do not come from our cage. You are not like us. Tell me what you are, and I will call my friend off."

"*Laysi*," the light one rasped from the corner, rising to his paws. He shook himself, unsteadily, and stretched. His bones popped loudly and he winced. "We are *laysi* for the *Ukeshu.*"

Laysi? White One puzzled over the word for a moment, as it was not immediately familiar to her. She understood the components, and recognized it as a rank, but had never heard the term used that way before. *Run, find, see.* They were…runners, then. No, explorers. Scouts. Not a rank they would have in a cage setting, of course. White One smiled a little grimly. Now that they mentioned it, she supposed she too was a *laysi.*

"Scouts, then," she replied, and tested out the term on her tongue. She liked the sound of it, and filed it away for future use. "And who is this *Ukeshu?*"

The wild rat floundered, clearly not understanding the question. He stared at her, maw working quickly and eyes boggling in awkward uncertainty. Dumbo, still seated upon the larger male, dug her claws into the skin of his neck, and he squeaked in protest.

"Don't hurt him," White One said. She wasn't sure why she felt Dumbo should spare him any pain, as he would certainly not extend the same courtesy to them if their roles were reversed. Still, she was now confronted with something of a puzzle, and White One was incapable of walking away from a problem needing solving. "You don't understand 'who,'" she said, thinking out loud. She remembered that the wild ones had said that, when they first approached, and it had made no sense to her then—but now, she tried to understand it so she could properly phrase her question. How could they have no sense of 'who'?

Something occurred to her, then, and she looked up, eyes narrowed shrewdly. "What are your names?"

"Names?" the male echoed, looking more baffled than ever.

Dumbo, who hadn't quite caught on and who hardly had the patience for word games, snapped, "Yes, your names. What are you called?"

"We are called *laysi*," he said, his expression now totally bewildered and a little desperate. There was an unspoken plea in his eyes for them not to hurt him. White One felt herself softening toward him immediately. "I told you."

"That's *what* you are," White One said, patiently, cutting off Dumbo before she could say anything else. "Not *who* you are. Who you are is…you, specifically. What are *you* called? What do the Great Ones call you, to separate you from the others?"

"We know no Great Ones," the dark one said, in a hiss—not so much because he was angry as because Dumbo's weight was choking him. "We know none of what you say. We are only *laysi*. Maybe—maybe you speak with *Ukeshu*, then we understand better?"

White One and Dumbo exchanged uneasy looks.

"Do you have *nosobo*, in your colony?" White One asked.

The lighter male, apparently overjoyed at being asked a question he understood, boggled so enthusiastically that his eyes looked like they would bulge right out of his head. He ran his paws over his ears and face in a nervous gesture, shaking himself afterward. "Yes, yes. *Nosobo*."

Dumbo gave White One a questioning look, but White One ignored her. The cluttered buzzing in her head had finally settled, and she realized that she had a plan—a solution. A piece to the puzzle

"Well enough, then. If you can take us to a *nosobo* in your colony, we will speak with your *Ukeshu* and answer whatever questions they wish us to." She returned her attentions to Dumbo, and there was something fierce and blazing in her expression. "Let him up, Dumbo, and go gather the others."

"I…don't think Sniffles is up for a journey," Dumbo said, uncertainly. She seemed uncomfortable, as though not sure what to do now that the fighting had finished. "And besides, we're trapped here, aren't we? Until the Big Water goes down?"

White One looked to the wild ones for comment.

"We know paths," the *laysi* said, still nodding enthusiastically. "We know safe ways. We can get you there, safe, dry."

White One and Dumbo exchanged another look, and Dumbo relented, stepping away from her captive. He remained on his side for a moment as though dazed before finding his way back to his paws. He shook himself vigorously and peered between them, then back to his companion, looking off-put. This, clearly, was not going as well as he would have wished. Dumbo made her way to White One's side, touching her nose to her cheek.

"I don't trust them," she whispered. "Not at all."

"I'm not sure if I do either," White One admitted. "But if they know a way down, we have to take it, don't we? I for one don't want to be stranded up here with no idea where the others are or if they're safe. If nothing else, let's stay with them long enough to find the safe paths, then if we need to we can give them the slip." She grinned, because Dumbo was looking dubious, and she bumped her shoulder. "Don't look so uncertain. I'm the cleverest rat you know, and you're the daughter of an *usoothe* and apparently a scrappy fighter. We can get through anything."

Dumbo smiled uncertainly. "If you say so," she said. Her eyes became serious again. "I want to stay here, then, and keep an eye on them in case they try anything. And," she added, casting a cold glare at the others, who were now huddled together licking their wounds in the corner, "so they don't follow you down, and see where we've set up the nest."

"I'm sure they know—" White One started, but was cut off by Dumbo.

"Just, trust me. Sniffles is in no position to go on a journey anywhere. If you're getting anyone, get Cookie."

"Cookie?" She laughed, incredulously. "What good will she be if a fight breaks out?"

"And what good would she be protecting Sniffles while we're gone?"

White One sighed. "Fair enough. I'll be just a moment, then," she said, and without further delay, made for the path down to the lower shelves to explain the situation to the others.

Chapter Ten

It was a dream—the same dream that Monster always had. She was back with the snake. She could smell it, the rancid scent of *ushu*, the pressing odor of death. The snake moved with maddening slowness, slithering forth with confidence and precision. It knew she was vulnerable. It knew she was trapped. It could take its time.

The serpent was huge, unfathomably huge compared to her. She was so tiny, so fragile, so lost and confused and alone. The snake wouldn't just kill her. It would devour her. Its jaws would open and swallow her up until there was nothing left. They both knew it, and the inevitability of the thing hung heavily in the air between them.

The snake moved its body over the wood chips that made up the floor and its scales rasped against them. It stared at her with deep black pits for eyes. She looked into his eyes and saw the endless descent into death, and she felt her heart flip over in her chest.

The snake crept forward, its tongue flicking out, emitting a long hiss. It stayed there, inches from her, staring at her with those depthless empty eyes, before it lunged forward.

It moved too fast! Monster tried to dodge but was unable to. She felt its mouth close around her neck and within a fraction of a second it was around her, the long coils of its body pressing her chest and squeezing the life from her. Rows of tiny, sharp teeth held her in place. She couldn't breathe. Blood dripped from her nose. She felt her ribs strain under the immense power of the snake's coils, felt them begin to crack, and she screamed and kicked and squirmed with everything that she had.

She thrashed and clawed and bit, and she felt her teeth collide with his scales and she tasted his blood on her tongue and then there was air again, fresh air as the snake retreated from her and she tumbled head-over-heels and rolled and ran for escape. She panted and clawed at the glass and shivered and screamed and there was no way out.

Monster was hurting.

The pain was constant and intense, a deep-seated ache that crept deeper than her torn flesh and reverberated through her bones, her insides. She hurt in parts of herself that she had never known existed. Some of it was the pain from her torn skin, where Bitey had bitten her. Some was from the soreness of muscles grown stiff from over-use and the awful penetrating cold. Some, too, was hunger.

It was the hunger that woke her. She had been hovering, lost between sleep and wakefulness, in the gray place that divided life from death and reality from the Spirit Realm. Between dreams and memories, where memories become dreams and dreams become reality. She was caught in limbo, reliving the hell that had shaped her life.

With great effort, Monster opened her eyes. They were heavily crusted with porphyrin and felt glued together. She couldn't smell much, her sinuses so deeply impacted with mucus and floodwater and mud, her own body reeking so badly of blood and muck that it flooded her senses and drowned out all other odors. She was mostly blinded by the dark and her crusted eyes, and she lay senseless and confused and vulnerable for a time as she tried to remember what had happened and how she had come to this place.

She had been hungry like this before. She remembered. She had been hungry when she was with the snake. That had been three days. Three days of waiting for death, of stealing sips of water from the snake's bowl and having nowhere to hide. Three days of escaping and throwing herself desperately at the glass. Limbs shaking. Bones bruised, some broken, and so desperately hungry. Just one attack…of lunging, biting, coiling, squeezing. One time of the snake's blood on her tongue and his flesh in her teeth and beneath her claws. One time and she struck back again and again and wanted in her heart to kill the beast.

And then she had received her name, and had been pardoned.

What a worthless pardon, what a miserable existence, to be thrown back into captivity to relive the memories, to re-experience the horror. What mercy was there in that? Death still followed her—the snake still watched her. She could smell it, always. She could feel the brush of scales against her skin and hear the hiss of its approach. Its teeth digging into her shoulder and its muscles coiling around her body. She could feel it always, in her dreams and in that place between waking and dreams, and the snake waited and watched her from beyond the spirit walls with black pits of eyes that reflected her body and foretold doom.

"Monster?" a voice said, from near to her ear. "Monster, are you okay?"

"I'm fine," she muttered, feeling sense slowly creep back into her, reality slowly gaining more hold than dreams. "Would be better if it weren't for the hole you put in my shoulder." The bite, in the same place as the snake had gotten her, memory of pain, old wounds breaking open. Death was coming for her. She could feel it.

"Sorry about that." Bitey lay near to her, still damp and crusted with muddy water. Her scent was stronger even than Monster's; she reeked of fear. "Seemed like a good idea at the time."

"Right," Monster muttered, forcing her eyes open the rest of the way, forcing her thoughts back to reality, to pragmatism. She shook herself and relished in the pain of her skin tearing further. Pain like this was real. Pain like this didn't live in the world with the snake. She took a moment to collect her bearings, and to understand where she was.

Big Water. Rising Big Water, and the tear of skin on wire and of teeth against flesh. The bitter cold and wet and the flood of liquid into her nostrils and lungs and then pain and then freedom and then the snake.

No…not the snake. That part had been a dream. Always the dream.

"Where are we?" she asked.

"Above another cage, like ours but…higher."

Monster looked at Bitey, clearly baffled. Above the cage? What madness was that? There was no 'above' the cage, there was only inside and outside—and here was neither. This was some sort of maddening limbo, maybe, some barrier between life and death, a proving ground. But there was no above.

"White One found the way out," Bitey added, apparently noticing the expression on Monster's face. "There's a whole world out there, larger than anything. And food, more food that you can imagine. And no Great Ones, anywhere."

Monster scoffed. "I've seen the world," she said, irritably. "It's just a bigger cage, a trick from the Great Ones." She said this last phrase with contempt.

"I don't think so," Bitey said, a bit meekly. "This isn't like when Soft Hands puts us in that other place, when we want to bite. This is…this is different. Our own place. Free of them. For rats, alone." She paused, wanting to go on, and sighed. "Besides, just now we don't have many other places we can be."

"You pulled me from the cage, before the water rose?" Monster asked, abruptly, rising to her paws and stretching. The bite mark on her nape, and the scratches along her side, gaped open and she let out a quiet squeak of pain before collecting herself. "You pulled me out so I wouldn't drown?"

"Yes," Bitey said, tone still slightly apologetic. "The others had a chance to escape, but you didn't know it was coming. It didn't seem fair to make you stay and die."

I wouldn't have died, Monster thought bitterly. Her fate lay elsewhere. Her fate was in the eyes of the snake, and she would be alive until she met it head-on and was torn from life into death by its jaws and those terrible coils of flesh and muscle. She said nothing for a long time. Then, rather than address the topic, she directed her attention through the mesh beneath her paws, pressing her nose against it. She sniffed, deeply, trying to smell through the putrid stench that clung to her own body. "There's creatures near. Not rats. Not *ushu*. Something else."

"I know," Bitey said. "I told you—we're atop another cage. I've heard them talking, but I don't understand them."

"Wonder if they have any food?" Monster said, nose pressed through the mesh. She smelled fear. "Probably not. You said there was food outside?"

"Lots," Bitey said. "But I don't know how to get there without going under the water again." And she shivered then, as though struck in her heart by an awful memory.

Monster looked at her, shrewdly. She scratched at the mesh below her paws, and it did not give way. The animals below her moved about and made small frightened noises.

"I wish Nezumi were here," Bitey said, and winced, as though expecting to be attacked, reprimanded. "She could speak with them, is all. Find if there's another way out."

Monster allowed this thought to fester for a moment in her brain, contemplated it a long while. She changed the subject again. "You say we can get out under the Big Water?"

"Well, yes," Bitey said. "But…I wouldn't want to. It's awful."

"Do you know any other way out?" Monster asked, and crept forward toward the open space inside the unit, sniffing curiously at the open air. It smelled of tepid water and spoiled food. "Or where else we could find food?"

"No," Bitey said, and reluctantly came alongside her.

"Then we go the way you know how," Monster said. The snake was gone, for now. She could no longer smell it, could no longer feel it leering at her. "We get out, and find food, and find the others. Then…" she trailed off, not knowing what to do 'then'. Still, it was a better plan than lying on the wire, listening to frightened beasts below. "How do we get out?"

Bitey explained to her, as best she could: they would need to jump, and fall for some time before they hit the water. Then they would need to dive beneath, and go under a dark, heavy place, and emerge on the outside. And once they came to the surface, they would find the others. It wasn't far back to White One, if she was still where Bitey had left her.

Monster nodded, and at Bitey's order, she jumped in.

* * *

The snake had no name.

Even if the humans had given it one, the snake would not care. It had no need of such things. Names were a trivial concoction of social animals, beasts that needed to separate their ego from the collective. Animals that had need of rank and authority and individualism. The snake needed no name. It simply was. Eternal. Independent. It was the beginning and the end of its universe. An Ouroboros made flesh.

It had taken refuge on the lower level of a shelving unit, curling among bags of something or another and sleeping, for a time. It had swum, and hated it, and was in no hurry to return to the water. Instead it lay, and waited, and felt the ache inside.

The snake was hungry. It was cold, also, and the cold made it sluggish. Part of it wanted merely to curl up in the meager warmth it had found and sleep until the water dissipated, until heat returned. But the hunger was awake in him. Moreover, the hunger was primal.

Its tongue flicked at the air, tasting. It smelled weakness. Prey. Smelled the inevitable approach of death.

It wanted it.

The instinctive desire to hunt...tear...kill...crush and destroy and consume. The hunger welled inside of it, and it found its way slowly up the shelf, crawling tight-skinned up the shelving unit in a coil of muscle, seeking the source of the smell.

Chapter Eleven

"White One, I don't like this," Cookie whined. She lagged behind, shoulders hunched and fur rumpled. A wild, fearful look flickered in the depths of her eyes—the look of a rat who's been cornered and is about to bite. "I don't like this at all."

"Shh," White One said, flicking her ears back. "I know. It's not ideal. But we'll be fine, you'll see."

Cookie fell silent, save for the slight wheeze of her heavy breath. White One supposed this was the most walking Cookie had ever done in her life. The patchy female had always been too big to use the wheel—not that she'd shown much desire to do so.

The wild ones led them along a strenuous path: climbing down from the shelving unit, leaping from one island of debris to another, scrambling up the line of shelves that lined the side wall of the building. By the time they pulled themselves up onto the final row of shelves, even White One was panting. Her sprained paw ached terribly, and her lungs burned. She could taste floodwater in the back of her throat.

The wild ones gave no notice. They walked balanced on the edge of the shelf, moving with unwavering military precision. Their ears swept back, occasionally, perhaps to assure themselves that they were being followed, but otherwise they stayed trained on the path ahead. On one side, a display of cat furniture and pet kennels lined the wall. On the other side, the shelf dropped off sharply into the muddy gray flood water below. The current had stilled, and the water now lay stagnant and dark, seemingly depthless.

White One wished she had brought Dumbo along. With each step, it became clearer that they were at the mercy of these wild rats. Their journey so far had left them both exhausted and disoriented, and she wasn't certain she could make her way back to their nest on her own. The stench of the flood had washed over their trail, and her paws would never remember the safe places amid the debris.

"Are we nearly there?" Cookie asked between pants. She was so tired that she couldn't hold her tail aloft; she drug it behind her, leaving a damp trail along the shelf.

The dark *laysi*, who was foremost in the lead, let out a noncommital snort, but said nothing else.

White One considered contingency plans. There were only two rats. She and Dumbo had easily subdued them, but could she do it on her own? Could she count on Cookie to help in a fight? She doubted it. And now there was no way they'd be able to run. On her own—maybe. If her paw would hold up to the stress. If she could find the way to safety. But she already had Squeaker's death on her conscience. She couldn't abandon Cookie.

She glanced over the edge of the shelf. The water was deep and dark, and she couldn't make out its depth. Could they swim? Would the wild ones follow them into the water? Or did something lurk in the depths, waiting to pull them under, swallow them up the way it had swallowed Squeaker?

Ahead, the wild ones paused. Whiskers swept forward. Ears pricked up. One rose to his haunches, raising his twitching nose to the sky. The other crawled between two dog kennels, passing out of sight. He didn't return, and the second followed with no explanation.

White One paused at the opening between the kennels, sniffing at the air, and tried to make sense of the information her nose delivered to her. The smell of rat was heavy on the air, but she couldn't figure out why. It was a fresh smell. Immediate. But she and Cookie seemed to be alone; even the wild ones had disappeared entirely.

Before she could ask Cookie's opinion, a furry brown nose poked out of a hole in the wall. The hole was so perfectly concealed that White One hadn't seen it at first, but now it made perfect sense. It was like the gap in the wire, she thought.

The rat at the opening clicked his teeth together. "Come," he said, and then backed away, disappearing into the wall.

"Should we follow?" Cookie asked, pressing in close to White One. Her thick body nearly filled the narrow crawlspace, and she trembled slightly. "Is it safe?"

White One sniffed the wall. If they were going to make a break for it, they would do it now. She considered her paw, the burning in her lungs, the wheezing undercurrent of Cookie's breath. She thought of Sniffles and Dumbo, and about the way the water had swallowed Squeaker. A *nosobo*. She couldn't leave without a *nosobo*. "It's like the hole in the wire," she said. "That's all. Look."

She climbed through the hole. It opened into a narrow tunnel, a space gnawed open by teeth and worn smooth with use. It was close, and dark, and felt immediately comfortable —homey. She took a moment to get her bearings. She stood atop a broken cross-beam. The wooden ledge tilted downward, like a ramp, and she could feel open air before her. She crept forward. Up ahead, she could smell the agouti males that had led her here, but she could smell other rat-smells, dozens of alien odors affronting her nose.

"Many of our tunnels were flooded out," a voice—light-agouti, she thought, from the sound of it—said from up ahead. "But not all of them."

White One felt Cookie behind her. The beam was wide enough to hold them abreast, but Cookie fell into pace behind her. Her whiskers occasionally brushed the tip of White One's tail. Together, they walked down the ramp, working their way finally to solid ground. It was slightly damp, but there was no standing water, and as White One pressed forward she began to realize that she was no longer within the wall but was, rather, underground. She had never been underground, of course, but she recognized it—a gift of the collective unconscious, a memory from the Spirits. Warm, damp earth, the smell of rats. It felt right.

Ahead, the tunnel opened into a chamber. It was a large open space, the size of the old cage—perhaps even larger. Tunnels broke off from this central space like spokes of a giant wheel, but every tunnel was blocked by furry bodies. Dozens of glittering black eyes peered at them from every angle. The smell of wild rat—male and female—was heavy in the air, and it seemed that every rat in the colony had congregated here. Dozens of rats—maybe hundreds. More than White One could count, more rats than she imagined could ever inhabit the world, all of them crammed into this single cavernous space.

"Don't be frightened." The light-agouti male said from near to them. "Many of our tunnels and burrows collapsed in the flood. There is little room left for us, so we've gathered here. I imagine they're all very curious about you." He smiled, a soft twitch of whiskers. "Like I am. We've never seen a white rat before. Nor..." his eyes flicked to Cookie, who stood out terribly in her soft fawn-and-white patches and her corpulent body. "Well. Come. My brother is with the *Ukeshu*. He will want to meet you and see for himself."

Cookie pulled away, creeping tentatively toward the mouth of one tunnel. Her ears and whiskers swept forward, questioningly, toward the wild rats. They were all varying shades of black, grey, and agouti, and many were male. Cookie approached one, a dark grey-brown young male, and smiled at him. He hissed, baring his teeth, and she squeaked in alarm and nearly fell over herself as she scurried back to White One's side. She whimpered.

"Hush," White One said, irritated but also afraid. "They haven't hurt us yet. We'll be fine."

The light-furred agouti led them through a longer tunnel that opened out into another chamber. Rats crowded the opening, but they moved aside to make room for them as they passed. White One was uncomfortably aware of the brush of whiskers on her flank, the warm exhalations of breath, the cool dampness of noses. It set her fur on edge, but she tried to push down her terror. For Cookie. For herself.

This chamber was smaller than the one they had just left, and it was heavy with the scent of maleness and authority. White One stopped, whiskers trembling, and sneezed. The alien odors invaded her nostrils unbidden. She rolled back to her haunches to run her paws over her face, but Cookie stopped her, butting her shoulder into her and knocking her back to her paws. She blinked, and realized that she was in the company of the largest rat she had ever seen in her life.

He was larger even than Monster, which White One would have thought impossible. He filled up the space they were in, not just with his physical bulk but with the sheer volume of his presence, the resonating authority. He was solid black, without a hint of color or whiteness, and his fur was tattered and well-worn with age and battle. Scars crossed his pelt, the fur along his back and sides was worn so thin that his flesh could be seen through it—long, puckered lines of gray skin that twisted over old wounds. One of his ears was torn and lay flat against his head. When he spoke, his voice seemed to resonate inside of them, as though coming from their hearts rather than their ears. "My *laysi* tell me you were found outside. Explain yourselves."

White One exchanged looks with Cookie, who seemed in no rush to step forward and take the role of diplomat. Probably for the best. "We come from inside a cage," she said, choosing her words carefully, afraid that if the enormous male did not understand her explanation that he may decide to kill her just to simplify things. "We give thanks to the Great Ones for our survival, but they abandoned us to die in the Big Water, and we only survived from the guidance of an *usoothe*." And her own cleverness, but perhaps it was best not to mention that. "We are greatly divided, and frightened, but we mean you no harm."

"There are more of you?" he asked, in a way that suggested he hadn't cared at all about any of what she had just said.

"Yes," White One said, a little reluctantly, her mind racing. "One of us has taken very ill. I had hoped you have a *nosobo* who could—"

"I am asking the questions!" the *Ukeshu* snapped, and White

One quailed, falling immediately silent. "There are more. How many?"

White One hesitated.

Cookie, apparently unnerved by the silence, squeaked in alarm. "Many of us. Eight of us, in all, although we are separated and I don't know where the others are or if they're alive." Her eyes widened, realizing what she just said, and she squeaked again and buried her face in White One's shoulder. She trembled a little, and White One could not hold much anger towards her.

"Very well." The *Ukeshu* smiled. It was an alarming, wicked smile that glittered in the inky depths of his eyes. He turned his head to bare his teeth at the guard behind him. "And the others. Are there males among you?"

A sudden, uneasy feeling caught in White One's gut, and she kicked Cookie hard as a warning not to speak.

But their silence was damning. The large rat smiled. Behind them, they could feel many other rats pressing in near to them, cutting off their escape, and the girls huddled together for protection. "We lost many of our females to the Big Water," he said, and clicked his teeth together in an intimidating fashion. "They drowned in their nests, along with their *jask*. Lucky, then, that you should come along." He let that hang, with no further explanation. His one good ear flicked forward and back. His long whiskers brushed the tip of White One's muzzle. His nose twitched. "They're not ready yet. Take them to an unused chamber, and guard them until they are."

A sudden throng of rats—mostly male, some female, all of them battle-worn and reeking of the wild scent—pressed against them. They absorbed them into a wave, a furry mass that moved with the same strength and deadliness as the Big

Water. They ushered them with nips and shoves through a side tunnel. This opened into a small chamber, no larger than the space inside the igloo back home.

It smelled of amniotic fluid and blood. A birthing chamber, a long-forgotten nest. It was lined with a variety of trash objects, things stolen from the Great Ones or gathered from the garbage, and it felt slimy and unclean. As soon as White One's paws touched the ground she wanted to groom herself, but she could not. The rats shoved them both into the nest and leered at them, backing away to block off the doorway with their bodies.

"What do they want with us?" Cookie squeaked.

White One sighed, because she knew, yet could find no way to explain. She didn't have words for it, only instinct, and instinct wasn't something you could share. Not that she would, even if it were possible. The creeping horror in her heart wasn't something that Cookie deserved to feel. It wasn't something that anyone deserved to feel.

"We'll find a way out," she said, instead, in as soothing a voice as she could muster. "We'll find a way back home in no time."

She didn't believe a word of it, and for the first time in her life, White One's confidence in her own cleverness began to falter.

Chapter Twelve

"Did you hear that?" Top Ear halted, ears perked up, whiskers quivering. Her brow furrowed.

"Hear what?"

"Shh!" Top Ear rose to her hindpaws, sniffing furiously at the air. "Something is happening. A level up, I think. Above our heads."

"All the better reason to stay down here," Smeeze muttered.

Top Ear shot her a glare. "It's…I can hear it."

"And now I can smell it," Smeeze said, jerking suddenly to attention. "What is that?"

The odor came to them, rich and oily and stinking of *ushu*, and the rats froze in place. It was ferret-smell—the smell of the creatures they had seen Bitey free from their cage before the Big Water. What had Bitey decided to call them? *Shujisk*? Top Ear cocked an ear forward, and the sound came into sharper focus. Laughter.

The *shujisk* were laughing—a loud, chirping, maniacal sound that ricocheted off the walls and reverberated in Top Ear's chest and made her heart seize up with instinctive fear.

"We should run," she said, in a low voice, but her paws wouldn't cooperate.

"Run where?" Smeeze demanded, her tone angry and

skeptical. "There's nowhere to run to."

She was right. They stood on a narrow ledge in the shadow of scratching posts and cat trees. The shelf dropped away to one side, falling into the water. The other side, by the wall, was bathed in shadow and reeked of foreign smells. There were places to run—to hide—but there was no promise of safety anywhere.

Before either rat could make a move, two ferrets bounded into view.

They were chasing someone—another rat, but not one that Top Ear recognized. It was a grayish-brown female, built thin and lean, but younger than Top Ear. She looked like she had barely molted into her adult fur. Patches of soft baby down still poked through the guard hairs of her adult pelt. She ran from the ferrets, scaling cat furniture, scurrying in jagged zig-zags, but the weasels stayed on her heels. They were much larger than her. One could probably snap her in half with one bite. All three were coming their way, closing in with remarkable speed.

Top Ear stood frozen in their path, instincts screaming for action but paws unwilling to comply.

"What are you doing?" Smeeze hissed. She shoved Top Ear's shoulder, bowling her over with the impact. They rolled together, end-over-end, away from the ledge and into the open space inside of a cat perch. Smeeze kept her body over Top Ear's, pinning her with her bulk, but it was unnecessary: Top Ear was still too dazed to move.

From her vantage point beneath the cream-colored rat, Top Ear watched the small circle of the world that was visible beyond the opening where they crouched. Outside, the wild rat realized that there was nowhere to run. She paused, considering her options, and made a leap for higher ground. She jumped for the side of the cat condo where Top Ear and Smeeze now hid, throwing herself at its carpeted sides as she tried and failed to jump into the top entrance. Her paws scrabbled at the carpet. Top Ear could see her tail lashing out for balance, the flailing of hindpaws as they lost their foothold on the short-cropped carpet.

The ferrets, sensing an opportunity, closed in on their prey. The front-most bounced forward as though its body were a spring; it radiated joy and hunger, and its breath still carried the words Top Ear had first heard it say: "Hunt. Kill. Eat. Play."

The second ferret bounded at its heels, closing in at its companion's side. They were just inches away, now, and the heavy scent of their musk pervaded the small space where Top Ear and Smeeze crouched. The rat outside tried in vain to pull herself up, but the carpet was too hard, the fibers too small even for tiny claws to catch a safe foot-hold. She slid back, tail brushing the shelf as she tried once more to pull herself to the high ground.

The ferrets, focused on their target, didn't seem to realize that there were two more rats within reach. They closed in instead on the small female who clung for a paw-hold on the outside. The young rat, unable to hold herself up, fell back onto the shelf, inches from the ferrets' waiting jaws.

"No!" Top Ear yelled, surprising herself with the word as it tore from her throat. She squirmed out from under Smeeze and bolted for the opening of their hiding place.

"Top Ear!" Smeeze lunged, but not in time to stop her. Her paws brushed the fur of her flanks, and then she was out of reach.

Top Ear barreled into one ferret. Its fur felt oily against her and she realized how big it truly was, how solid. Its body was sinew and muscle, and it enveloped Top Ear and overpowered her easily. She realized, as it pinned her beneath long, dull claws, that she had no defense against it. Bitey had said that these foul-smelling beasts weren't *ushu*, but Bitey hadn't felt their hot breath and seen the long knife-points of teeth flash inches from her face.

The ferret laughed again. Its hot breath—smelling of kibble and blood—hit Top Ear in the face and made her whiskers quiver. The laughter was oddly joyous, the mirth of a maniac.

"Top Ear!" Smeeze yelled again, from the mouth of the cat perch.

The other ferret shifted its attention to her, a grin splitting its pointed maw as it dove toward her. The young wild rat, caught between them, screeched in alarm and scrambled to get out of the way.

From the shadows, a pair of furry faces appeared. Other rats. Larger than the young female, and both having a wild look. They moved with the grace of Spirits. Before Top Ear knew what was happening, they had converged on the battle. One jumped forward to bite at the flank of the ferret that loomed over her. The other aimed a bite at the throat of the ferret that was closing in on Smeeze.

The ferret on Top Ear's chest pulled back, whirling around to bite at the rat that attacked it. It hissed, baring needle-sharp teeth, and Top Ear took the opportunity to squirm from its grasp and recover her paws. The ferret no longer seemed interested in her; it was locked in battle with her rescuer. It was another female—large, built like Bitey or Smeeze, but without the layer of fat from a coddled lifestyle. She was solid muscle, and her pelt was tattered with scars. She was missing an ear, and she moved faster than any rat Top Ear had ever seen. Her jaws flashed, powerful incisors leaving a half-dozen fresh crimson wounds on the ferret's sides in the expanse of a blink.

The ferret, realizing it was overpowered, let out a cry and tried to withdraw. The rust-colored wild rat followed, single remaining ear thrust forward, dark eyes glinting with excitement.

"Enough."

Top Ear started. The word seemed to come from inside her mind, the way her mother's voice sometimes spoke directly into her thoughts. The fur along her spine stood on end.

The voice spoke again, but now it was aloud—and in words that Top Ear didn't recognize. It was the wrong language, the same alien chittering and hissing of the ferrets themselves, and it sounded strange coming from the mouth of a rat.

Top Ear didn't understand the words, but the ferrets seemed to. Both withdrew, stumbling away from the rats. The one that had attacked Top Ear was bleeding profusely from multiple bites and scratches; the other had only one wound, but it tore a deep, jagged line down its neck and shoulder. The enthusiasm and swagger had disappeared. The game was over for them, and they shuffled away in opposite directions to lick their wounds and recover from their ill-fated hunt.

"What..." Smeeze swayed on her paws, looking like she might faint. "What is it with Nezumi's children and jumping into danger? Is this hero complex genetic or something?"

Top Ear ignored her, and turned her gaze to the newcomers. The rat who had come to her aid settled on her haunches, grooming the ferret's blood from her muzzle. The small gray-brown female crept to her side, nuzzling against her, but the larger female paid her no heed.

The tan-colored male approached Top Ear, smiling. A white blaze cut a lopsided swath across his face, and he was blind in one eye. His other eye was soft and gentle. There was something wrong about his scent, something confusing, but Top Ear couldn't make it out.

"We knew that you were coming," he said, in a reedy voice—the same voice that had sounded in Top Ear's mind just moments ago, the voice that had spoken to the ferrets in their own tongue. "We knew you would come, and so we came to find you before the guards could capture you."

"What are you talking about?" Smeeze asked. She shuffled closer, looking off-put at being excluded from the conversation. "Who are you?"

"We do not know who." The odd-smelling male turned his attentions to Smeeze. He weaved his head, back and forth, trying to get a good look at her through his remaining good eye before he went on. "We were taught to know no who, only what, but we have defied that. We have names, and the power of the names has marked us. We cannot live among the others now, and so we wander."

Smeeze, who had little patience for riddles, bared her teeth at them.

The large-bodied, heavily-scarred rat bared her teeth back.

"Please. There is no need to fight," the blazed one said, stepping between them. "I am Usoothe. This," he gestured to the heavily scarred female, "is Ukeki. And our companion, Allaysi."

Smeeze scoffed. "Those aren't names," she said. "Those are titles. Ranks. Names come from the Great Ones."

The scarred female—Ukeki—bristled. "We have no need of your Great Ones," she said. She spoke the word with the same measure of disdain as Monster always did. "We are named by Usoothe, and he is our guide."

"I see," Top Ear said. Hardly a word of this made any sense to her, but she knew that she owed her life to them. That was enough for her. "Well, fine enough then. Greetings." She pulled away, edging closer to Smeeze. "I am Top Ear, and this is Smeeze."

"You're the *usoothe*'s daughter," the white-blazed Usoothe said, and something flickered across his features. "I can smell her in your thoughts."

"Um. I suppose?" Top Ear glanced uneasily at Smeeze. None of this made any sense. "I mean—yes. My mother was an *usoothe*. Nezumi."

"She does not walk in this world."

"No." It wasn't a question, but Top Ear felt it required an answer. "She…she died. Before the flood."

"She walks with the Spirits," Usoothe agreed, but that same incomprehensible expression flickered over his features as he spoke.

Top Ear and Smeeze exchanged battled looks again.

"You jumped in, to save me from the *ushu*," Allaysi interrupted. "Why did you do that?"

"Because it was the right thing to do?" Top Ear blinked, not at all sure why anyone would question what seemed like a very clear motive. "You were out-numbered, is all."

"It runs in the family," Smeeze said. "Like I said earlier. Nezumi's children—they're crazy, every one of them." There was fondness in her voice as she said it, warmth. "You should have seen her sister jump into the Big Water. It was…." she trailed off.

Bitey. Something clenched in Top Ear's chest. A moment ago, when they were cowering in terror from the ferrets, it had been so easy to forget about the others—but now it came crashing back. She and Smeeze had been walking for so long with no sign of their friends. Would they ever find the others? Were there even others left to find?

Usoothe smiled. "We have much to learn from each other, I feel. But for now, you must listen to me. You are all in terrible danger."

Smeeze tilted her head. "You mean, more than we already were? How's that work?"

"You have companions." He said, flicking his gaze back to Top Ear. He had the habit of making statements from things that should have been questions—as though he had already plucked the answer from their heads before speaking. "Females. One, like you, but with different ears. A white one, and one with patches of pale color—like your mother, but golden."

He looked at her, long and hard, waiting for her to answer. She shifted uncomfortably and said nothing. Perhaps it was a trap. But the details chilled her. How could he possibly know all of this?

"They were found," Usoothe pressed on. "By our scouts, and two are being held prisoner in the chamber of our leader."

"You're real heroes, then," Smeeze said, finally, snapping her attentions back to Usoothe. "What sort of rats are you, taking prisoners? And come to find us so we can come along? Hardly!" She hissed, lunging forward, but Ukeki stepped into her path, fur bristling and teeth bared.

Top Ear nipped her shoulder in reprimand. "Hear them out,"

she hissed.

"So then why are we sitting here talking about it? And why didn't you help them escape, if you're so noble?" Smeeze asked, glancing between Usoothe and Ukeki.

"Because we are not welcome there anymore," Ukeki said, with a growl. "They banished Usoothe, for speaking against the *Ukeshu*, and nearly killed us all."

"But we followed him, because we know his is the better way," Allaysi said.

Top Ear let out an agitated noise, rubbing her paws over her face. "None of this is making any sense. You say our friends are in danger. Why? What is the matter with them?"

Ukeki gave her a long, haunting look, a look that chills bones. "They are female," she said, simply, and left that hanging in the air.

Chapter Thirteen

In the nest, Dumbo pressed her body against Sniffles. She didn't know how long they had been alone, but it was longer than she was comfortable with, and she began to wonder where the others were and if they were alright. Sniffles was quiet, save for the rasping sound of her breath. Dumbo groomed her sister, having nothing else she could do. She ran her tongue over her face, clearing her nose as best she could, and her eyes. She was no *nosobo*, but it hardly mattered now.

Death would come soon for Sniffles. Dumbo wished it would hurry. That was a terrible thought, but one she could not deny that she felt. Death would be better than this terrible rasping limbo.

Was that true for all of them?

The thought rose in her mind, unbidden, but it took root there and refused to go away. Alone with her dying sister—a rat that could almost have been her twin, if not for the shape of her ears and the mark upon her brow—Dumbo felt lonelier than she had ever been in her life. She had never been alone before. There was no concept of privacy within a cage. Now she was alone, and she might be alone forever.

What if the others never came back? Had she made a mistake

in sending Cookie with White One instead of going herself? Should she have let them leave?

And the others—would she ever see them again? She thought of Top Ear, of how the two of them had always been inseparable from birth. Bitey had befriended Smeeze, and Sniffles had Squeaker—but Top Ear and Dumbo were true sisters. They had always been like two halves of a greater whole. And now….what good was Dumbo on her own? Was she anything at all?

Something rustled beneath her. She heard the breathing of rats, the sound of claws on plastic and metal as someone climbed the shelf.

She froze. Her nose twitched, but she could make nothing out over the stench of tepid floodwater and the pervasive smell of encroaching death. She pressed close to Sniffles. Was it more wild rats? Had they come back to finish what they had started? She wasn't sure if she could fight them again. She'd had an advantage last time, catching them by surprise—but now, she had no upper hand. And what if there were more?

But what if it was White One? What if she'd found a *nosobo* and was coming back to help them?

"Guys?" A voice—familiar, though thick with congestion— rang out, and Dumbo jumped in alarm. "Is anyone here?"

"Bitey?" Dumbo asked, shocked, poking her nose out of the opening.

It was, indeed, Bitey—and, incomprehensibly, Monster.

They looked awful. Both of them were filthy, covered in blood and slime, and there were heavy crusts of porphyrin still clinging to their eyes despite both of them being soaking wet. Monster especially looked like she had been attacked by something; her pelt was torn ragged in places around her shoulder and nape. Both had a haggard, desperate look in their eyes, and Bitey's sides heaved with effort as she struggled to catch her breath.

"Where is everyone?" Bitey asked. She flopped down unceremoniously. Monster, sides sucked in with pain, settled down next to her.

Dumbo took a deep breath and, in a faltering stream, explained everything that had happened. The Big Water swallowing up Squeaker, Sniffles hovering near to death, White One taking Cookie and disappearing with the wild ones, the whereabouts of the others still unknown.

They all fell silent for a time, once she had finished explaining. Dumbo could think of nothing better to do, so she started grooming the others. She nibbled at mats and ran her tongue over mud-encrusted fur. Bitey and Monster didn't protest against the attention, though it hardly seemed to make much difference to their grubby pelts. When she could groom no more, Dumbo rolled back to her haunches and looked them both over uncertainly. They looked almost as grimy as they had when she started.

Bitey let out a quiet, defeated noise, somewhere between a whimper and a sigh. "Too much," she said, eyes rolling in her head, exhaustion overtaking her. "I feel like I should go look for the others, but I'm just...I can't go back into the water."

"Don't," Dumbo said, licking her between the ears. "We can't risk anyone else getting sick, or swallowed by the water." *And I don't want to lose another sister*, she thought, but didn't say.

But Bitey seemed to guess what she was thinking. "Do you think Sniffles will make it?" She asked.

Dumbo didn't trust herself to answer. Her silence spoke volumes.

Silence settled between them for a while, before Dumbo finally hesitantly asked the question that had been nibbling at her thoughts since their arrival. "Bitey. How...tell me everything that happened. How did you get here?"

Bitey snorted. "I...I don't know if you'd understand, or if I could explain," she said. She nibbled at the fur on her wrist. "I don't have words for things, not the way White One does. It doesn't matter. We're alive. That's all."

Monster withdrew, limping away from the nest and settling in the corner of the shelf nearby. She looked pensive but not as surly as she generally did. She found one of Cookie's *chusim*, and began meditatively gnawing on a lab block. "Something's coming," she said, ears twitching. "The snake. The snake is coming."

"The snake isn't coming, Monster," Bitey said, patiently, without looking up from her paws. "It's just a feeling you get, sometimes."

"No," Monster said. Something was wrong with her voice. It sounded hollow – and young, petulant, like a child's plea. "No, no, no."

Bitey met Dumbo's eyes. Her brow furrowed, and she rose tiredly to her paws. Dumbo followed her out of the nest. Monster sat, hunched over, against the corner of the shelf. Her fur stood on end, and she gazed down at the water with wild, bulging eyes. She quivered.

Dumbo looked past her, trying to see what she saw. At first, there was nothing. Then, like a shadow, it appeared—pulling its long, lean body over the lip of the shelf. Water glistened on its sides. Its long black tongue flicked out, tasting the air, and it emitted a low hiss as it lowered its body onto the cold metal of the shelf, just a foot from Monster's trembling form.

Ushuzu-sim.
The snake.

* * *

"We're trapped, aren't we?" Cookie said, pressing in close to White One's side.

A dozen pairs of cold black eyes gazed hungrily upon them. Guards blocked the exit, made a circle around them. They had not moved from their posts since their arrival. They simply sat and watched, barely blinking, barely breathing. Only the slightest quiver of whiskers proved that they were alive—that, and the hungry gleam in their eyes.

Rats should not be so deathly calm and so utterly still. It was unnatural.

"Looks like it," White One said, but she was only half-listening. The whole thing was so illogical. These rats were waiting—patiently biding their time. But why? What was the point in holding them hostage? Why not kill them? What did the wild ones want from them that was worth waiting for? White One thought she knew; she felt the understanding tug at the back of her brain. But when she tried to pin the thought down, to put words to her dread, it made no sense at all.

More unnervingly, something stirred deep down in White One. She had no name for it. It was a resonating excitement, an uneasy nervous desire for something. Like the desire to run, or eat, or drink—a basic, instinctive craving.

White One cast her gaze toward the guards, suddenly hyper-aware of their masculinity. Their scent filled her nostrils and clung to her whiskers and her heart beat faster—in fear? Or from something else? She felt something stir in her, like the discovery of something hidden deep inside. The only coherent thought in her mind repeated itself, over and over, but it didn't help because she wasn't sure why she was thinking it. Perhaps it was a thought from the Spirits.

Not now. Not with them. I don't want them to do it.

"White One?" Cookie asked.

White One shook herself away from her contemplations. "What?"

"What are you thinking about? Do you have a plan?"

White One hesitated. Could she begin to explain what she was feeling in her heart? In her body? The emotion was too complicated. Desire and dread, restlessness and fear. She couldn't sort out her feelings from the terror. Finding no words for the uneasy sensation that spread through her, she merely offered a smile to ease Cookie's worries. "When I find us a way out of here, I'll tell you."

Cookie returned her smile, clearly relieved. She touched her nose to White One's side. "I'm glad you're here. If I have to be captured…you're the rat I want at my side," she said.

White One wished she had as much faith in herself as Cookie had in her.

Chapter Fourteen

The snake slid over the lip of the shelf—slow, agonizingly deliberate, terrifying in its confidence. Its tongue flicked out, tasting the air, and it slid over the edge and onto the shelf, long coils of muscle and sinew piling up behind it. The snake was a behemoth, four feet long and as thick as a human arm, its head the size of a grown rat.

It's come for me, Monster thought.

It loomed there, a tremendous leviathan, but it did not strike at Monster. Instead, it shifted its path, sliding its scaly body over the shelf between her and the others. Its sides rustled against the bags as it uncoiled and crept forward. Its target became clear: The nest. Sniffles.

Nearby, Dumbo and Bitey both stood as still as statues, frozen in terror. They had never seen the *ushuzu-sim*, and Monster's stories could not have done it justice. Monster knew what was going through their minds. It was the snake's eyes, the way they bore into you, hypnotized you. She remembered freezing in terror before its mesmerizing gaze. But she remembered what came after. The bite. The squeeze. The wet crunch of her ribs cracking. The taste of her blood in her throat.

Bitey and Dumbo stood together outside the mouth of the

nest. Just a few inches away—but enough. Monster, from the corner of the shelf, could see clearly what was about to happen, even as she saw the others watching with dumbfounded expressions.

It happened quickly.

The snake lunged into the nest, striking at Sniffles. Its jaws clamped around her prone form.

At the same time, Monster leaped across the shelf. She cleared the distance between herself and the snake in two bounds. Running on instinct and rage, she shoved past Bitey and Dumbo and threw herself at the snake's broad scaly back.

The terrible hunger, the hours of waiting, the desperate feel of death upon her back. The snake, always watching, always desiring, the soft slither of its body over bedding.

She struck. Teeth tore through scales. Blood crept around her claws, pooling up from beneath the surface of the reptile's flesh. Monster curled her toes and dug in, feeling the shift of muscles beneath her paws.

The snake, startled, released its hold on Sniffles and whipped around to strike back at Monster, but she was too fast. Its teeth grazed her side, but she was out of its range before its jaws snapped closed. She climbed up its neck, toward the base of its head, to the place it could not reach. It thrashed, and she slid down, tearing gashes in its side as her claws caught in the scales, but she did not lose her foothold. She bit it, digging her teeth into its leathery hide. She dug her teeth in further and tasted coppery blood and rancid scales and hard, unyielding flesh. Every muscle in her body quivered with effort as she pulled herself further upward, clawing her way back for the snake's head even as it twisted upon itself in an effort to reach her.

The feel of crushing bones. Blood spurting from her nose, the taste of death in her throat. The terrible squeezing, air gone from her lungs. The slow approach of darkness.

Bitey, released from the terror that had frozen her, rushed forward to join in the attack. She bit its throat, struck at its exposed underbelly. The snake thrashed and tried to bite her, but it labored under Monster's weight. Its size worked against it; the snake was too large, and too cold, to move with the speed needed to counter the onslaught.

Monster did not relinquish her hold, but instead jerked her head, wrenching at the flesh. She felt the blood of the snake bathe her in cool crimson spurts, and the snake trembled and fell still. Bitey rolled away from it as the snake sprawled across the shelf. Monster took the opportunity to attack its face, biting rapidly at its eyes, until they burst, bleeding, from the snake's face.

The rancid taste of flesh. The snake, always watching, biding its time, waiting for another opportunity to strike. Always watching. Always waiting. Haunting her dreams.

The snake twisted in agony, shaking like a thing possessed. It trembled from fear or pain, or perhaps a spasm just rolled through it as it died. Monster couldn't be sure. Was this real? Was it the nightmare again?

It thrashed, no longer in control of its powerful body. Its tail fell over the edge, and its body, unresisting, followed it. Monster released just in time, jumping from its face before it drug her down, and the snake fell over the lip of the shelf into the water bellow.

It landed with a splash and disappeared, swallowed by the Big Water. Monster ran to the edge of the shelf to peer down at it. She couldn't see the snake below the brown surface, but she could feel it there, as if part of her had fallen with it.

Bitey came up beside her. She trembled. Monster felt the flutter of twitching whiskers against her side. "We did it," she said, and there was an edge of laughter in her voice, a nervous chitter of excitement. "We killed that dirty *ushu.*"

"It's not dead," Monster said, voice hollow. She, too, trembled, but not with the electric rush of excitement. "It's never really dead."

Behind them, Dumbo made an odd noise. Bitey turned, leaving Monster to peer over the edge of the shelf and into the muddy water below.

"Dumbo?" Bitey asked. "What…what is it?"

Monster's ear flicked back, but her eyes stayed fixed on the water. She waited for the shadow beneath the surface. Perhaps when the snake returned, it would be even larger. The size of a Great One. She could almost see it—rising from the depths, water glistening on its sides, jaws the size of a cage opening to swallow her. Her heart hammered in her chest. It would come. It was still waiting for her.

"…Dumbo?"

"She's gone," Dumbo said, quietly.

So the ushuzu-sim had drug someone into the depths after all, Monster thought. Not in body —but in spirit. Four rats rested on the shelf, but only three drew breath.

* * *

Rats mourn in a silent, subdued way. They do not draw attention to their tragedy, and do not linger in sadness. They cannot afford to lower their guard for the luxury of pain in a world full of *ushu.*

They huddled around Sniffles, all of them—even Monster—forming a quiet circle around the body, silence filled with respect. Sniffles lay lifeless, the last of her blood seeping from an open bite wound on her shoulder. From the moment of the black rat's birth, everyone had expected her young death. Yet, somehow, the shock of it was deep and visceral. It was worse than Nezumi. Worse, even, than the water swallowing up Squeaker. This was not the natural order.

Monster was fated to die by the snake. Not Sniffles.

"It's a mercy, really," Dumbo said, the emotion in her voice subdued. "She probably felt nothing. It saved her from… lingering."

"Lingering," Monster said, the word thick on her tongue. She wished she could have moved just a little faster, a moment sooner, could have killed the snake before it had the chance to strike. That, now, would haunt her dreams also. "She'll draw attention to us, if we don't…" she fell silent, then, knowing what had to be done but not wanting to say it aloud. Sniffles was not her kin. She shared blood with the others—it should be their choice.

Rats don't always consume their dead, but they often do. In part, it serves as a way to protect themselves from scavengers. It is also a way to stave off disease and decay. In dark, close tunnels, a corpse breeds sickness. More than that, though, it is a way to pay homage to the dead. Consuming them gives their Spirits rest; their living kin absorb their knowledge, their soul, and keep the Spirit from wandering. Through this, knowledge can pass through generations into the collective consciousness of the rats, joining with instinct to create something else, something unique to their experience. Knowledge, understanding of the world, delivered by the

Spirits into their very hearts.

So, in reverence and necessity, the rats silently lowered their heads to consume Sniffles— not from hunger, but from love.

Chapter Fifteen

The flood waters began to recede. Outside, the rain had stopped, and the cloud cover slowly dispersed. The first hint of stars gleamed just behind the pale gray blanket of sky. The clouds glowed, backlit by the moon. Inside, the floodwaters had dropped to six inches and trickled slowly through the open doorway. Goldfish, temporarily liberated by the flood, thrashed in the shallows. Stranded, with no way of making their way back to their aquariums, they flopped and gasped for oxygen in the stagnant water. A stench settled over the pet store: the smell of death, of dying fish and tepid water and the first hint of mildew.

Atop a cat condo, gathered in a lopsided circle, was an odd assembly of rats. Smeeze and Top Ear sat on one side, huddled together. The three wild ones sat opposite. Their eyes were blank and inscrutable. Everyone was hungry.

"There's food back at the shelf we nested in," Top Ear said. "We can get some for you, if you'd like."

"I'd like that," the smallest one—Allaysi, whom they had saved from the ferrets—said, and then looked uneasily at her companions. Her ears folded meekly to her skull. "If that's okay," she added in a mumble.

"There's not much time," Usoothe said. He sat back on his

haunches and ran his paws over his oddly marked face, the blaze shining against his tan fur like a beacon, pointing to the blue-white milkiness of his blind eye. "But it may be a good opportunity to get some food and rest, and concoct a plan."

"Why are you helping us?" Smeeze asked, for probably the hundredth time.

"As I told you, we do not align ourselves with the *Ukeshu*. He has grown mad with his power and can no longer maintain his colony. It has grown too large, and cannot support itself with the resources available to it here."

Top Ear, trying to ignore the gnawing hunger in her gut, attempted to wrap her mind around this. "So you left because the colony got too big?"

"Not precisely," Usoothe said, with the same long-suffering patience in his voice that Nezumi had often had. "We left because the *Ukeshu* cannot survive when the Great Ones return. I have foreseen it. There is only one way—and that is to side with you."

"Foreseen it?" Smeeze said, and bristled. "Foreseen what? Stop playing games and tell us what's going on."

Top Ear tried to make sense of this. "You want us to help you because you foresaw us coming, and we are the path of your salvation." But that didn't make any sense. They could barely fight off a pair of *shujisk*. The wild ones were stronger, faster, more experienced. And at least one of them could see the future, talk in foreign languages and possibly read minds. What, exactly, could Top Ear and Smeeze offer that would be of any help to them at all? "So why help rescue the others?"

Ukeki smiled with a grim twitch of whiskers. "The *Ukeshu* will have discovered by now that your companions are female," she said, and the bitterness burned in her voice. "He has little love for females, but he desires above all to swell his ranks, and so they are in constant demand."

Top Ear and Smeeze exchanged confused looks, but an uncomfortable sensation was welling in Top Ear's gut, as though some deep instinctive part of her did know precisely what was happening and was not pleased.

Ukeki, frustrated with their ignorance, let out an agitated huffing noise and continued. "Your sisters will almost certainly be pregnant when we find them. And we want those kits to be born outside of the colony, in our care, not under the *Ukeshu.*"

"Oh," Top Ear said, still feeling a bit out of her depth. "I see." She cast a furtive, sidelong glance to Smeeze, who looked at her with a mirrored expression of bafflement. Top Ear felt immediately better about her confusion.

"I want to build a new colony—a better colony, one that doesn't exist simply to feed the ego and the belly of the *Ukeshu,*" Usoothe said. "But I cannot sire litters myself, so I must resort to theft."

At first, Top Ear had no idea what he was talking about— but looking again at Usoothe, who was still sitting upon his haunches, paws raised to groom his face, she noticed a scar she had not seen before. It was a long, twisting line of bare flesh down his underbelly and across his scrotum, which was itself slightly shriveled and malformed.

"The Uesheku distrusted my genes," Usoothe said, with a wry, knowing smile, as though there were something else he desired to say but was holding back. "And so he made sure that I would not further taint the colony with my blood."

"Because you can see things?" Top Ear asked. "Or because of the blaze on your face?"

"A bit of both, I'm afraid," he said. "But enough talking, now. Let's get some food in our bellies and devise a plan, shall we?"

Smeeze snorted. "What's to say we'd let you take their *jask*?" she demanded. "What right do you have to them? If what you say is true—if they're really going to be pregnant when we find them—you would be nothing more than a thief."

"You were taken from your mother, were you not?" Usoothe asked, mildly, tilting his head. "And raised by another as her own?"

Top Ear wished he would stop doing that—climbing into people's thoughts where he wasn't wanted. It wasn't fair for him to have that kind of power. Nezumi had never done that. If she knew what others were thinking, she'd kept it to herself.

Smeeze bared her teeth. "It's not the same. Don't twist this back on me. Why should we help you steal from us?"

"Because we know where your friends are," Ukeki said. She lifted a paw to scratch at the stump of her shredded ear. "And you don't."

Top Ear's gut squirmed. White One and Cookie. If these wild rats were telling the truth, then refusing their terms would be like abandoning them. If they were lying, then... what? What was the end goal in any of this? "This colony," she said, trying to find something about these rats to understand. "That you want us to help you build. Why? What's it like?"

"It will be wonderful!" Allaysi burst out, then ducked, ears folding back. She looked nervously at her companions, then added in a quieter voice, "Everyone will have names. And when the Great Ones return, they will see us, and love us, and bless us."

Smeeze snorted. "Please. They've abandoned us. Why do you think they'd care about you?"

"They didn't abandon you," Usoothe said, lowering himself back to his paws. "It's a test. The best—those that pass the test—will be taken with them into the Beyond."

"The Beyond?" Top Ear echoed. This was getting more ridiculous by the second. "But…that doesn't make any sense. We're in the Beyond. This is it."

Usoothe laughed. "Oh, no child. You don't understand. This is nothing." He tilted his head, gesturing with his nose at the open space of the store. Somewhere very far away was an open door, though none of them could see that far. "That is the Beyond. The world outside—where the Big Water came from. The source of light, and air. All of this is nothing but a cage."

Cages within cages, Top Ear thought. When did it end? How could you ever know if you were really in the Beyond or if it was just a bigger cage? Still—Ukeki had a point. They couldn't abandon the others. Not when nothing else made sense any more. "Let's go back to where the food is," she said, finally. "We'll eat, and make our plan from there. Hopefully it will all make more sense."

"An excellent plan," Usoothe said, and something flickered in his one good eye.

Top Ear suspected that he was in her mind, poring over her thoughts, and she tried to shut him out. It might have worked. He said nothing, and she rose to her paws and sought out the safest path down from the shelf, looking for enough rubble to cross the water without dipping into its muddy surface. The others followed in silence.

Chapter Sixteen

They were a miserable bunch. The three of them pressed in close, but none of them said anything. Though their bodies touched, Bitey had never felt so alone. Words hung over their heads, unspoken. Bitey kept grooming, though the blood from the snake—and Sniffles—had long since been washed from her fur. She could still feel it. Nezumi. Sniffles. Squeaker. Her kin and her friends—lost, now, and where were their Spirits? She couldn't feel them. If they were there, they said nothing to her.

A terrible thought occurred to her: What if the Spirit Realm was a lie?

They had already done the impossible. They had crawled out of their cage, away from their known world. They had inherited the Beyond—but this was no paradise. The Great Ones had abandoned them. The snake was here, just as Monster had always said it would be. Everything she had been raised to believe was a lie.

So what if the Spirit Realm was, too?

She licked her paws until the skin was chapped and raw, then she kept licking. She didn't know what the others were thinking. She wished she could find words to ask them, but she didn't dare break the silence.

She wasn't sure how long they sat there, huddled damply in the space they had reserved as a nest. It was dark in the store. The water had begun to recede, though Bitey could no longer see it in the gloom that fell over them. Somewhere, below, the snake's body lurked in the shallows. Dead. Or was it? She wasn't sure of anything anymore.

From the shelves below, near the water line, something moved. Bitey made out the sound of paws over plastic packaging, the rustle of a rat climbing the shelf. She tensed. The others either hadn't heard or didn't have the energy to move; neither of them stirred. Perhaps they were asleep. Or perhaps they had slipped into that place, the frightened fugue state that separates brain from body when a creature is too exhausted and terrified to fight. Either way, when Bitey crept out of the nest, she was alone.

Her nose twitched, and she caught a familiar scent. It was mingled with unfamiliar smells as well, and her brow furrowed in temporary confusion before she rushed to the far end of the shelf. She wasn't sure what she would find. What if there was another snake? What if the wild ones came for them, like Dumbo had said they might? What good would anyone be while they were busy feeling sorry for themselves? Bitey was hardly in any condition to fight. She hadn't slept properly since before Nezumi's death. Every muscle in her body screamed in pain, and her skin was torn and scabbed. Her heart ached from loss and her head ached from exhaustion. She wanted to lay in a stupor like the others and let the grief immobilize her.

But she had to be strong. She had to be the one to fight, because no one else would.

A brown-smudged nose came over the edge of the shelf.

Bitey froze, uncertain, every aching muscle taut and ready to spring into a fight if this was a trap. A large, ivory-colored rat climbed up, a pair of tired ruby-red eyes landing on her.

They stood, nose-to-nose, both frozen and uncertain.

Then Smeeze let out a joyful squeak and heaved herself forward, slamming into Bitey, laughing and showering her neck and face with kisses. For a moment, Bitey forgot where she was, utterly transported with joy, and they wrestled, tumbling end-over-end, the way they had played together as weanling *jask*. Bitey pinned the other rat and licked her affectionately between the ears.

"I thought you were dead!" Smeeze said, squirming under Bitey and kicking her off, rolling back to her paws.

"I thought I was too, for awhile!" Bitey said, half-dancing on her paws. "You'll never believe it! I went under the Big Water—twice! And there was a snake and we killed it and—" she stopped, suddenly, remembering about Sniffles. The joy drained out of her once more.

Smeeze's whiskers twitched, and she opened her maw, apparently considering pressing the issue, but stopped. Instead, she said, "We've had a crazy time, too. The others are coming…I just came on ahead, because I was tired of listening to them." She grinned. "Is Monster with you?"

Bitey nodded back to the nest. "She's been in an odd way. Since the snake." *And Sniffles*, she added, silently, but couldn't say it aloud. Because she didn't want to hear it spoken. She shook herself, and redirected her attentions to Smeeze. She registered what Smeeze had said—others. *Them*. "Who's with you?"

"Top Ear," she said, grooming herself for a moment before starting for the other end of the shelf. "And three wild rats."

"What?" Bitey started, genuinely surprised.

"Yeah," Smeeze said, pausing in place. "Just…well, you'll see." And, without further explanation, she made her way toward Monster.

Bitey tensed, prepared to follow, but the others arrived just then. They heaved themselves over the crest of the shelf, single-file. Bitey's sister, looking so much like Sniffles that her heart wrenched to see her. On her heels were three agouti rats. One was hardly full-grown. One was large-bodied and heavily scarred; she cast a surly glance at Bitey as she came over the edge of the shelf. The last was male, and his face was marred by a large white blaze and a mangled scar that crossed over one blue-white eye.

Bitey looked between them, taking a defensive step back, feeling her tail lash behind her almost involuntarily. Her teeth clicked together in warning.

"It's alright, Bitey," Top Ear said. "They're with us. This is Usoothe, and that's Allaysi and Ukeki."

The two females pulled away, distracting themselves by browsing the food available along the shelves. The smaller one climbed on top of a bag, gnawing open a corner, and slipped her whole small body inside. The larger one, who was missing an ear, rolled back onto her muscular haunches and gnawed at a peanut shell. The male, however, stayed quietly behind.

Bitey snorted. What ridiculous names—and now barging in here like they owned the place, after she and White One and the others had gone to such lengths to secure it as their own new territory. "And what do they want?"

"They came for some food," Top Ear said. Then, perhaps sensing Bitey's agitation, she added, "They say they want to help us. They say the others are in danger, and they can help us rescue them."

"Dumbo said they left with two wild rats," Bitey said, uneasily. "Wild rats—like them."

"It's complicated," Top Ear said wearily. "You...wait. Dumbo's here?" Her ears swept forward, a sudden light gleaming in her eyes. "Who else?"

"Monster," Bitey said.

Top Ear's brow furrowed. "Oh. The wild ones said there's just two of us, kidnapped," she said, slowly, ears twitching. "What about Squeaker? And...and Sniffles?"

Bitey looked away, still unwilling to say it aloud.

Top Ear's eyes widened, in alarm. "They're not dead," she said, but there was no real disbelief in her voice.

Everyone had always known that Sniffles lived on borrowed time. But, of course, Top Ear didn't know the truth. She hadn't seen the snake plunge its teeth into her. She hadn't stood, frozen with shock, while the *ushuzu-sim* tore into her. Bitey raised her eyes to meet her sister's, and the hollowness in them spoke more than any words could say. Yes, Sniffles was dead. Bitey had consumed the body herself, but could never tell anyone that, not in a thousand lifetimes. She couldn't tell Top Ear about the snake. These were secrets she would carry with her until she walked among the Spirits.

"Not to interrupt," Usoothe said in a voice that suggested that was exactly what he meant to do, "But I believe there are more pressing matters at hand."

Top Ear looked at him, expression carrying rather more scorn than perhaps was warranted. "Stay out of this," she said, coldly. "Unless you have a plan—unless you know how to make things better—then shut your maw."

Bitey cast a curious sidelong look to her sister. Top Ear—the rat who had always been so keen to follow rules, the rat who had danced with uncertainty about anything that questioned authority—when had she gotten so bold?

If Usoothe was bothered, he didn't show it. "No plan, precisely. If all is as I suspect, then they will be held until they wean kits that the *Ukeshu* can use. Then he will be satisfied to neglect them, the way he does all his servants." His whiskers drooped. "But we don't have that kind of time, and I don't think you would want to wait even if we did."

"Time for what?" Bitey asked, feeling her patience slipping further with each passing minute.

Before anyone could explain, Dumbo appeared on the shelf, glancing curiously at the gathering. Her eyes flicked from Usoothe to the two wild females, both of whom were now grooming after their meal, and then back to Top Ear. Her face lit up with delight, and she bounded forward. "Smeeze said you were here," she said, pouncing on her sister, "But I wanted to see for sure."

Top Ear squeaked and nudged her sister fondly, but it wasn't the exuberant dance of glee that Bitey had expected. Her brow furrowed, looking between the two of them, trying to understand what was going through Top Ear's head. Was it a pang of loss for the third black-furred sister? Or was something else weighing too heavily on her mind to make room for joyous reunions?

Dumbo settled in next to Top Ear, pressing herself close to her. "So," she said, as she rested her chin on her sister's shoulders, "what's everyone talking about?"

Usoothe, who looked as though he may soon begin losing patience with these interruptions, said, "As I was explaining, I fear that your companions are being held by the *Ukeshu*. I don't think you have much time." He looked around with his single good eye. "Rescuing them after they've been bred will be much more difficult. I imagine they'll be kept under higher security."

"Bred?" Bitey's ears flicked back.

"Yes," Usoothe said, with impatience now clearly in his voice. "So that the *Ukeshu* can begin rebuilding his colony."

Dumbo squeaked. "I should have gone instead of Cookie..." she whispered.

Bitey ignored her. There was nothing that regret could help with now—not with the snake, and not with the wild ones. She looked up sharply at Usoothe. "...You're telling me that someone is going to put his *jask* inside of White One and Cookie."

"I suspect so."

"Whether they want them or not."

"I would imagine."

Bitey rose to her paws, ignoring the scream of pain in her muscles and torn skin. "Then why are we still sitting here?"

"And there it is again," Smeeze interrupted. She made her way out onto the shelf, followed by Monster—who had a sleepy, far-away look in her eyes, and seemed to find nothing at all strange about the sudden swell of their numbers. Perhaps she didn't even notice. "That hero thing that all of you have."

Now that they were all assembled on the shelf, Bitey was fully—painfully—aware of how ridiculous and futile they were as a group. All of them were exhausted. Some were wounded. But that wasn't a good enough excuse. She ignored Smeeze and looked back at Usoothe, glaring at his good eye. "Where do we go?"

"To the point. I respect that," Usoothe said, with gentle irony.

He glanced at Top Ear. "I can show you the way there, but I won't be able to go much further. I'm afraid showing my face there would cause more problems than it would solve. I am not the *Ukeshu*'s favorite rat."

"Then do what you can," Top Ear said, rising to her paws. She met Bitey's eyes, briefly, before looking back to Usoothe. "Show us to the entrance and we'll find a solution ourselves."

Usoothe nodded. "Well enough."

He began to detail the layout of the colony and its tunnel system. The tunnels, the chambers, the location of the entrances and the bolt-holes, all of the tunnels built into the very foundation of the building beneath the floors and inside the walls.

Top Ear and Bitey listened intently. The others seemed less interested. Ukeki and Allaysi lay in a small heap, snoozing. Monster stared over the side of the shelf, gazing into the water. Dumbo and Smeeze both tried to listen, but it clearly didn't fully sink in. Smeeze's ears kept flicking as she tried to listen, but she was distracted, constantly looking between them and back at Monster. Dumbo kept shifting uneasily from paw to paw, an uneasy expression clouding her features—guilt, perhaps, at the role she played in causing this.

"There is one last thing, that will prove an added challenge." Usoothe's whiskers twitched ironically. "Or, perhaps, an opportunity, depending how you choose to see it."

"If the others are ready for breeding," Bitey said, shrewdly, "Then so are we."

"Indeed." Usoothe's ears waggled, playfully, a little suggestively. Top Ear shot him a dirty look. "Use that knowledge as you will."

Bitey ignored his flirtation. "I'd like to see them try. Still—

for all of our sake, we'd be better off going in a small group rather than all at once."

"I'll show you the way in," Allaysi said, speaking for the first time. She yawned, stretching as she crawled toward them. Bitey wondered how long she had been awake. "The others won't recognize me as easily as they would my friends, and I know all the entrances better than anyone."

"Fair. Bitey and I will go with Allaysi, then," Top Ear said, quickly.

Bitey nodded. "Usoothe and Ukeki should stay here, then, in case there's any trouble. Dumbo, you stay here to make sure they don't cause any trouble. Monster, Smeeze, will you stay or go?"

"Smeeze will go," Monster said quickly, and gave Smeeze a look that challenged her to defy it. "And I will stay, in case the snake comes back."

"The snake won't be back, Monster," Bitey said, quietly—but she didn't know if she believed that. There were no further arguments, though, and they collected themselves to eat and rest for a brief interlude before heading into the unknown.

Chapter Seventeen

"Do you feel funny?" Cookie asked. She pressed herself so closely against White One that she practically crawled beneath her. "I feel funny."

"Yes, Cookie," White One said, and the resignation in her voice terrified her. She had been through all her options a dozen times, but she could see no way out that didn't end in death. "I feel it too." And, indeed, she did. Her heat cycle had begun in full force, and an event she had until now viewed as a simple restlessness had—in the presence of so many males and their reeking stench of testosterone—heightened to a feverish desire. She held herself steady, terrified of the wild rats and not knowing what to do with the feeling anyway, and realized how thoroughly miserable she truly was. She could smell it on the Cookie also, the unmistakable scent of female in rut, a scent that makes males of any species go crazy.

In the entrance of the largest chamber, a large dark-furred wild one turned attentive, excited eyes toward them. His whiskers trembled and he stepped forward, bridging the gap between them with long, easy strides.

He sidled up against White One, the oily fur of his flank brushing her side. His touch was electric and her body shuddered despite herself. She had never felt that way from a touch before, and it frightened her. She jumped back, even as her haunches moved, acting against her will; she felt the muscles tense in her legs and tail and her knees quivered.

"What do you want?" she asked, forcing herself away from him. It took tremendous effort, as something seemed to hold them together, some magnetic bond of attraction that superseded her disgust. "What do you want with us?"

Other males had pressed in, surging between the girls, pulling them apart. A low hum of excitement filled the chamber. Wordless vocalizations of desire echoed from the walls, throaty hisses of territoriality and pure animal want. The stench of male, of desire and violence, hung in the air and mingled with the earthy smell of estrus. Males butted shoulders as they vied for position, sidling and kicking, biting each other and scrapping among themselves even as they climbed over each other in the effort to get close to the two huddled females in the tight space.

The dark male pressed himself against White One's side, laying his mouth along her cheek. She could feel the warmth of his breath against her whiskers, and when he spoke it was in a low voice that made her ear twitch. "Don't fight it," he said. His voice was husky and low, and there was a wild, desperate look in his eyes. "Don't struggle. Don't fight me. You want this—I can smell it."

And she did want it. That was the terrible, incomprehensible thing.

She did want it—but not from him.

She squeaked in protest and struggled away from him, but found herself unable to escape. Wherever she turned, she found herself surrounded. Rats pressed in from all sides. Too many to fight against. There was nowhere to run.

The dark male closed in on her. Within a microsecond, his jaws clamped over her nape. His body moved to cover hers.

Her mind reeled. She was confused and frightened, and receiving signals from her body that made no sense at all. The only thought in her mind was the repeated scream: *Not now. Not him.*

She whirled around, snapping at the approaching male. Her teeth caught his shoulder, and he sprang back in surprise. It afforded her enough space to press her advantage, and she pushed forward, landing another bite on his face.

He screamed, recoiling. The others closed in around her. There was no way she could fight them all. But she could try. Rats spilled in from both sides. Everyone wanted to get to her first. It was a jumble of confusion and bodies. Males tore into each other. Squeaks and cries and the sound of fighting resonated from the walls. The smell of blood mingled with the other scents on the air.

Bodies crawled over her. Someone bit into her nape, shoving her face down into the dirt. She felt her tail being shoved aside, and her haunches lifted instinctively before she came to her senses. *Not them,* she thought, clinging to this thought— the only thought that made any sense—and crawled forward, kicking up with her hindpaws.

She could make out Cookie ahead of her, and she pushed her way toward her. A large, tawny-colored rat was clawing at her sides, trying to get a firm paw-hold as he climbed onto her, but he kept sliding free; she was too large and her sides were too soft for him to get a good grip. Cookie squirmed away, crawling out from under him, but was immediately accosted by another rat, and White One let out an angry screech and pressed forward through the crowd.

She shoved her shoulder into the male, whirling around to bare her teeth at any others who came close. She pressed in close to Cookie. "Have they taken you yet?" she asked, from the corner of her maw.

"No. Not yet."

"Good." White One stayed close to her, afraid that if they were separated she would be unable to fight her way back to her side. "Don't let them. We can fight them."

"Okay," Cookie said, uncertainly.

Together, the two of them backed into a corner. There was no tunnel here. It had been a bolt-hole, once, but it had caved in—during the flood, perhaps, or earlier. The earth was damp, and the tight space could hold only one of them. White One shoved Cookie into it, tail-end first. "If anybody comes this way, if they get past me, you bite them, alright?"

She stood, fur on end, outside the mouth of the small gap, and bared her teeth at the rats that approached. She knew it was hopeless—that their position was indefensible—but she had to try.

The crowd of rats in the room milled. Many seemed to have forgotten that they were there; there was much fighting, and many had retreated to lick their wounds or simply avoid the onslaught of claws and teeth. Not everyone forgot about the females, though, and a small crowd pressed forward, blocking off escape. White One and Cookie were cornered, and a rat pressed his oily pelt against White One's body.

White One squirmed, squeaking desperately, but was quickly overwhelmed. She wheeled around, to lash out at one male as he approached—but this one's scent was familiar. The light-colored agouti, the rat who had brought her here. The one that had seemed almost kind…almost apologetic.

She hesitated.

"I'm sorry," he said, quietly, as he came up to her. "It's the only way."

White One, who had always prided herself on her cleverness, saw that it was true. "Stay with me," she said, urgently. "So the others…"

"I know." He shoved another rat away, kicking out with his hindpaw and catching the intruder across the face with his claws. He climbed onto her back. He was small, for a wild rat, but larger than she was, and his body pressed her down with its weight. She felt the bulge of muscle against her spine. He had no fat anywhere on his body; just bones and muscle and knotted sinew.

She readied herself for the inevitable. She closed her eyes, ready to go somewhere else, to let her thoughts take her away until it was over—but nothing happened. He merely lay upon her back, breathing into her ear. "What…"

"Not here," he said, repeating the thought that had echoed through her brain. "Not like this."

"Are you an *usoothe*?" she asked, in a low, awed whisper.

"No," he said, his whiskers brushing her ear. "Later. I'll explain…later. Just now, keep quiet, so they won't understand."

White One didn't know what was happening, or why, but she understood that she had been spared. She lay, quiet and still, against the floor and felt the heartbeat of the rat upon her back, a nameless scout who shielded her from an onslaught of guards.

Chapter Eighteen

"Do you think we can trust this?" Bitey asked. She stood just outside of a small hole in the floor—a gap between the tiles, mostly hidden by the shelf above it. To a human eye, the gap was basically invisible. The rats recognized it immediately, though, from Usoothe's description—and from the smell of rats that came from inside. It was a bolt-hole, a secondary entrance to the network of tunnels below. "It could be a trap."

"It could," Top Ear agreed. "But do we have any other choice?"

"It's not a trap," Allaysi said. Standing beside Bitey, her small stature was quite obvious. The silky patches of baby-fur poked up at odd angles beneath the guard hairs of her adult pelt. She looked ridiculous. Top Ear wanted to groom her, smooth down all of the patchy fur, but she restrained herself. "Usoothe wouldn't do that."

"If it were a trap, I really don't think any of us would expect you to tip us off," Smeeze said. She settled down next to them, running her paws over her face. Mud clung to the damp, spiky strands of her usually cream-colored pelt. The floor was mostly dry, now, but deposits of sediment had settled along the ground, and it had stained her pale underbelly and legs.

"How do you know each other, anyway? I mean—why the three of you? Of all the rats Usoothe could have picked as followers…" Top Ear bent down to sniff at the hole. It was damp and close; the tunnel had caved in at least partway from the flooding. She started to dig.

Allaysi joined her in the digging. Her ears, which were still a bit too large for her, folded back against her gray-brown head. "Usoothe didn't pick us. We followed him. He told us about his vision—about the Great Ones, I mean—and we knew he was right so we followed him. Now we just watch and wait for the Great Ones to return and take us into the greater Beyond." Her whiskers twitched. "Well, that's why I followed him. I don't know what Ukeki wants, exactly."

"Maybe she thinks the Great Ones will give her a new ear," Smeeze muttered.

Bitey kicked her, but she smirked all the same.

Allaysi ignored them. "He's really smart, you know. Usoothe taught me everything. He told me about how names work. He taught me what 'who' means, and who I am."

Top Ear tried to comprehend the significance of this. It was such a small thing for her, being an individual—having a name, even if it wasn't yet a True Name. She couldn't imagine what kind of life the wild rats lived, or what sort of rat this *Ukeshu* must be to force them all into it. With everything that had happened, she wasn't sure what she believed about the Great Ones—but she knew they were definitely better than the life that Allaysi seemed to have come from. Given the choice, she would have followed Usoothe, too.

They dug in silence, taking shifts as they excavated the partially-blocked bolt-hole. Allaysi and Top Ear did most of the digging. Bitey and Smeeze were both too large to maneuver comfortably in the tight space, and neither of them had the patience for that type of work. Bitey kept getting angry and striking out at the sediment as it caved in around her, and Smeeze worked at half the pace of the others.

Top Ear didn't mind the labor. It was almost like running on the wheel: By keeping her paws busy, she could keep her mind busy as well. The harder she worked, the less she had to think about what they were coming up against—which was good, because she didn't really know what to expect. Her universe, whose borders were once so clearly defined, had expanded so much in the past two days, and it seemed to become more dangerous the larger it grew.

"We're in!" Allaysi squeaked from down inside the newly-excavated tunnel. "I can feel the open air on my whiskers."

Top Ear settled at the lip of the tunnel. She waited for someone to speak up and start giving out directions, but it never happened. Bitey was undoubtedly brave and powerful, but she wasn't the alpha yet—and she certainly didn't seem to be in a hurry to come up with a plan. Top Ear remembered the fiasco with the *shujisk* and the Big Water all too well; Bitey's idea of "planning" seemed to be jumping in and winging it. That wasn't something Top Ear was comfortable with.

When no one said anything, she ground her incisors together nervously and took a deep breath. "Here's the plan. Allaysi goes in first to see what we're up against. Bitey and Smeeze, you two make a diversion, and get ready to fight our way out if you have to. I'll go on ahead with Allaysi, find the others, and we'll all get out of here. Got it?"

Bitey smirked. "About time we saw some action," she said.

Without further response, Top Ear crept into the tunnel and followed after Allaysi, heart pounding in her ears.

* * *

White One hadn't realized she'd slept until she awoke. She blinked, pawing at the porphyrin that crusted the corners of her eyes. Cookie still pressed against her back. White One could tell from her heavy breathing that she was asleep. On her other side, the male who had protected them lay curled on his side, grooming his underbelly and genitals. He was wounded, and blood smeared his sides; a few patches of fur were missing altogether.

"You're awake," he said.

The crowd of rats had abated. They weren't entirely alone, but the other males seemed to have lost interest for the moment. Most stayed crowded around the entrance. A few cast surly looks toward the male.

"You're hurt."

"Just a few scratches." He straightened. The nervousness that had marked him earlier seemed to have dissipated. He seemed, almost, to be an entirely new rat, and White One could hardly understand why. Perhaps it was the absence of his larger, gruffer companion. Or perhaps a Spirit had nested inside his mind and taken control of his actions. Either possibility seemed equally likely in this strange world she had fallen into.

"Why are you helping me?" she asked. White One wasn't one to mince words.

"To atone," he said, flicking an ear back toward the opening of the tunnel. "For bringing you here. For ignoring the words of Usoothe, and staying under the paw of the *Ukeshu* instead."

"Usoothe?"

"He…he was marked. By the Spirits. He saw things—knew

things—and he was driven from the colony for his blasphemies. He said so many things that didn't make any sense. But he also said that a great white rat would come and mark the beginning of a new, changed world. I thought he was lying…but then I saw you, and I brought you here, and…" He trailed off uneasily.

"And you think I'm that rat?"

"You must be."

"I notice he didn't say a better world," White One said. "Only new, different. These prophecies are always vague, aren't they? How do you know me being here isn't going to make everything worse for you—for your colony?"

"I guess I don't."

Silence fell between them for a long while. Cookie grunted in her sleep. At the entrance, some of the rats began to shift uneasily, perhaps regrouping for another onslaught.

"You can't keep us safe forever," she said, matter-of-factly. "Eventually, they will kill you to get to us."

He made a low, noncommittal grunt.

White One's ears folded back to her skull. She rose to her paws, still feeling the shifting uneasiness that spread through her and made her skin crawl. "They all want to put a *jask* in me, right? That's what this is about. They won't stop until someone does."

"The *Ukeshu* must rebuild his colony."

"You should be the one to do it, then."

"What?"

"I can't speak for what Cookie wants. But, for myself." She pressed against his side, touching her nose to his cheek. He trembled, either from fear or anticipation, at her touch. "If it will make them stop—if someone has to do it—I want it to be you."

* * *

At the end of the tunnel, where it began to open into a wider chamber, Allaysi pulled ahead of the group. "I'll meet with you outside," she said, briskly, before scurrying out of sight. She was small enough to pass by most guards unnoticed, and she knew the tunnels well; having her run ahead was vital to their plan. Top Ear just hoped she could be trusted.

"Are you both ready?" she asked in a low voice as she crouched in the tunnel.

"As ready as we'll ever be," Bitey said.

"Yes. Hurry, though, before I change my mind," Smeeze muttered.

"Be safe, both of you." Top Ear hesitated, ears folding back. "And Bitey..."

"Save it for when you get back," Bitey said, wryly.

Top Ear smiled and crept forward, belly low to the ground, ears and whiskers swept forward. The chamber was largely empty. From Allaysi's description, this bolt-hold hadn't been used in quite some time—not since it had caved in—and it wasn't generally guarded. This chamber was largely disused, but it stood adjacent to the holding cell where Cookie and White One were likely to be kept. Allaysi was infiltrating that space; it was Top Ear's job to draw away the guards between here and there so they could escape.

The overwhelming stench of maleness assaulted her senses as she reached the far end of the chamber. It smelled as though the tunnel outside had been packed full of them. It was an angry, violent smell—greasy and foreign—and it made her recoil. She fought back her agitation and pressed forward.

A guard was sitting on his haunches outside the opening to a side corridor. He was carefully grooming the fur of his armpit and sides, and he seemed unaware of Top Ear's approach. She took advantage of his inattentiveness to draw in close, keeping an eye out for others. There was one more—a second guard, larger-bodied and with a dusky yellow-gray pelt. She took a deep breath and pressed forward, walking past the first guard and moving deliberately toward the second. "Hey, boys," she said, lifting her tail and waggling her ears suggestively.

The guard at the far-end perked up immediately. The other dropped to all four paws, looking agitated at being caught by surprise. They met each other's gaze for a flash of a second, an expression of stupefaction passing between them.

"Is that one of the prisoners?"

"There wasn't a black one, was there?"

"She's not one of us…"

"You're not the brightest bunch, are you?" Top Ear marveled, turning nimbly before reaching the far end of the tunnel. She swept within inches of the far guard, flicking her tail close to him. He darted forward, to pursue her, as she had hoped he would. "Let's see how fast you are, then."

She didn't feel as bold as she sounded. Her heart pounded in her chest, and her limbs trembled, but there was no time for fear. She took off at a run, blazing past the first guard and heading, full-tilt, for the chamber where she had left Bitey and Smeeze.

As anticipated, the guards chased after her, sounding an alarm. Their screeching cries bounced off the tightly packed earthen walls of the tunnel system, and Top Ear had a fleeting, terrifying thought that every rat in the colony might come pouring in to help them —but it was too late to worry about such things. The important thing was creating a diversion so

Allaysi could reach the others and get away.

Top Ear felt warm breath at the edge of her tail. She squeaked in alarm and surged forward, throwing herself through the opening of the chamber. The first two guards shoved in behind her, followed by two others that had come in response to the alarm.

Their attentions focused entirely on Top Ear, the four wild ones didn't even notice Bitey and Smeeze until they closed in from the sides.

* * *

When he was finished, the male curled protectively against White One's side. He needn't have bothered; the other males were rapidly losing interest in her and Cookie. The scent of their estrus was fading, and the battle to get to them was too fierce for most of the males to bother with.

Though he didn't need to stay, he did, and White One was grateful for it.

"Usoothe," she said, after a time, thinking back to what he had said before. "This seer who foretold our coming. You said you could have joined him?"

"Yes. He was banished, but he took some followers with him. He gave them names."

From the way he said that, White One could tell it was significant. It intrigued her. The power of a True Name was something all of White One's colony had been raised to respect. But it had never occurred to her that a wild rat might long for a name as well.

"You deserve a name, too," she said, impulsively. She wasn't sure why she said it, but she knew that she meant it. "I'll call you…Jetak."

His brow furrowed, perhaps not certain that she was serious. Then, a smile twitched his whiskers. "Jetak?" he repeated, and chuckled. "You would name me Safe?"

He laughed again, but White One could tell that he was pleased. He kept whispering it to himself, under his breath, when he thought she wasn't paying attention.

Time passed. It was hard to tell how much. White One dozed, intermittently. Jetak slipped away, once, to try and bring back some food, but he stopped at the opening and returned.

"White One," he said, in an urgent whisper. "Cookie. Wake up. Something is coming."

He didn't need to tell White One—she had caught the subtle change in scent and was already on her paws—but she nudged Cookie awake. Most of the males had given up, realizing that they had been beaten to their goal. It would be easier, now, to claim false fathership than to attempt to plant their own *jask* in the captive's bellies. A few still lay scattered around the chamber, but they slept uneasily, aching from the open wounds caused by in-fighting and the relentless attacks of the females themselves.

"Is it a guard?" White One asked

"No," Jetak said, drawing away, ears warily swept forward.

Before they could speculate further, the interloper appeared at the entrance. It was a wild female, small and still quite young. Her bright eyes took in the scene at an instant, and she smiled with familiarity at the male. "Brother." Her attention shifted to Cookie and White One. "You two. Come with me."

Cookie pressed close to White One, looking uneasily at the newcomer. "Who are you?"

"No time," the female said, hesitating at the chamber's opening. She didn't seem baffled by the question of 'who,' which was encouraging, but she shifted impatiently from paw to paw. "We have to hurry. The others are making a distraction, but it won't last for long once the other guards hear."

"Others?" White One asked, looking up sharply.

The female lashed her tail in agitation. "Yes. Others—tame ones, like you, that ask just as many irrelevant questions. Now come on!"

A terrible cry came from further down the tunnel—a warning, or a scream of pain. Perhaps both. It was followed soon after by the sound of fighting. This roused the slumbering males in the chamber, and they awoke, bleary-eyed and agitated.

"Go," Jetak said, nudging White One forward. "She is with Usoothe. Go with her."

"Aren't you—"

"Go!"

The freshly-woken males rose to their paws.

Cookie stumbled forward, making her way to the entrance at the young female's side. White One hesitated just a moment before following. Jetak followed them to the opening before wheeling around, baring his teeth at the newly-awakened males and blocking them from the tunnel.

"This way," the female said, pulling back into the open tunnel. "We haven't got much time until more guards come."

The sounds of fighting broke out on all sides, and it filled the tunnel as Cookie and White One followed the unnamed scout away from their prison.

* * *

The chamber wasn't large enough for a full-scale battle. As the females withdrew toward the bolt-hole, the wild ones were forced to approach them single-file, and their larger size was a disadvantage in the cramped spaces. Bitey and Smeeze, meanwhile, were in their element.

The mink-hooded female moved with a speed and precision that caught even Top Ear off-guard. She had seen her sister nip at the hands of Great Ones before, but this was something different entirely. She moved the way Monster had moved when she'd killed the *ushuzu-sim*: swiftly, relentlessly, without mercy. Blood flecked the white patches of her pelt, her own wounds tore open and new ones appeared along her sides, but she did not ease up on her attacks. Smeeze, at her side, seemed to understand Bitey's wishes without speaking; when one moved, the other would take advantage of the opening and press the attack.

Top Ear, meanwhile, stayed clear of the fray. She pressed herself close to the bolt-hole, prepared to defend it if anyone broke through Smeeze and Bitey's defenses, and waited for a signal. It was hard to hear over the din of battle, but she kept her ears trained for the first hint of sound to suggest that Allaysi had been successful.

There—fighting sounds from the adjacent chamber. Top Ear waited a moment, making sure she had heard it correctly, but there was no doubt; rats were fighting beyond the battle currently raging before her. She couldn't be sure that the sound meant Allaysi had succeeded, but she couldn't stay here forever waiting to find out. "Bitey! Smeeze!" She yelled, before turning to run for the bolt-hole. "Fall back! It's time!"

Smeeze, who was holding a male down with her forepaws so Bitey could land a blow to his haunch, looked up. A smear of blood crossed her smudged nose, and her ruby eyes sparkled with amusement. "What, already?"

Bitey wrenched her teeth from the male and withdrew, nudging Smeeze toward the exit. "Come on. Let's see if they have the courage to follow us."

It's not in the nature of rats to fight to the death when it can be helped. Normally, the victor in a battle between rats is whoever can hold his ground; the loser retreats to tend his wounds or succumb to blood loss and infection far from the battlefield. When the females made their sudden retreat, then, the wild ones watched them leave with a look of conflicted stupefaction, clearly uncertain whether they had won or lost.

For her part, Top Ear was relieved that they did not follow them. Perhaps the wild ones knew that this narrow bolt-hole was in danger of caving in again if the larger males shoved through it. Maybe they just didn't think to press the battle beyond the confines of the burrow.

Or, Top Ear thought grimly, perhaps they were simply falling back to gather reinforcements before launching another attack.

She broke through the surface of the bolt-hole, crawling out from beneath the shelf that hid the entrance, and felt the others at her heels. Her legs trembled, and she wanted to give in to the exhaustion that pressed over her, but she forced herself to stay on her paws. If she gave in now, she might not be able to get up.

The others burst out behind her, panting a bit with the effort of squeezing themselves free.

"We'd best pull away a bit, in case someone follows us," Top Ear said, ears and whiskers quivering as she sought out Allaysi—but, so far, there was no sign of the smaller rat or their lost companions.

"Where is the little one meeting us?" Bitey asked, as if reading her sister's thoughts.

"I'm not sure. She said she'd be taking another exit," Top Ear replied, drawing away from the bolt-hole and moving instinctively back toward the shelves they had claimed as their new territory. "It might be some distance from here, if their burrow is large."

"Let's head back, then, and hope she has the sense to meet us there," Bitey said, limping alongside her sister. The wound in her shoulder had been torn open yet again; it looked as though I may never properly heal. The edges were dry and cracked, and the muscle underneath looked damp and shiny. "Either the others escaped or they didn't, but there's no more good we can do waiting here."

"Oh, good," Smeeze said, clearly relieved. "I was afraid you were about to suggest something heroic again. That plan is much more sensible."

Chapter Nineteen

White One kept her ears folded back, waiting for the sound of a fourth rat to follow them, but Jetak never came. She followed after Cookie and Allaysi, the young stranger, and with each step her doubts began to grow. Had something happened? Was he overpowered by the other males? Had the guards caught him? Perhaps they had learned of his actions—which were surely treasonous—and taken him before the *Ukeshu* to be dealt with.

White One had never been a particularly imaginative rat, but she could not help the frightful images from blossoming in her mind, nor the twisting feeling in her gut that suggested her dread was warranted.

My gut, she thought, with a sudden jolt. Fear wasn't the only thing building there. The thought of the *jask* he had planted there felt like claws pricking into her heart. At the time, it had been a matter of cold necessity, of survival; but now she had escaped, and he hadn't, and the significance of the unborn pups seemed to suddenly swell.

Spirits be with him, she thought, trying to force her attentions back onto the more pressing matters of survival. Whether Jetak lived or died, she had greater concerns. She had to remember that.

Allaysi moved confidently before her, leading the way without pausing to glance behind. For a small rat, her pace was brisk and graceful, and keeping stride with her was like running over the top of a wheel already in use—if you stopped running, you'd never catch up. Cookie trailed after them, huffing and panting. She had not complained once since they had escaped, not even when the narrow spaces of tunnels had pressed against them and it had looked as though her bulk would not allow her to pass.

"We're nearly there," Allaysi said, without bothering to look back. "If the others got away, we'll know soon enough."

So much uncertainty. White One had never felt so lost.

The shelving unit loomed ahead, as massive and immovable as a mountain. The floor was damp, but the flood water had mostly receded. In its wake, it had left a generous layer of detritus and sediment. A few wayward fish, swept from their aquarium, lay still and dry on their sides—and, in the shadow of the shelf, the long corpse of a snake lay stretched and deflated.

The rats gave it a wide berth as they passed, though White One could not keep her eyes from straying back to it. Monster has faced her *ushuzu-sim* after all.

Was it a terrible omen? Or a sign of their strength?

"White One! Cookie!" A familiar voice broke through her thoughts, and White One's whiskers twitched in recognition. Before she could react, a dark-furred bullet darted to her side. Top Ear squeaked in relief and elation, touching her nose to White One's cheek and ears. "It took so long, I wasn't sure if you were coming."

"The tunnels were slow going," Allaysi said, moving past the others without paying them much heed. "Washed out in places, and narrow. But we're here. I told you we would be."

"You did," Bitey said. White One's attention snapped to her; the mink-hooded rat was nearly unrecognizable through the tattered fur and fresh wounds that now dotted her pelt. Something in her face, too, was new: something hard and determined. "I'm sorry to have doubted you."

"Don't be," Allaysi said, jumping onto the bottom shelf and beginning the ascent. "Skepticism will keep you alive out here."

Her tail flicked out of view as her small body disappeared among the items on the shelf, and the others were left alone: three sisters and an outsider, four refugees from a dwindling colony. Cookie flopped down, exhausted, and refused to move for a time, so the others stayed close. "Smeeze is up top, with the others," Bitey said, rolling gingerly to her haunches to run her paws over her face. "Monster, Dumbo, and two other wild ones. Once you've rested a bit, we'll go up to meet them. They'll be happy to see you both."

"It feels like it's been forever," Cookie said, struggling to groom her swollen hindpaws. One had a small, blistering sore. "So much has happened…and I'm so hungry."

The conversation lulled as they passed food around and ate their fill. Cookie was right: So much had happened, to all of them, and it was all too big to be shared in words. In time, perhaps, there would be stories to tell. For now, there was only exhaustion, uncertainty, and guarded relief. The rats pressed in close to each other, taking meager comfort in the warmth of bodies and familiar scents.

"It's not over, you know," White One said finally, wearily. "With the *Ukeshu*. He will come."

"I'm counting on it," Bitey said, with a flash of incisors. Her eyes strayed toward the shadowy corpse of the snake, its hide torn open, its innards a bloody tangle across the grubby tile floor. "Let him come."

* * *

They slept in fitful shifts, taking turns staying awake to keep watch for the wrath of the wild ones. When they slept, it was an uneasy slumber filled with troubled dreams. They sought each other out in the dark, pressing in close and drawing what comfort they could from the proximity of their friends, but the hours stretched on like shadows at dusk and fear spread through the group like a disease.

Why had no one come?

Bitey, on her shift, pressed herself close to a bag of food and ate in slow, half-hearted pawfuls. In the semi-darkness, everything was still but for the sounds of uneasy sleep. Distant sounds whispered just outside the open door, but the world outside was incomprehensibly far away, a distant galaxy that bore no consequences on the world inside.

This is what Monster must feel like, Bitey thought. *Always waiting for the snake.*

Usoothe was awake, also. He lay near Bitey's place, his head hung over the edge of the shelf, and stared pensively at the world below. "You need not be awake for my benefit," he said, without looking up at her. "If you'd rather go back with your kin, I can continue my watch."

"I can't sleep, anyway," she said, slowly masticating a peanut without tasting it. Usoothe said nothing, and she waited in silence for a time before asking, finally, "Why aren't they coming for us?"

"I...don't think they know how many of you there are," he

said, after a moment of hesitation. "It was a surprise, I think, for them to run across you at all. I know it was for me, when I met your kin." He lifted his head and pulled away from the shelf's edge, shifting his attention to meet her gaze with his own single dark eye. "We have lived most of our lives with only the vaguest understanding that there are rats in cages. It's hardly something we dwell on."

"We didn't know that other rats existed at all," Bitey said. "Or any of the rest of this. The Beyond…it's not quite what I'd expected."

His whiskers twitched with a smile. "The Beyond? Is that what you call the world outside your cage?"

"It was meant to be a paradise," she said, holding another morsel of food but not bothering to eat it. "The place we would be taken when the Great Ones deemed us worthy."

"And did you believe that?"

"It's what my mother told me," Bitey said, uncertainly. "But… no. I guess part of me always knew better."

His whiskers twitched, and he fell silent for a time, before he said, "I don't know, for certain,what is taking so long. But if I had to guess, the *Ukeshu* is likely gathering an army of his strongest guards, so that he can attack once and for all with no fear of failure. He will not abide being made a fool again."

"That's comforting," she said, wryly. "How many?"

Usoothe shrugged. "Countless. His army surely suffered in the flood, but I doubt it suffered much. He has many warriors. We will be unable to hold them off from here."

"I was thinking that. This place is good for a look-out, but not for fighting. It's too open, and there's nowhere for us to run." She sighed, scratching at her ear with a hindpaw. "Maybe I should wake White One. Surely she knows what to do."

"Let her sleep," Usoothe said, tentatively picking up a food pellet and examining it critically. He sniffed it, considered it, and then took a thoughtful nibble. "She'll be needing the rest. Her and the *jask*."

Bitey started. She had nearly forgotten. "Do we know…?"

"I can hear them settling in her belly," he said. "They are not the only burden she carries, but they weigh heavily upon her."

Somehow, Bitey had not taken the time to appreciate whether the half-blind seer was true to his name. Now that he was on his haunches, eating the kibble he had found, the scar that twisted along his belly and groin was impossible to ignore, and Bitey found her gaze following it. It was unlike any scar she had seen: deep, deliberate, and cruel. Not the incidental toothmark of a battle, but…something else. An action of malice.

"A parting gift from the *Ukeshu*," he said, noticing her attention. "Shortly before I was expelled from the colony."

"Why? For being a traitor?"

"No. For being a curse." He swallowed, dropping back to all fours and hiding the scar once more. "I sired a few litters. He wanted to see if the *usoothe* gifts would pass on to future generations. Whether they did or not, I do not know. But this did," he said, lifting a paw to run it along the large misshapen blaze of white that crossed his face. "And the *jask* born with the mark died soon after leaving their mother's sides."

"All of them?" Bitey asked, incredulous.

"Yes." He smiled bitterly. "I was deemed unfit to serve the *Ukeshu*, and the evilness of my bloodline was prevented from spreading." He hesitated, then, as if prepared to say something further—but he stopped. When he spoke again, Bitey was sure he it wasn't what he had first meant to say. "Though I was already hardly his favorite, going on as I was about a future where the Great Ones would embrace us and the rule of rats would fall. Which, I suppose, is why he was so eager to replace me."

"Do you still believe the Great Ones will come?"

"It's what I have seen," he said. "I have seen that they will return, and the world will change. The rule of the *Ukeshu* will end. If I am wrong, then perhaps the Spirits have lied to me; but I have faith in what I have seen."

Bitey wasn't sure she could believe him. Of course, after everything that had happened—Nezumi, the great water, the snake—she could hardly doubt anyone. But to think that, after everything, the Great Ones might truly return…it was impossible to comprehend. Still, she knew he was right about one thing: The *Ukeshu* would come, and when he did, they would need a more defensible location. And an army to rival the *Ukeshu*'s wouldn't hurt, she thought, and an idea began to fall into place.

Hints of light came from outside, pouring through the windows and the high skylight to cast the building into an early morning gloom. There was little time to spare. *Jask* or no, Bitey decided, it was time to awaken White One.

IV

Faith in Gods

Chapter Twenty

The weather had cleared, and Lori was in a hurry to return home. Now that they were away —staying in a hotel in the next county—the evacuation had seemed premature. Clouds still hung in the sky, and another storm was possible, but the worst seemed to have passed.

On the morning of the fourth day, Mr. Haskins called.

"It looks like the flooding has cleared," he said. "I'm going to go do an inspection for the insurance company and take a few pictures. I'll let you know how it looks, but judging from what I've been seeing on the news, I think we're probably looking at a total loss."

Lori had seen the images on the news. In some places, it looked more like the town had been hit by a hurricane; there were downed power lines and washed-out streets everywhere. The low-lying areas around the shop had been under six feet of water at a few points. So it wasn't surprising that the shop might be totally unsalvageable—but the idea was incomprehensible.

"Do you want me to come with you?" she asked.

"Oh, no. Don't worry about it." He hesitated, then said, 'I'll let you know if any of the animals made it. Hell, if you want, you can take them all home. I'm getting out of the pet shop business, I think, once I get this shit worked out with the insurance."

Lori glanced over at her mother, sitting on the other hotel bed, watching the news. She wondered what her mom would say about taking home animals from the shop, if any were even in any shape to bring home. If Mr. Haskins wanted her to do it, surely her mother couldn't fault her with that? And it was only a few more weeks until summer was over, a few weeks before she could move.

"Don't get your hopes up," Mr. Haskins said, perhaps sensing Lori's excitement in her silence. "It's been four days. If they're not drowned, half the animals are probably starved. But I'll let you know what I see when I get there."

* * *

"This is never going to work," Smeeze said.

"It'll work," White One replied, irritably. Since her time with the wild ones, she had grown more agitated and, if possible, more flighty than she had ever been. She wanted something from the others, something that she wasn't getting, and she didn't know precisely what it was. Sympathy? Apology? Gratitude? Something.

She wished she could discard that gnawing desire, as it did nothing but make her angry. She had told no one of what had happened—the male she had named, the way he had protected her, his *jask* that now dwelled inside her—and she had no intention of telling them. So it was unreasonable to expect them to treat her in any special way. Even if she had told them—what was the point? So she had suffered. They had all suffered. And yet, no matter what she told herself, the feeling refused to go away, so she did the next best thing and ignored it.

"Trust me, Smeeze. Have I ever steered you wrong?"

Smeeze was silent, and White One chose to take the silence as an affirmation.

Early this morning, Bitey had approached White One with a request: Find a safe place to move the colony. Somewhere defensible from the wild ones. Somewhere they could make a stand if the *Ukeshu* sent an army after them, no matter the size. White One had discovered just that, though no one else seemed entirely to understand that she had.

Along the side wall of the pet store, not so far from where the *shujisk* had been found, were rows of empty cages. They smelled of *ushu*, but long-since faded to a ghost. The hint of their odor clung to the steel, a heavy stench of urine hidden beneath years of cleaning solution and dust. The bottom cages, level with the floor, were large and made of wide steel mesh. Those above were smaller, with thinner mesh—but just wide enough for a slender female rat to squeeze through.

White One had discovered, through trial-and-error, that she could climb over top of one of the dog crates and, from there, squeeze through the bars into the smaller cage above. The inside of the cage was roomy and vacant, with no shelves to hide within, and all the walls were made of the same drafty mesh—but it was secure.

"I don't like it," Smeeze said. "It's all out in the open. No place to hide, inside."

"Well, we'll fix that then," White One said, with an agitated and dismissive shake of the head. "We'll bring in bedding. We'll build nests."

"We can't get a nest box in there," Cookie added. "How could we make it fit?"

"We don't need a nest box," White One said, with as much patience as she could muster. "We'll build our own nest. I know it's not perfect, but…well, we'll make it work. It'll be just like home." She sighed. She wondered how it was that, of all the rats available to her, she had been given Smeeze and Cookie as her partners in building a defensible fortress while Bitey led the others to grow their army.

It wasn't that she disliked either of them. They were just the two slowest-thinking rats she knew. Literal-minded, maybe, was the kinder way to put it. And, at the moment, infuriating. "Here. Watch. Let me show you why this is a good idea."

Sighing with long-suffering resignation, White One stepped toward to her newfound discovery. She scaled the lower dog crate—perhaps not as smoothly as she would normally have been able to, given the penetrating soreness in every inch of her body, but with enough grace to prove that it was easy. Then, she scampered over top, where the smaller cage pressed against it, and squirmed through the bars.

She turned her attentions back to Smeeze. "Now then," she said, from behind the bars of the cage. "Come attack me."

Smeeze looked at her, a little stupefied, but did as she was told. She clambered laboriously up the side of the dog crate and pressed her head through the one-inch bar spacing of the ferret cage, beginning to squeeze herself inside. White One approached her calmly and nipped her nose.

Smeeze squeaked in alarm and jerked away, nearly falling through the broader, three-inch gap of the dog crate's mesh. "What was that for?" she asked, rubbing a paw over her bruised face.

"An illustration," White One said. "To show you that for any wild rat who tries to approach us, we'll have the upper hand. They'll be slowed by the wire—if some of the larger ones can get through at all—and we'll have plenty of time to tear them apart in safety."

"But what if we can't fit?" Cookie asked, from the ground. She stood on her hindpaws. She had lost some weight over the last few days of hardship, but she hardly looked emaciated.

She may still have a difficult time in pulling through an inch-wide gap, White One knew, but she had a contingency plan for that. "We'll get as many as we can inside this cage," she said, tapping her forepaw against the floor before squeezing her way back through the bars. "The others will have stay down here, where the wire is further apart." Then, before Cookie and Smeeze could interrupt by pointing out how much less secure it was, she continued, "If it comes to it, we'll post our best guards here—Monster, and Bitey, Ukeki and Smeeze, if she wants. The rest of us will be up top. And, if we can get the *shujisk* on our side, like Bitey wants, they'll be down here too. Remember that."

"I wonder how they're doing, anyway," Smeeze asked.

White One shrugged, climbing down the last of the way to the ground and nudging Cookie encouragingly on the shoulder, displaying higher spirits than she felt. "We'll see soon enough," she said. "Now, come on. We have to get food and bedding in here quickly, if we're all going to get moved in before Bitey gets back."

* * *

"I'm really not sure this is a good idea," Top Ear said, warily.

"The *Ukeshu* will come with army of 'countless warriors,' or so Usoothe says," Bitey said. "We don't have an army at all. We need what we can get."

"Yes, I understand that, but…they're *ushu*."

"Also, the last time we saw them, they were trying to eat me," Allaysi added. "I'm with Top Ear. This type of alliance is unnatural."

"Rats in cages are unnatural," Ukeki said. "Of course they'd come up with unnatural ideas."

Bitey sighed. She should not have taken so many rats with her, that much was obvious. But it had seemed like the safest plan at the time: bring as many as possible as defense in case the *shujisk* were hostile. But she'd hoped they wouldn't be. Of course, she hadn't been around for the attack that Top Ear and Allaysi spoke of, so perhaps she misunderstood the nature of her would-be allies. She didn't think so, though. She could remember their restless energy in their cage, the way they had crawled over each other and struggled to follow her awkward instructions.

She had saved their lives. They owed it to her.

She led an odd group. Top Ear, Allaysi and Ukeki walked with her. Dumbo, Usoothe and Monster had been left behind as look-outs for White One and the others; if the wild ones were to return earlier than they'd anticipated, they were supposed to intervene until Bitey could return. She truly hoped it would not come to that. Though she had little doubt of Dumbo and Monster in a battle, the thought that her friends might be in danger while she tried something that may prove hopeless was unbearable.

"I don't even think they're still here," Top Ear said, anxiously. "Let's just go back."

"They're here," Ukeki said. "Can't you smell them? Their

stink is everywhere."

"Yes, but their stink isn't going to help us fight."

"Quiet, both of you," Bitey said, pulling forward. "We'll never find anything if both of you are chattering away like fools."

Grudgingly, they fell silent, and the four of them walked slowly down the devastated aisles of the pet store, searching for any sign of the *shujisk*. They had been looking for some time without much luck. Everywhere they looked, things had been destroyed, and it was difficult to tell if it had been only the flood that had caused that damage. Bags of food were torn open. Collars and leashes lay in tangled knots on the floor. Things were knocked over or shredded or torn through. And, as Ukeki had pointed out, the entire area stank with their oily scent.

Just as Bitey was prepared to give up and turn back, she heard something move nearby. She froze, ears swept forward, fur standing on end. A *shujisk* appeared from beneath a shelf, squeezing its lean body through the gap and gazing out at Bitey from shining black eyes set within a dark mask. Bitey tried to recall if she recognized this creature—if it was one of those she had met previously—but there was little time to consider it before he was upon her.

He moved with stunning speed, as if a snake and rat had been fused into a single deadly machine. All of the laughter was gone; now he was only an *ushu*, and she was beneath him, feeling his hot breath and long blunt claws. She let out a surprised cry, squirming to get away, to find an opening to attack—and then, just as quickly as he had bowled her over, he was gone.

Bewildered, Bitey rose to her paws. Ukeki had pinned him down, her nose in his face, teeth bared and tattered ears folded back to her skull. *She's fast*, Bitey marveled, and then said, "Don't kill him."

"I won't if he doesn't make me," Ukeki responded, her face still touching the ferret's larger nose.

Top Ear and Allaysi exchanged uneasy looks.

"Where are the others?" Bitey asked, circling around to come close to the ferret. He gazed at her impassively from his dark eyes, his jaw hanging slightly open now that he was forced onto his back. It looked as though he were smiling in a rather grim way. The tips of sharp teeth poked out from below the corners of his lips. "Your friends. I freed you—all of you. Do you remember?"

The ferret did not answer, but he did not struggle away from Ukeki.

"I helped you get out of your cage. I saved you all from the Big Water. You would have drowned."

"Bitey, I don't think he can understand you," Top Ear said, anxiously.

Bitey ignored her. She knew the *shujisk* wouldn't understand every word, but she suspected that at least part of it was getting through. "I'm going to tell my friend to let you go," she said, attentions still focused entirely on the ferret. "When she does, you will not attack us. Is that understood?"

"Yes, yes, yes," the ferret said, in its odd accent. "No bite, no tear. Friends."

"Ukeki."

"I'm not letting him up. He's an *ushu* and a liar."

"Ukeki," Bitey repeated, with warning in her voice.

The large-bodied warrior growled but relented, slowly withdrawing. The ferret squirmed, struggling to right himself back onto all four paws before looking between them, head hung low. He seemed to count them, quickly, and realize that he was entirely outnumbered. "No bite," he said, again. "No kill."

The rats slowly encircled him, prepared to intervene if he attacked again, but he made no move to do so.

"No bite," Bitey agreed, with a grim smile. "But you'd like to, wouldn't you? You'd like to chase…hunt…kill." Her stomach turned at the implication of what she was saying, but there was no way around it, not if she wanted to stand a chance against the *Ukeshu*. "I know a way."

The ferret tilted his head, curiously. His ears piqued forward.

"Tell your leader he owes me a favor," she said. "I helped you. Now, you can help me and my friends."

Chapter Twenty-One

They were coming. Bitey didn't need any *usoothe* to tell her that—she could feel them. Smell them. Hear them. They consumed her senses and she trembled. No matter how well they had prepared for this moment—no matter how inevitable it had felt—she wasn't ready.

She stood just inside the wire of the bottom cage—the larger kennel—alongside Smeeze, Monster, and Ukeki. The others were above, in the smaller cage. Cookie had managed, somehow, to squeeze in, and she was in surprisingly high spirits considering the circumstances; once given the task of building shelter inside, she had happily taken to weaving nests from scraps of plastic, paper, and fabric brought by the others. By the time Bitey and her retainer had returned from their journey, the cages almost looked like home.

Good thing, Bitey thought. *If we survive this, it* will *be home.*

Above, the rats were huddled together, awaiting the onslaught. If they were lucky, the fight would not go that far. Not a rat among them was truly built for battle, though Dumbo was able to hold her own. They may be able to ward off attacks through the bars, but if the *Ukeshu's* guards broke through, it would be over quickly.

All the more reason to make sure that doesn't happen.

Below, the guards were restless, wandering or pacing or grooming. None looked at each other. Smeeze shifted uneasily from one paw to the other and kept casting uncertain glances up at the top cage as if regretting her post. Only Monster seemed unfazed; her blood-colored eyes were glazed and distant.

Outside the bars, the ferrets wrestled and bounced, chasing each other around the cage. They seemed to be enjoying themselves. Bitey was glad; she wasn't certain that they knew what they had been brought here for, and she feared they may leave if things stretched on much longer. They didn't seem to be particularly patient creatures.

They waited this way for a long time. The sounds of the *Ukeshu*'s army grew nearer, but did not become more urgent; the warrior-king of the wild ones was confident and unhurried. Besides, they had been forced to cross the store in the open, and their progress was slowed by caution. Rats, even those on a mission, can never let down their guard; they can never forget that they can at any time become the prey of nearly everything else. Survival and caution first. Anger and violence second.

The approaching rats did not quite march. They crept along walls or darted across open spaces. They pressed themselves low to the damp tile and moved with the cautious, jerky footsteps of those on unfamiliar ground. A few, scenting the *ihujisk*, started and tried to draw back. The rats behind them, though—the largest and most powerful of the party—nipped at their haunches and urged them forward.

They were an impressive army. They totaled perhaps twenty in all, each one as large and heavily-scarred as any in the *Ukeshu*'s service. The smallest of them were gaunt and angular with shrewd faces; the largest rivaled the ferrets in size. All of them reeked of maleness and the promise of violence.

At the rear of the group, moving with the terrible deliberation of one who has never known fear, the *Ukeshu* stood a head taller than any in his army. His sleek dark fur caught hints of light, illuminating his muscles, and the twisted scars that crossed his sides stood out in stark contrast to his sleek pelt. As they came within sight of the domestic colony's stronghold, the *Ukeshu* rose to his haunches and hissed out a warning—a wordless threat that made even the skin of his allies crawl.

The wild ones halted at the sound of their alpha's cry. They stood in a tense line, a jumble of bodies that seethed with tension, and waited for a signal. At their paws, an expanse of two feet stood between them and the cage where Bitey and her kin had chosen to make their stand. Between them there was only an empty expanse of tile—and a small handful of *shujisk*.

The ferrets—who had seemed listless and ready to leave just moments before—suddenly snapped to attention. A harsh predatory gleam lit in their eyes. They whipped their blunt heads toward the approaching rats and gave out a piercing, joyous cry. Before the wild ones could react, the first *shujisk* had darted forward with the speed and grace of a demon, and the others soon followed. Some, attracted by the sound, bounded free of hiding places beneath shelves or within cages. Creatures who had moments ago been playing amongst themselves were suddenly converted to a single purpose: violence, for the simple joy of slaughter.

Bitey, holding her position behind the bars of her crate, was caught off-guard by the ferocity of their action. She could merely gape at the simultaneously vicious and playful way that they conducted themselves, her thoughts temporarily torn from the enemy. What had she done? What kind of allies had she chosen?

"Snakes," Monster said, in a low voice beside her. "They've all been turned to snakes."

They leaped. They clawed, they dodged and bit and struck and tore and the wild rats screamed and tumbled over each other. They fought back and ran in equal measure, scattering as they broke rank and bolted. The instincts of prey overrode the orders of even the most fearsome alpha, and the blind terror of *ushu* was enough to daze and disorient even the most stalwart warriors. The *Ukeshu* screamed at them to stay—to stand and fight— but they paid him no heed.

Some got away.

Others were not so lucky. Bitey heard the screams of the rats as they were overcome, strangled cries that were cut abruptly short by the snapping of necks or the tearing of throats. It turned her stomach, even knowing that the survival of her colony depended on them. There was something unnerving in the cheerful bloodlust of the ferrets, something terrifying and primal.

She hoped that they would not turn on her when they were done.

Despite her fear, her resolve strengthened. She had not come this far only to recoil at the last moment; as long as there were threats outside, she would hold her position.

"Think they'll get scared and run?" Smeeze asked, hopefully.

Bitey didn't bother to answer; despite the threat of the *shujisk*, several of the wild rats rushed forward. They were the largest of the crowd, the *Ukeshu*'s private guard—rats whose incisors were already stained with the blood of their more cowardly kin. The ferrets now were so distracted with their prey that they paid the others no heed, and Bitey knew that the fight was now hers to finish.

Spirits help me, she thought. The collective consciousness of the dead had once taught her to swim—a task she would have thought impossible before she'd done it. Now she hoped they could guide her on just one more impossible task.

The first of the rats squirmed through the barrier, pulling his bulk free of the bars and rushing at Bitey. His eyes were wild and he bared his teeth; his incisors were long and orange and filed to sharp points. For a moment, they met nose to nose; the stand-off lasted only a moment before he broke the stillness with his first attack.

He lunged forward, and Bitey dodged him, aiming a kick at his side as he came along her haunch. She wheeled around once more to face him, ignoring the searing pain of old wounds on her side; her heart pounded in her chest, but her mind was utterly, blissfully blank. She moved as a creature of instinct, not consciousness—acting as though her body were a conduit for the Spirits themselves, countless generations of rats who had fought with teeth and claws for their survival in a world where they were merely prey.

Bitey and her opponent rose to their hindpaws, whisker to whisker, and hissed wordless threats at each other, caught in a terrible moment of stasis. The male ducked his head and darted in to aim a bite at her underbelly, and she moved quickly, leaping over top of him and sinking her teeth into his haunch. She tore his flesh and he screamed; she tasted his blood, and she bit him again and again. He struggled, breaking free of her, and retreated. She pursued him, and she nipped at his haunches and his tail as he squeezed clumsily back through the bars. The tip of his tail caught in her teeth and she spat it out as she watched him flee.

All around her, the battle raged on. Ukeki battled with a slender, tawny-colored male who circled and darted around her, his sinuous body more like a ferret than a rat. Smeeze pressed herself against the bars, scratching at the eyes of one particularly large male who had gotten caught between the wires; he screeched and scrabbled at the ground with his paws in every direction, clearly not sure whether to press forward or retreat. Monster screamed and wheeled around, taking on two warriors at once. Blood poured from her nose and the tip of her tail was missing, but she seemed not to notice; her dark ruby eyes held the same glazed, distant look they had since her fight with the snake.

They're all snakes, Bitey thought, Monster's own voice echoing in the back of her mind. *They've all been turned to snakes.*

They struggled on like this, battle and chaos everywhere. Deafening. The scent of blood and fear and urine and testosterone clogging the senses. The fight seemed to exist in its own time; each movement occupied an eternity, and it seemed as though there had never been any time outside of this moment. The fight could have taken minutes or days; it was all the same.

"You fools!" The *Ukeshu* roared, standing outside the cage; his cold dark eyes fell upon the warriors inside—and those scrambling, beaten and bloody, to escape. His force had dwindled to a half-dozen rats still willing to continue fighting, and his displeasure was obvious. His whiskers quivered with rage. "Climb over the top!"

His warriors halted, bewildered. Clearly, Bitey realized, the wild ones had the same problems with understanding space as she had overcome when leaving her cage for the first time.

Just as climbing outside of a cage was incomprehensible to her, scaling the wire was an insurmountable task to these rats who had lived all their lives underground. The *Ukeshu* shoved them aside and led the way himself, climbing the side of the dog kennel with surprising agility for his size.

"Smeeze!" Bitey yelled, struggling to free herself from the rat who had engaged her. "Get him! Stop him!"

Smeeze reached her paw through to snatch at him, her claws scraping his belly. He carried on, unfazed, and before she could climb up to pursue him from the inside, one of the remaining guards had rushed to his alpha's aid. Slamming himself against the bars, he caught hold of Smeeze's extended paw in his teeth. He bit down, and the audible crunch of shattering bone was only partially obscured by Smeeze's scream of pain. She fell back, clutching her forepaw to her chest; blood blossomed from the wound, staining her pelt as it poured from the gap where two of her fingers had been.

The warrior, pressing his advantage, squirmed through the bars and threw himself forward.

"Smeeze!" Bitey yelled, aiming a kick at her opponent's face as she struggled to free herself.

Monster, whose own opponent had just been sent reeling into Ukeki's side by a particularly brutal kick, darted forward. She jumped, arcing through the air and landing on the male's back. The two tumbled, end-over-end, like two kits at play— but the screams of protest from the wild one shattered that image. Monster's teeth flashed and tore. When they came to rest, only one rat rose to her paws; the male lay, bloodied and still, on his side.

Overhead, the *Ukeshu* continued his steady ascent of the cage. "You're mine," he rasped, climbing atop the larger kennel and reaching for the bars of the smaller cage where the rest of the domestic rats sat huddled together. "All of you. You may fight me now…you may even win today…but the *Ukeshu* will not be defeated."

"You just keep telling yourself that," Allaysi muttered, bounding forward to boldly snap at his paws as he clung to the side of the cage. "Your time is over, old-timer."

Below, the last of his retainer had caught on. Three rats followed him up the side of the cage, scaling the dog kennel's outer walls and moving to flank him on the side of the cage, struggling to shove through the smaller mesh. Rats surged forward to claw at eyes and nip at noses as they appeared.

Even the *Ukeshu*, driven back by the relentless onslaught of rats pressing themselves against the mesh, fell back to stand on the roof of the larger cage, teeth bared and whiskers twitching swiftly as he contemplated a new strategy.

"This was brilliant, White One!" Top Ear said, reaching through the bars to swipe at a rat's eyes. "You're a genius!"

White One grinned. "We can't hold them off forever, if they keep coming," she said, but it was impossible to hide the pride that touched her voice. "But it really was one of my better ideas." She rushed the bars, snapping at a paw that broke through. The rat squeaked and jerked his paw away; she aimed for his scrotum instead. She thought Usoothe would appreciate it.

Below, the last of the wild ones on the lower levels had retreated. Only the *Ukeshu* and his most loyal retainer remained, and so far White One's defenses held firm. Victory, it seemed, was not only possible— it was eminent.

Then the *Ukeshu* froze. Perched precariously on the edge of the larger kennel, he reared back on his haunches and stood as stiff as a statue, eyes bulging and ears swept forward. Only the tips of his whiskers trembled. A sudden hush fell over the wild ones. Noses twitched. Whiskers flicked forward.

All at once, they fled.

They scrambled over each other in their rush to escape. One jumped clear of the cage and landed with a sickening crack as his leg broke; he tucked the limb against his belly and struggled forward anyway. Below, the injured scrambled over each other, crawling over the bodies of those too damaged to escape. Even the *Ukeshu* seemed forgotten in the sudden chaos; he lagged behind his panicking crew.

"*Ushu!*" they screamed, illogically, loud enough that even the ferrets started with surprise. "*Ushu! Ushu!*"

White One's ears folded against her skull, eyes wide. She drew away from the bars, huddling close to her companions. "Something is coming," she said. "And I don't think we want to be here to see."

"Do we hide? Or do we run?" Top Ear asked, her muscles tensed for flight. "What do we do?"

"White One," Bitey asked, warily, from beneath their feet. "What's happening?"

"I don't know!" White One snapped, still watching the wild rats flee as though the Spirit gates had opened and the ghosts of all time were mad on their heels. "We hide," she said, not knowing if it was the right answer, but feeling that it was. "We hide. NOW! Everybody, find cover!"

With effort, they squeezed back through the bars. Dumbo, who was in line behind Cookie, gave her sister an impatient shove; the tan-speckled rat squealed in protest but emerged on the far side of the cage, sprawling. Top Ear picked her up by the scruff, lifting her to her paws, and they scaled down the sides of the cage as quickly as they could, jumping clear and rolling to safety. Bitey and the others shoved through the wide bars of the dog kennel and joined them as they ran for cover.

They fell in with the wild ones, all of them united by their fear.

All except Usoothe. He fell behind the others, standing stock-still in the floor, eyes lifted to the threat as it came. A hopeful smile upon his face, his folded back in obeisance; hope glimmered in his remaining good eye. "They've come," he whispered, quietly to no one, as none had stayed behind to hear.

Chapter Twenty-Two

Bob Haskins heard the crunch of glass under his boot as he stepped over the threshold of his store. The stench caught him first: the smell of decay, of dead fish and growing mold. His eyes watered and a hand rose to his mouth. For a moment he thought he would retch, but he didn't, and he pressed his way in.

The store was a mess.

Trash and dirt and fallen merchandise littered the floor. The tile was still wet in places, but in others the silt had begun to dry, creating drifts of sand against the base of shelves. There were dead goldfish everywhere. Some still gasped desperately in shallow puddles. The stock on the lowest shelves was strewn all over the floor—broken aquariums, soaked bags of pet food, molding pet clothes, a tangle of damp collars and rusting chains.

The goddamn snake—the python he'd spent so much money on, the store mascot—was sprawled on the floor as limp and lifeless as a garden hose.

Bob walked slowly, deliberately, past the cages and tanks. Most of the fish—the ones that had not been swept away in the flood—were dead in their tanks. Some of the other animals, too, were lying dead in their cages, and others were in sad shape from thirst and hunger. The latch of the ferret cage had, somehow, been opened, and the cage was bare.

The rat cage was waterlogged and empty, except for the decaying body of a single black and white rat. Curious, he bent down to examine it for a moment, before making his way toward the rear of the store. The wall of empty cages stood like the last forlorn memories of a once-glorious shop. Something squeaked near his feet and he glanced down, seeing a brown-gray rat run past him, a ferret hard on its heels. Bob Haskins blinked, not sure if he had seen that properly. The animals disappeared as quickly as he had seen them, and he continued on.

What he saw made him do a double-take. His eyes traced over the sight, but his brain refused to compute what he was seeing. Along the wall where the large display cages were, a dog crate sat below a smaller cat cage. And, swarming over both in a seething, furry mass, were dozens of rats.

They ran, blind and terrified, in every direction. By the time he was near they had largely disappeared—running along the baseboard or squeezing beneath nearby shelves. It was almost as if they'd heard him coming and called out an alarm.

One of the little bastards, with a big white blaze up his nose, actually walked up to him, staring up at him like it wanted something.

Like a dog begging for a treat.

Like a bold, presumptuous little shit.

Bob Haskins kicked it with the toe of his boot. It squeaked and went airborne. He heard the crunch of bone as it hit the baseboard, and it didn't get up.

"Goddammit," he swore, disgusted.

Time to call the exterminator.

* * *

"I don't understand why we have to hide," Cookie whined, her voice a breathless wheeze from trying to keep up with the others. Her sides were bruised from being shoved through the bars of the cage, and her paws had begin to swell, the tiny sores on the soles spreading with each step. "The Great One is back!"

"It's not safe," Top Ear said.

Ignoring her, Cookie crawled forward, drawing away from their hiding place near the baseboards to make her way into the open.

Out on the floor, Usoothe cried out rapturously, the joy trembling in his voice: "At last! At last they've come! Our salvation! The prophecy fulfilled!"

A tremendous shadow passed over them, a god of incomprehensible size.

"Join me, sisters! Come out to greet the new dawn!"

An immense foot sailed through the air, making contact with Usoothe with a terrible thud. The prophet flew, head-over-heels, and slammed into the baseboard with a crunch of bone.

He landed just inches from their hiding place. Blood seeped out of his ears. His one good eye went dark.

Cookie screamed and ran back to the others, scrambling back beneath the shelf.

"And that," White One said, "Is why we have to hide."

Chapter Twenty-Three

The night was quiet and still. An odd foreboding had fallen over them since Usoothe's death. It was like the day of the flood, but magnified by terror. Two *usoothe* had died, now, as bookends to disaster. It felt like a terrible omen. In their quiet way, they prayed to the Spirits for strength, or guidance, but nothing seemed to change in their condition. Perhaps the Spirits had given all the gifts they could give. Perhaps even they did not know how to confront this new, tumultuous world.

Or, perhaps, they too had been murdered, dashed against the wall with the brains of their final prophet.

Most of the wild ones had vanished after the appearance of the Great One, and had not returned. A few stayed behind, huddling miserably near the hiding place of their enemies, too scared to press their rivalry. All of them were too frightened to venture out of their hiding places. No one knew exactly where the *shujisk* had gone. Worse, Great Ones occasionally entered the store. Each heavy bootstep sent thrills of fear through the hearts of the refugees, and they pressed together tightly in their hiding place and trembled until the noise had stopped and the shadows ceased moving outside.

That was not the worst of it, though. The worst of it came

later, when the hunger set in.

They were too frightened to venture far in the open. Scampering across open spaces had been one thing when they were emboldened by their solitude. It was another matter entirely when Great Ones moved outside like shadowy behemoths and the constant threat of boots hung over everyone's heads.

Snakes, Monster had said. *Everything had turned to snakes.*

There was little food near their current hiding place. Several times, small scouting parties had gone to retrieve what they could find, but the best stashes were far away—and then, one day, they were gone completely.

"Taken away by the Great Ones," White One explained, sensibly.

"They never keep food in the cage when the snake is coming," Monster added.

Soon after the food disappeared, the traps began to arrive. The first of these they avoided. Allaysi had seen them before, tucked away in the corners of the storeroom. She quickly explained—as best she could—about the spring-loaded trap and how it could snap the spine of any who ventured too close. The rats gave that one a wide berth.

What Allaysi hadn't warned them about was poison.

In their hunger, the rats had failed to be cautious about their food. The Beyond had always supplied them with *uchu*, food of high quality, and it never occurred to them that this might change. And so when Dumbo had found a new stash of food, tucked away in a hidden place, she hadn't thought twice about digging in.

Now, inside their hiding place amongst the shelves, the rats huddled around Dumbo, who lay shuddering on the floor. Her extremities were swollen with blood and her eyes were glazed.

It had been nearly a day since she had eaten the poisoned food, and her condition worsened with a slow, miserable inevitability.

Death was near, and she had been talking nonsense for hours. First, she had begged for water. Then, she had begun to cry out for Nezumi, and she'd started talking as though her mother were there with her. She'd been talking in a low voice, her words a mere jumble of sounds, and even Top Ear—who lay over her, inconsolable in her grief—couldn't make out what she was saying.

Suddenly Dumbo cried out, startling her sister and waking the others from their troubled half-waking dreams.

"The air!" she screamed, and the voice that tore from her throat sounded like Nezumi's. "The air is nothing but death."

She began to shudder, then, and writhe against the tile. Her tail thrashed. Her jaw worked, uselessly. Her eyes slid closed and she was still. Finally, still.

* * *

The media got wind of the situation, the way they always do, and soon the place was swarming with cameras, and reporters, and newspaper writers. Mr. Haskins didn't know where they'd come from, or what they wanted, and he spent a lot of time not talking to them when they called for an interview. The police put up yellow tape around the building. The place was considered a health and safety hazard. A disaster area. That was fine by him. The headlines cropped up that night. "Pet store infested with rats!" the headlines declared. "Little pet shop of horrors!"

"I never saw a rat in there aside from the ones I sold," Bob

Haskins said, again and again, every time they called.

"But they must have come from somewhere," they insisted.

He'd hang up on them. When he wouldn't talk to them, they made up things to say; when he did talk to them, they made things up anyway.

He didn't want to call Lori, but he'd promised, and she had kept leaving him voice mails.

"I saw the news," she said, immediately, when she answered.

"Yeah, I know." He sighed. He could already hear it in her voice. She was going to call those PETA assholes, or the ASPCA, or the National Guard. Someone. Goodness and righteousness and the sanctity of all life or some bullshit. "The store's going to be closed for good after this. I'm getting out of the business, like I said. Just so you know."

She sounded genuinely disappointed, and it made him smile a little. At least somebody other than him gave a shit about the place.

"The rats," she said, after they discussed the matter for a while. "Some of the rats…they're ours, aren't they? They'd have to be."

"I'm done with it," he said, wearily. "The exterminator's been laying out poison, and the big crew is coming in the morning. They'll gas the building, kill everything in it. The insurance is paying for everything and then we'll be free of all of this. I'll let you know if I open a new store. Tell you what—I'll give you the first job opening I get."

"…You can't just kill all of the animals," she said, sounding horrified.

He smiled grimly. "If you want to save them, you have until 8:00 o'clock tomorrow morning," he said, and hung up.

She'd be there with have-a-heart traps and an arm full of

cookies within the hour, and he knew it.

* * *

Lori had never broken the rules of her house. All her life, she had taken care to be respectful of her mother's wishes, even when they had run contrary to her own. She had agreed to attend the state college when her heart had been set on the pricier art school out of state. She had put aside every penny of her earnings from the pet store so she could pay her way without putting a burden on her mother. And she had, all this time, heeded her mother's firm "no animals in the house" rule.

But there was a time and a place for following rules, and a time for breaking them.

She glanced over her shoulder, slowly easing her mother's car from the parking spot. So what if she wasn't supposed to be driving? There was no way her mom was going to let her follow through with her plan, and she wasn't going to let Mr. Haskins murder the rats without at least trying to help them.

Behind the car, Lori's mother stepped into her path, arms crossed over her chest.

"Shit," Lori muttered, hitting the break too quickly and feeling the car shudder and threaten to stall out. She shifted it into park.

"Where do you think you're going?" her mother asked, circling around the car and speaking through the rolled-up window.

Lori rolled the window down and attempted to explain. It poured out of her in a confusing jumble: the rats, the flooding, the exterminators. Her long-lasting plan to sneak the rats into her dorm room at college. The way she had been hiding toys and cages and supplies away while working at the store, preparing for this, and how it would all be pointless if Mr. Haskins succeeded in killing the rats in the store.

"You're serious about this?" her mother asked. "You're going to go through all this trouble for some vermin?"

"Yes," she replied, firmly, and moved to shift the car back to reverse.

Her mother's face was inscrutable, but Lori thought she saw a hint of something—maybe pride, or respect—in her eyes. "Stop the car. If it means that much to you, I'll drive you."

Chapter Twenty-Four

Cookie's nose twitched. She smelled food—not stolen kibble, not rat chow, but good food. Human food—*uchu*. Her belly growled. After Dumbo, they had all been too frightened to eat anything. She could feel the weakness creeping in from her extremities. The others might make fun of her for it, but she felt that the awful gnawing in her gut was worse than anything that could happen. Even death—writhing in pain and delirium like her sister—would be better than slowly starving in a dank hovel.

The scent tantalized her and, despite everything, she could not resist. She crept out of the cover and toward the smell.

The Great One was there. Not the terrible ones with their boots and angry voices, but the other one. Soft Hands, the one who brought the cookies, the one who had given them all names. She had cages in her hand, strange cages with doors that only opened one way, and she was laying these on the floor near their hiding place, putting food in them. Cookie's heart thudded with excitement and she darted forward, bounding up to her, delighted, fearless.

"Cookie!" Top Ear hissed, from her hiding place. "Cookie, what are you doing?"

"*Uchu*," she said, exuberantly. "And the Great One! Look!

She's come for us! I knew she would."

"Don't be stupid!" Bitey said, lunging to catch her before she could escape. "She'll kill you! Don't you remember Usoothe? Dumbo? She'll crush you! It's poison!"

Cookie ignored them. "It's Soft Hands!" she replied, exasperated. "She won't hurt us."

She nimbly sidestepped Bitey's grasp and scampered out into the open, leaving the others huddled in the hollow beneath the shelves.

Lori knelt down and extended a hand, holding a wafer cookie between her fingers. Cookie tentatively sniffed her fingers and took the treat, retreating a few steps to eat it. It was good—no, delicious, amazing—and she ate it with boggle-eyed bliss. Lori's hands gently scooped her up, cradling her against her chest, and Cookie snuggled into the warmth in the crook of her arm. She struggled only briefly against being picked up, the unnerving sensation of weightlessness, and then she swallowed the last of her treat and buried her muzzle in the warm place and gave herself fully to her.

She dozed for much of the journey. She was dimly aware through her exhaustion of having been put into a cage, and of motion, alternating lights and the intermittent touch of fingers against her. She awoke from her exhaustion, at length, and found herself in a cage unlike any she had been in before. It was large and furnished with not just one nest box, but several, and soft fabric hammocks, and a myriad of shelves for climbing on. The food bowl was overflowing, and she set in on the bowl, greedily stuffing her face, relishing in the taste of each item as it slid over her tongue.

This was paradise. Not a paradise filled with lies and danger, but a real one, the way The Beyond was supposed to be.

Chapter Twenty-Five

"She's gone," Top Ear said, hollowly. It felt odd to say it aloud. Gone. Nezumi, Sniffles, Squeaker, Usoothe, Dumbo. And now Cookie, taken up in the hand of the Great One, and no knowing what had happened when she passed out of sight. An age ago—in a time when the rats still dwelt within cages and the rules of the world still made sense—this would have been cause for celebration. Rats had gone to the Great Ones before. It had once been the ambition of all of them.

But the world was different. The Great Ones had never abandoned them, then. They had never murdered a prophet with a careless sweep of a boot. In those days, they were infallible. But today, they brought with them nothing but doubts, ominous and terrible.

Cookie was gone. Dumbo was gone. Nothing made any sense any more.

"I should have stopped her," Bitey said. "If I'd gone after her…followed her into the open…"

"Then you might have been taken, too," Top Ear said. She pressed close to Bitey—the last of her sisters, the only family left in a world that had gone insane—and tried to quell her trembling. "Don't blame yourself."

They fell into miserable silence.

"What do you think Dumbo meant, the air is death?" Smeeze asked, haltingly, as though unsure whether it was safe to bring it up.

"It means we have to get out of here," White One said. She ran her paws over her face, slowly, deliberately. The swell of her belly was beginning to become visible. "Something awful is coming."

"Something awful already came," Monster said. "Something awful is already here. It's always been here."

Despite her insanity, Monster had a point. Top Ear shivered.

"Then maybe Cookie is safe," Smeeze said, uncertainly. The wound on her forepaw had begun to heal, scar tissue knitting itself together over her missing toes. "I mean. There's a chance. What if…" her jaw worked, her teeth gritting together as she wrestled with ideas too big for words. She fell silent.

"There's a chance that she escaped whatever is coming, and we didn't." White One said, shrewdly. "There's a way to find out. But there's no coming back from it, if we're wrong."

"What do you mean?"

White One nodded toward the trap Lori had left behind, which stood just a few feet from their hiding place. Her whiskers twitched. "The food, in that funny cage—it's *uchu*, like Cookie always ate. It's from Soft Hands."

The others looked at her in confusion.

She pressed on. "She must have left it here for a reason— must want us to go in there. We go in the cage, maybe she'll come back for us. Take us where Cookie is."

"What if she wants to hurt us? What if it's a trick?" Bitey asked.

"Then we made the wrong choice," White One said, grimly.

"But maybe we'll have the chance to make it right," Top Ear said. "Save Cookie, if that's what happens."

"It's a trap!" Bitey said. "A trick! After everything that's happened, you expect me to willingly climb into a trap?"

"We can't stay here, either," Smeeze protested. "The air is death, remember? And even if it's not, we'll starve. The *shujisk* will eat us. The wild ones will come back to kill us."

"It's just another cage," Monster said wearily. "No matter where you go, there's only cages and snakes."

Nothing had changed, Top Ear realized. They were trapped, once more, without food, huddled together against a warning from the Spirits. Before, the only way to survive had been to climb outside of their cage; now, perhaps, they needed to climb into one.

"Allaysi, Ukeki," Bitey said, desperately. "Talk some sense into them. Tell them they can't trust this."

"I've never seen that trap before," Allaysi said, uncertain. "But there are many things I've never seen."

Ukeki, who had not spoken a word since Usoothe's death, gritted her teeth and remained silent.

"I can't tell you whether it's the right choice," White One said. "But it's what I'm going to do."

Top Ear touched her nose to Bitey's shoulder before pulling away to follow White One. Together, they crept out into the open, bodies pressed low to the ground, ears and whiskers perked forward and twitching at every hint of sound.

"Ignore the food," White One said, sniffing the wire. "In case it's poison."

Smeeze stood behind them, reluctantly, frozen in place halfway between the trap and the hiding place. She held her ruined paw against her chest and waited with quivering whiskers.

Taking a deep breath, Top Ear slipped inside the cage. Just inside, she froze, waiting for something to happen, but nothing did. White One followed behind her, nose and whiskers twitching. They avoided the bait and waited.

"It's safe," Top Ear declared, finally.

Smeeze, outside, took two hesitant steps forward before bounding ahead, limping heavily on her maimed paw. She darted inside, pressing against the others in the cage, the three of them huddled close to where the bait had been laid.

"Okay, guys," Bitey called, her voice shaky and uneasy. "That's enough. Get back here."

Someone shifted, an errant paw was placed, weight pressed against the pressure plate inside the cage. The trigger snapped. The cage's fourth wall, a solid plate, slammed shut.

"Wait!" Bitey let out a cry, too late, and darted out from her hiding place. She temporarily forgot her terror of the world outside. She ran to the cage, circling it, searching for an opening. She pressed her nose through the bars and shoved a paw inside, grasping desperately for the others inside. Top Ear snatched at her paw, reaching for her.

The choice had been made, two fates divided by cage bars.

Whatever happened next, Bitey would be on the outside.

* * *

When White One slept, she dreamed of Nezumi. It was a strange thing, dreaming about the piebald *usoothe*. She'd never had much of a relationship with her, and she had mourned her death less than the others in the colony. She had given her little thought since escaping their cage, since finding the

Beyond. And yet, as she curled up in a ball on the floor of the humane trap, she dozed and dreamed of Nezumi.

In the dream, Nezumi was curled up in a cage very much like this one. A handsome brown-furred rat with a white blaze across his face approached the bars, and he looked in at her with a gentle smile. Inside the dream, Nezumi touched her nose to his, and he squirmed inside the cage bars. White One recognized him, but as soon as she did the illusion was shattered. The dream broke apart, replaced by memories: Nezumi's bulging eyes and gasping final breaths; the blood seeping from Usoothe's ears.

So that was her secret, White One thought, sleepily, feeling in her heart that the dream was true. *I hope they've found each other, in the Spirit Realm.*

When White One awoke, she wasn't sure that the dream was over. She opened her eyes to see a tan face outside the wire of the cage, and she stared at it blearily for some time before she realized it wasn't Usoothe.

"Jetak?" she asked, incredulous.

He offered a small, meager smile, his whiskers twitching. "I only have a moment," he said, with the same nervousness as he had shown at their first meeting. He was wounded, carrying scabs and hairless patches from a struggle against the other wild ones, and his ears folded back as though waiting for someone. "But I heard…I heard what happened to Usoothe. I heard about the Great Ones. I wanted to see you before…"

White One couldn't think of what she was supposed to say. Behind her, inside the cage, Smeeze and Top Ear burrowed together in slumber. Smeeze muttered something in her sleep.

"You said before, that maybe the world wouldn't be better… that maybe it would only be different…"

"Something terrible is coming," White One said, wearily. Jetak hadn't come here out of affection, she realized. He came here because she was a fabled white rat, the last herald of the new era. She was the last symbol of whatever faith he could cling to. He came to her for hope and all she had to offer was uncertainty. "We're going Beyond, with a Great One, to see whether we can escape."

"Can I come with you?"

A terrible ache pierced through her heart, and she groomed her face and whiskers to keep him from seeing the look that passed through her pink eyes. "There's no way into this cage now," she said, wearing her pragmatism like armor. "It's sealed behind us."

"The Great One…"

"Might kill you, like a Great One killed Usoothe."

His whiskers drooped.

Something bad was coming. But something bad was *always* coming. That was the lesson of The Beyond, the truth that she could see. There were wonders here, greater than the imagination. And terrors, too. Braided together, nested like the scales on her tail. She could see it, make out the pattern, find a grim sort of beauty in it—but it was sparse, cold comfort for Jetak.

He deserved a better answer. They all did. But she could not give it to him any more than she could know what would happen to her unborn *jask*. She was no *usoothe*. And even if she were, it wouldn't make any difference. All the *usoothe* she had known were dead. Knowledge and wisdom couldn't save them, in the end.

But they'd tried, hadn't they? And it had made some kind of difference, hadn't it? A day of life was still life. And a glimmer of hope was still enough to see by.

White One extended a paw through the wire, touching his nose. "There are others. Friends of ours—Allaysi, Ukeki, Bitey, Monster. They're hiding. Go to them, see if you can help them. And anyone else from your colony that you feel is worth saving. Find a way out, into the Beyond. The real Beyond. Before...whatever bad thing is coming, can come."

He stared at her, uncomprehendingly. The irony of it all was too thick for her to stand. All her life, White One had yearned to climb out of a cage, to venture into the Beyond. And now she was the one in the cage, of her own free will, and it was a decision she could never undo. Just days ago, she had struggled to explain the concept of "outside" to Bitey and Smeeze...and now, Jetak struggled with the same idea.

He caught on more quickly, though. "I'll do my best," he said, finally, and she believed him.

She had chosen to name him "Safe." She hoped that he could live up to his name.

Chapter Twenty-Six

itey smelled the male before she saw him, and she was on him within moments. Although the area beneath the shelf was narrow, she had enough room to push him to the floor, and she stood over him with bared teeth and twitching whiskers. "Did the *Ukeshu* send you?" She demanded.

He squeaked in alarm. "N-no! It was…White One…please don't…"

"Bitey, let him go," Allaysi said, beside her. Despite the tension of the situation, there was a hint of laughter in her voice. "It's just my brother."

"Your brother?"

"Yes. Well. I think he's my brother. We have the same mother, but different litters. Anyway—let him up. He won't hurt you."

Bitey hesitated. Nearby, Monster let out a low growl, and Bitey knew that the older rat felt the same way she did. They had been through far too many unpleasant surprises to accept this intruder with open arms. "Did you say, White One?" Bitey asked.

He nodded enthusiastically. "Yes! I'm…she calls me Jetak," he said, in a nervous squeak. "I was the one…I found her, and…and the other one. And I'm the one who…" he trailed off. "Ask Cookie! Or Dumbo! They know who I am."

"Cookie and Dumbo are gone." But Bitey caught the gist of what he was saying. She wasn't an idiot. Usoothe had told her that White One was carrying *jask*, and if she was, they were likely the product of this squirming idiot. "What do you want?"

"White One told me to help you. To take you somewhere safe."

Bitey snorted. The significance of his name had not passed by her unnoticed. But she withdrew, letting him roll back to his paws. "What safe place?"

"I don't know," he said, and flinched, clearly expecting to be attacked again. "She just said to take as many rats as I could and to get out of here. Outside. Far away from here."

By now, the concept of "outside" no longer baffled Bitey, although she still could not fully wrap her head around the scale necessary to make sense of it. "So you came to bring us with you?"

"If you wanted to come," he said, backing away nervously. "I wanted to go with White One, with the Great Ones, but she said it was impossible. And Usoothe is dead. I was too afraid to join him before…and now it's too late. But maybe we can start again…where he left off…"

"Usoothe was a fool," Ukeki said, her voice hoarse from being disused since her leader's death. "A dead fool who put his trust in the wrong place."

Jetak's whiskers twitched. "Fine," he said, a little impatiently. "But if White One said something terrible is coming, and told me to try and get out, then I'm going to do what she said. If you want to come with me…come with me. There were tunnels that didn't get wet in the Big Water. Maybe they'll be safe now, too."

Allaysi squeaked in approval. "I'll come with you," she said, at once. "It can't hurt."

Bitey smiled a little sadly. Ukeki, despite her reservations, moved to follow the young scout and the slender sandy-colored male. Now it was just Bitey and Monster lingering in the shadow of a shelf, hiding from the inevitable, while the rest of their surviving colony hid in a cage and awaited an unknown fate.

They had gone through so much, and yet it seemed it was all for nothing.

"Monster…" she started, but she guessed the other rat's answer before she even asked.

"I'm tired of running," Monster said. "It's all just wheels in cages."

Bitey sighed. Jetak lingered, but eventually left, the females in tow. He told her where she could meet up with him if she chose to follow them.

* * *

She spent a long night in contemplation.

All her life, Bitey had struggled with her instincts. She had proven to herself that she was strong and capable. She had led the *shujisk* and driven off the onslaught of the wild ones. She had swum in the Big Water and rescued Monster. And now she had an opportunity, perhaps, to get away from it all; to start all over again as a wild one, living the way rats had lived for centuries.

And yet, faced with the choice, Bitey wasn't sure that it was the right one. Like Monster, she was tired of running. And she was tired of everything around her turning to lies. She had run out of things to believe in.

There were only two things Bitey could still trust: herself and her colony. And just now, the last of her colony were in a cage, awaiting an unknown fate. She couldn't leave them to that. Even if their choice was wrong—even if Cookie was gone forever and Soft Hands was just another liar—Bitey would rather face death with her sisters than risk being alone.

Nuzzling Monster on the cheek, the mink-hooded rat rose to her paws and crept out into the open. She curled up beside the cage and waited for Soft Hands to return.

Chapter Twenty-Seven

T he morning dawned too early. Three rats sat huddled inside a cage. Another hung back fearfully in the shadowed overhang of the shelf. Between them, straddling both worlds, Bitey pressed herself against the outer wall of the cage. She had neither moved nor slept, and the tendrils of gray light that crept through the skylight were the only hint of the passage of time.

Outside, footsteps crunched over gravel and debris. Voices spoke and drew near as the echo of footsteps grew. Great Ones, a pair of them, unlike any Bitey had seen before. They wore orange suits and carried with them the machines of death. They smelled like death, too; they smelled of snakes and floodwater and poison. Bitey, caught in the open, froze, every hair standing on end. Competing messages—Run! Attack! Help the others!—flooded her mind and held her immobilized.

"Hey, look at that," one of the Great Ones said, in the deep lumbering voices made of sounds and earthquakes. "Bold little thing, isn't it?"

"Not for much longer it won't be."

Top Ear rushed at the side of the cage. "Bitey!" she yelled, hopelessly. "Bitey! Do something!" She threw herself at the mesh and squeaked miserably.

Outside, Bitey found that she could do nothing. It wasn't like facing the Big Water or fighting off the *Ukeshu*—times when the only choices were fear and courage. There was not enough courage in all the Beyond to save her from this. The feeling of being out in the open —of vulnerability—fell over her, and she shuddered; it was the most terrible feeling. The others might be in a cage, but she was every bit as trapped as they were.

It's all just cages. Everyone has become a snake.

"What do we do with this cage?" the Great One's voice rumbled like the distant roll of thunder, like the approach of another flood-bearing storm. "There's a couple live ones in there."

"I think some girl's coming for it, is what the owner said. I don't know. Come on—help me lay down the tubing. If she's not here by the time it's done, we'll just keep going."

The air is nothing but death, Bitey thought, watching as the boot steps retreated. None of it made any sense, but she knew in her heart that Dumbo's words—no, Nezumi's words, the *usoothe*'s final prophecy—were coming to pass.

Another storm. Another flood. Another cage.

* * *

"Wait!"

Plastic sheets hung over the door, and Lori impatiently shoved them aside as she ran into the building, yelling for anyone who would listen. The exterminator truck outside was empty; she hoped she wasn't too late.

"Don't start yet! Wait!"

"Are you the one with the traps?" One of the exterminators

lifted his mask and gave her a curious look. He held a bundle of rubber tubes under one arm.

"You'd better hurry," the other one said. "We're on a deadline, here. Five minutes, and we're gassing the rest."

"Thank you," Lori said, not bothering to look at them before running to check her traps. The first two were empty, and her heart pounded painfully in her chest. The third, final cage had three rats. She recognized them. The white one. The top-eared Berkshire. The Siamese. They looked thin and terrified.

"Where are the rest of you?" Lori asked, looking down at them.

That was when she noticed a fourth rat—the mink girl, the one who liked to bite. She was cowering outside the cage, her back hunched and teeth bared. She was almost unrecognizable, the white of her fur stained with dried blood and a dozen scabs littering her pelt. When Lori moved close, the rat hissed and fumbled backwards.

"It's okay," Lori said, soothingly. "I know you're scared. But you have to let me catch you."

Outside, her mother honked impatiently. Lori didn't want to make her wait any longer—not when her chances of keeping them were already so slim. One of exterminators, standing at the plastic-covered door, looked at his watch and pointedly back at her. There was no time.

Lori sighed and turned for the door, scooping the cage up into her arms and leaving the fourth rat behind.

* * *

Bitey cowered in the shadow of the great one. Her fur stood

on end, and thoughts tumbled over in her mind in an uneasy stream of chatter, like the insane ramblings of the *shujisk*. *Run. Bite. Hide. Snakes and cages.* In her mind, she saw Usoothe; she heard the crunch of his bones against the wall. She was frozen with fear. Her insides trembled, but she could not bring herself to move—not to attack, not to run.

The trap holding her three companions rose in the air, drawing them away from her sight.

"Bitey!" Smeeze squeaked, desperately, snatching at the air with her paw. "Monster! Both of you! Come on! Please."

The Great One knelt down, extending a hand, and Bitey shied away. Her brain still jumbled, her body responded with panic and she stumbled back toward her hiding place to evade the hand that came from the sky.

"I can't," Bitey said, and she froze once more, paralyzed by doubt. It had been easy to decide to come along with her colony last night. Now, in the shadow of the Great One, her instincts screamed at her to stop. Maybe, if she hurried, she could make it back to Jetak.

"Bitey!"

"I—I don't know—I can't..."

Her breath quickened, her heart thudded.

The Great One stood and made her way toward the door, carrying the trap in one hand. It bumped and swayed, and the rats inside yelled out Bitey's name.

Under the shelf, a pair of ruby eyes peered out with a glassy, fearful look. Monster's nose twitched, but otherwise she was perfectly still, frozen in place.

"Monster?" she asked, tentatively, seeking an answer from the rat she had once viewed as her alpha, her mentor.

"Cages and snakes."

Something broke within Bitey's chest, something unable to withstand the walls built by fear.

She bolted for the door, chasing after the retreating footsteps of the Great One. She scrabbled for a foothold on the slick tile and ran like the Spirits and the wild ones, the snake and the *shujisk* and all other forms of death were behind her.

She came up even with the Great One's foot. Without thinking, she lunged forward to nip at her heel. Her teeth caught the fabric of her sock, just grazing her ankle. At first nothing happened, but finally Soft Hands stopped.

She bent down, setting the trap on the floor. Bitey flinched, expecting the worst, but no harm came to her. The Great One extended a hand, her fingertips gently brushing against Bitey's head and wounded shoulders. Bitey cringed but resisted her impulse to bite her. Her hand smelled like Cookie.

Lori fumbled with the trap, struggling to open a latch with one hand. Holding Bitey awkwardly, she dropped her inside with the others. Bitey, disoriented and unbalanced, screeched and tumbled into them; they fell into an uneasy heap and slid over each other as they struggled for footing on the cage's slick metal floor. The latch closed, and once more the cage was lifted. Bitey struggled with the feeling of weightlessness and she slid toward the far end of the cage, pressing her nose through the bars to look back toward the shelf.

"Monster," Bitey squeaked, in a whisper, extending her paw through the bars of the cage. "There's still time! Come on!"

Monster's ruby eyes stood out against the dark. They stared back at her, glassy and clear, and even her whiskers fell perfectly still. Bitey yelled at her to run: to follow the Great One, or to seek out Jetak and his offerings of safety.

But Monster did not respond; she merely stood and waited,

whiskers quivering, ears pricked forward, ruby eyes set on a distance that turned inward.

"She's still waiting for the snake," White One said, touching Bitey's shoulder with her nose. "But she won't have to, much longer."

The cage bumped against Lori's leg as she crossed the threshold outside. The exterminators closed the plastic flap over the doorway, sealing it against the fumes that would be pumped in.

The rats burrowed together, huddled against the cool draft of outside air.

The store passed out of sight, and the exterminators turned on the gas.

Afterword: Regarding Ratspeak

The language spoken by Nezumi and her companions is Ratspeak, the native tongue of all rats. For ease of reading, most of the dialogue throughout the story has been translated into its closest English equivalent, but due to the subtleties and intricacies of ratspeak, some meaning is perhaps lost in a direct translation. Allow me, then, to take a moment to explain the mechanics of the language, so that a better understanding can be gleaned of it and the characters who use it.

Rats, having no need of a written language, have no alphabet to speak of. Rather, their language is organized into a syllabry, each syllable being the smallest unit of meaning in the language. These syllables then are strung together to create a form of sentence, with meaning largely dependent upon inflection and context. There is little focus in ratspeak upon grammar, and much more emphasis upon the subtleties of communication: tone, gesture and emphasis.

The structure of ratspeak lends itself to constant evolution and creativity, allowing new words to be created as needed for a given situation. This is a double-edged sword; on the one hand, it is helpful for rats to be able to adapt to their ever-changing environment and communicate with each other within it; on the other hand, isolated colonies of rats can quickly develop a dialect so different from each other as to create enormous linguistic rifts. When a foreign rat ventures into such an isolated colony, he may quickly discover that he understands only the vaguest sense of their language.

By default, nearly all ratspeak syllables are nouns. Depending upon usage and the manner in which it is combined with other affixes, meaning can morph to other parts of speech. For example, the unit *ke* translates literally into "teeth", but can also carry the meaning of "bite" or "gnaw" depending upon context. *Ki* means, literally, "claws", but can also carry the context of "to claw/scratch", such that the ratspeak word *keki* comes to mean "fighter; one who bites and scratches."

Rats, being a social animal, are highly aware of rank and order, and their language reflects that. Many proper nouns in ratspeak denote the rank of the rat they are assigned to. The prefix *o*, for example, denotes a submissive or omega rat, whereas *u* denotes a rat of highly respected stature such as an alpha or particularly aggressive beta. Thus, the proper name *Ukeki* comes to mean "head warrior," or, more literally, "(respected one) who bites and scratches."

Rats also use prefixes to denote gender. The prefix "je" stands for male, such that Jetak's name literally means "safe male." The female prefix is "le."

A Word About Names

Ratspeak is a language of creation. It is comprised of a finite number of syllables, each with a discrete meaning, but these syllables and meanings can be strung together in a way that creates something new. Therefore, when rats confront something new in their world, they are given the task of naming it—and in so doing, they create an inextricable link between the thing that is new and all things that are known.

Rats believe that the world and everything in it was spoken into being by the Spirits, using words that have since been lost. If a rat could discover those words again, it's reasoned, they too could wield the powers of life and death.

And so, it's little surprise that rats hold names in high esteem.

For the domestic rats, those worshipers of The Great Ones, true names are the province of Great Ones alone. These names hold great power. It is said that once a rat is named, she is blessed by the Great Ones and granted immunity to the dangers of The Beyond. It would be blasphemy for a rat to steal this power.

Of course, rats do sometimes pick up nicknames, castaway titles offered by Great Ones in passing. These, too, are powerful—but it is known that their powers are limited, and that these titles are little more than placeholders until they are taken into The Beyond.

Wild rats look at this naming business differently. There is no place in a wild colony for individuals. They live and work together as one, for the good of the whole, and their language reflects this. Thus, a wild rat's identity is tied to his position: A rat may be a scout, or a healer, or a guard, but he shares his name and purpose with the rats on either side. Only one rat in the colony has a name: The alpha, the *usim-li*, who is a god among them.

The alpha chooses his own name, and in so doing, creates himself.

Glossary: Some Common Words

GLOSSARY: Common Ratspeak Words

WORD
Meaning

Allaysi

Scout; "chase and explore (with enthusiasm)"

Bozu

Fatally injured; dying

Chusim

Food stash

Churzu

Gone above; taken by humans

Jask

A child or infant rat

Keshu

Warrior. Literally, "enemy-biter"

Liso

"Well found," often meant as "good job."

Nosobo

Nurse/caretaker; "licks and touches the wounded"

Sazu

Running from death

Shujisk

Ferret. Literally, "laughing predator"

Taksim

Safe place; burrow

Uchu

Particularly high-quality food

Ukeki

Warrior name; literally, "bites and scratches"

Usim-li

Alpha. Literally, "good burrow maker"

Usoothe

Sage/wise man; "one who sees much"

Ushu

Dangerous predator

Ushuzu-sim

Snake. Literally, "Crawling death predator."

An Origin Story

In the beginning, there were only two rats in all the world: The Great White Rat, who was life, and The Great Black Rat, who was death. They lived together in the Spirit Realm and together they built a great nest, and that nest was The Beyond. When they were finished, they mated, and together bore the litter from which all rats are descended.

"There is room enough here for all of our children to live happily," The Great White Rat, who is the all-mother, said as she surveyed The Beyond. It was a huge nest, the greatest that had ever been built, and it was full of *chusim* and hiding places.

But The Great Black Rat saw things differently. "Our children must know struggle," he said, "Or they will be weak, and in their weakness they will not know how to use the gifts we've left for them."

The All-Mother saw that this was true, and so she gave her mate her blessing.

The Great Black Rat created *ushu*. He spoke words that have long been forgotten, powerful words of creation, and from those words came all the evil that dwells in the world.

"You have made the *ushu* too numerous!" The All-Mother cried, when she saw what her mate had done. "Who will protect our children from them now?"

But she had an idea. And so, while her mate was busy bringing evil into the world, she slipped away to speak the words of creation for herself. And so she created The Great Ones, vast titans with the wisdom and courage to protect her children, and her children's children. She gave them domain of The Beyond, and power even to defeat the *ushu*.

Her mate was not pleased with her decision. "You defy my wishes," he told her, when he saw what she had done. "Our children will be weak with these Great Ones watching over them."

But The Great White Rat, the all-mother, who is life, said, "No. Our children must earn the protection of these Great Ones. Only the most loyal and clever will be saved."

And so it has been since. Many generations have passed since the first litter, but The Great Ones still stand as guardians of The Beyond, and the *ushu* still lurk at every corner to test the strength and cleverness of Life and Death's children, and only the cleverest and strongest and fastest will survive. So it has been from the beginning, and so it shall be until the end.

* * *

That is the story that rats in cages tell to their *jask*. It is widely known.

But the Wild Ones have a different story. This is what they tell.

* * *

In the Spirit Realm, the Great White Rat Ule is mother to all. The world was born from her womb. She has many children, but the most important of these is Uzu the Trickster, who is death.

While his siblings were content to live within the Spirit Realm without complaint, Uzu had trouble in his heart. He was always playing pranks on his siblings. But he was Ule's youngest child, and her favorite, and her most powerful. Like his mother, he had the ability to speak things into being, and he used this power to craft his tricks. He created many things that had not lived before: things that crawled, and things that bit. The *ushu*. They followed his commands and terrorized his brothers.

"This boy Uzu is a nuisance," the spirits would say to Ule. "We do not want him living among us anymore."

Finally, after much complaining, Ule relented. She saw that he and his pets could not live in the Spirit Realm any longer. And so she called him and the hordes of his *ushu* and banished them all to the outerworld, to the places outside the barriers of her Spirit Realm.

He lived in the outerworld happily for some time. His creations flourished, breeding and multiplying, and for a time Uzu was happy.

But eventually, he grew bored and lonely. He missed his siblings. He missed having others to play tricks on.

And so Uzu sat down and spoke the words of creation, and with them he crafted himself a mate. They bred, and soon their offspring filled the world, more numerous even than the children of his *ushu*. And he loved his children, each and every one of them—but Uzu was, after all, a trickster. He showed his love through wickedness and mischief.

Ule, seeing what her child had done, felt a pang of regret for her grandchildren, who now filled the outerworld so plentifully. And so she resolved to allow them passage into the Spirit Realm, where they might live forever, if they were unlucky enough to fall victim to Uzu's wicked pranks.

And so it happens that the rats live in constant struggle with Uzu's creations. They must respect Death, for he is their father, but they must also outwit him. That is how the game is played. And when their time is come, and they have proven themselves worthy against the teeming thousands, Ule will accept them into her den for eternity.

About the Author

T.L. Bodine is the author of NEVEREST, RIVER OF SOULS, the Wattpad-exclusive THE HOUND, and many other tales of horror. She's interested in uncanny, fantastic things, and the way average people with human problems interact with them.

When not writing, she can usually be found watching horror movies, playing story-heavy video games, or experimenting in the kitchen.

She lives in New Mexico with her husband and two small dogs.

You can connect with me on:

◑ https://www.tlbodine.com

Subscribe to my newsletter:

✉ https://www.patreon.com/tlbodine

Also by T.L. Bodine

These Kids Are Not Alright
https://books2read.com/b/mq2V06
Childhood is supposed to be safe. But these stories know better.

Stray children roam in hungry packs. A school sacrifices its students to forgotten gods. Harbingers from a doomed future confirm a childhood superstition. These fifteen unsettling tales follow children and teens poised to inherit a world that has already left them behind.

Here, trauma and transformation bleed together, monstrosity becomes an inheritance, and kids sharpen their teeth on the bones of the adults who failed them. Rooted in fairytale and urban legend These Kids Are Not Alright is a love letter to the stories we tell to survive growing up, and the horrors we carry into adulthood.

www.ingramcontent.com/pod-product-compliance
Lightning Source LLC
Chambersburg PA
CBHW030902060726
47591CB00005B/1381